Praise for Claire Allan:

'Amazing. I read it in one go.'
Marian Keyes

'Utterly addictive! Literally couldn't put it down all day!
Compulsive, twisty, tense. And LOVED the ending.'
Claire Douglas

'A powerful and emotional psychological thriller that will
keep you guessing and leave you breathless.'
C.L. Taylor

'SUCH a good read! It made me feel so uncomfortable,
but I still kept gobbling up the pages.'
Lisa Hall

'*Her Name Was Rose* is heck of a read! It's a psychological
thriller with a heart; it's taut, emotionally challenging and,
unlike so many thrillers, each twist and turn is here because
it deserves to be and not for the sake of it.'
John Marrs

'An exciting debut that I couldn't put down,
Her Name Was Rose got under my skin in a way I wasn't
expecting. An intriguing and menacing page turner.'
Mel Sherratt

'The depth of characterisation and its fast pace is what
makes *Her Name Was Rose* stand out as a thriller.
It had me hooked until the end.'
Elisabeth Carpenter

'A tight and twisted tale with a set of seriously complex
characters – kept me guessing right 'til the end. This is
going to be one of 2018's smash hits.'
Cat Hogan

APPLE OF MY EYE

Claire Allan is a former journalist from Derry in Northern Ireland, where she still lives with her husband, two children, two cats and a hyperactive puppy.

In her eighteen years as a journalist, she covered a wide range of stories, from attempted murders, to court sessions, to the Saville Inquiry into the events of Bloody Sunday right down to the local parish notes.

She has previously published eight women's fiction novels. Her first thriller, *Her Name Was Rose*, was published in 2018.

When she's not writing, she'll more than likely be found on Twitter @claireallan.

By the same author:
Her Name Was Rose

CLAIRE ALLAN

APPLE OF MY EYE

avon.

AVON
A division of HarperCollins*Publishers*
1 London Bridge Street,
London SE1 9GF

www.harpercollins.co.uk

A Paperback Original 2019

1

A catalogue record for this book is
available from the British Library

UK PB: 978-0-00-827508-2
TPB: 978-0-00-832342-4
US PB: 978-0-00-832867-2

Set in Bembo by Palimpsest Book Production Limited,
Falkirk, Stirlingshire

Printed and bound in Great Britain by
CPI Group (UK) Ltd, Croydon CR0 4YY

MIX
Paper from
responsible sources
FSC™ C007454

This book is produced from independently certified FSC™ paper
to ensure responsible forest management.

For more information visit: www.harpercollins.co.uk/green

In memory of my grandmother, Mary McGuinness, who raised ten children with a fierce love and pride and who always had time and love in abundance for every one of her grandchildren and great-grandchildren. Especially the bookworms x

The king said, 'Bring me a sword.' So they brought a sword before the king. And the king said: 'Divide the living child in two, and give half to one, and half to the other.'

The Judgement of Solomon – 1 Kings 3:16–28

Prologue

Louise

As soon as I saw her I knew that she didn't deserve to be a mother. She was squeezed in behind a table in the café, her face pale, drawn. She rubbed her stomach for the briefest of seconds, as if it were something she'd just remembered she was expected to do. Act the part of the happy mum-to-be; rub your expanding stomach, push it out, flaunt your fecundity to the world.

Everything about her body language screamed that this wasn't a wanted or loved baby. That she didn't appreciate what she had. What a gift she'd been given.

She looked like a woman who saw pregnancy as an ordeal. Something to be endured. If only she knew.

When it was me, I'd welcomed every pregnancy symptom. Every single one. The sickness. The sore and swollen breasts. The bleeding gums. The swollen ankles. The backache. Even the acid reflux. It was proof I was doing something miraculous. Making a new life and bringing a new soul into this world.

I'd gone to sleep every night with my hands on my bump, whispering stories and hopes and dreams to my baby. Telling him or her of the life they'd have. Of the love that would be showered down on them. God, I was never as happy as I was when I could feel my baby wriggle and kick. I felt more alive with every movement. The symbiosis of my child and me as we shared each breath.

I deserved to be a mother.

This woman, tired and worn out and miserable, didn't. Not as much as I did, anyway.

Holding my breath, I watched her across the café as she pushed a loose strand of hair back behind her ear, listened as she sighed loudly.

The thing is, babies don't really need their mothers. Once they're delivered, all they want is someone to see to their every need. To feed them, change them, pat them gently on the back to bring up their milky-scented burps. To bathe them and dress and rock them gently to sleep.

Other people could do that.

I could do that.

CHAPTER ONE

Eli

The crisp white envelope sticks out from where it's been stuffed into my pigeonhole. I lift it, along with the rest of my post, and make my way to the staffroom.

It's probably a note from one of my families. I both love and hate receiving them. A note or thank-you card of course means I've done my job well, but it also usually follows a death. One of my patients will have gone, and a thank-you note will mark part of the admin for a poor family to complete while they're still shaken from grief.

My name's printed neatly on the cover. Almost as if it's been typed, but there's a small smudge of ink that betrays its hand-written status.

Eli Hughes
Senior Staff Nurse
Cherrygreen Hospice

I don't think much of it at first. I'm focusing on getting fifteen minutes to compose myself. To try to eat something before my hunger turns to nausea. Drink some coffee before my fatigue overwhelms me. Put my feet up before my ankles swell further. Yes, I'm at the retaining-water stage of pregnancy – seven and a half months – and still waiting for the sickness to pass. I've long ago given up on the notion that it's just morning sickness. Hyperemesis is beyond morning sickness. They should call it pregnancy poisoning. I'm only able to function because of anti-sickness medication, and even then . . .

There's a plain ham sandwich – white bread, thin layer of real butter – wrapped in tinfoil in the fridge. My stomach turns at the thought. I'll try a coffee, even though I shouldn't. Even though the smell makes me feel woozy and I've had my one daily cup already. I need caffeine.

I make a cup and sit down, a plain Rich Tea biscuit in front of me. Lunch. Once this baby's born, I'll never, ever eat plain biscuits again.

I turn my attention to the post, the neatly handwritten envelope first. It contains just one sheet of paper: small, blue, lined – the kind on which I'd have written pages and pages of letters to my pen pals when I was a teen. Unfolding it, I see just two lines of text, written in the same neat print:

YOU SHOULDN'T BELIEVE
EVERYTHING HE TELLS YOU

I look at the words and read them again. I turn the page around to see if I'm missing anything on the back page to put these words in context. I even check inside the envelope, peering in, shaking it out. A strange feeling washes over me. Is this some silly joke, or meant for someone else, or a clever marketing scheme for something? I hadn't the first notion what that could be, but wasn't that the whole point with clever marketing schemes these days? Get everyone talking. Then bam! The big reveal . . .

I shouldn't believe whom? What? I put the note down, then

gingerly bite on my biscuit, which crumbles into sawdust in my mouth. I know I won't finish it.

I don't have the patience for silly games or puzzles. But I can't deny my inner nosiness.

Rachel arrives, walks to the fridge, mutters about it being a long day and stares at the wilted salad she's brought in with her, closing the fridge door in disgust.

'I think I might run out and grab something from the shop. A sandwich or something. Can I tempt you?'

Rachel does this a lot. Brings in a healthy lunch and forsakes it for something laden with mayonnaise and cheese when push comes to shove. Still maintains an enviable figure – one I envy even more now that I'm expanding at an exponential rate.

'There's a ham sandwich in there you can have. It's good ham. I'm not going to eat it. Will save you nipping out.'

'And take food from a pregnant woman? Do you think I'm some sort of monster?' She laughs but opens the fridge anyway and lifts out my tinfoil parcel. She points it in my direction. 'Are you sure you don't want it?'

My stomach turns in response and the involuntary face I pull answers her question.

'You poor thing. You know, Eli, maybe you really should think of starting maternity leave early.'

I shake my head. 'Nonsense.' Keen to change the conversation, I push the note in her direction. 'Look at this note I got. Did you get one like it? Have you any idea what it's about?'

Sitting down, she takes the note and looks at it. I watch for a reaction on her face. Her eyebrows rise just a little but she shakes her head.

'I've no idea,' she says. 'But no, I didn't get one. Ooh! Eliana Hughes, have you got a stalker?'

She laughs but I don't. I force a smile but feel my chest tighten. She must notice my expression.

5

'Eli, I'm kidding. I'm sure it's nothing. Someone's idea of a joke or something. Or mistaken identity. Sure, it's bound to be that. Who would you have to mistrust? You and Martin have the most solid marriage I've ever seen. There's no way he'd play away.'

Martin.

It didn't even cross my mind it could be about Martin. Until now. I want to nod and say yes, we're the most solid couple people know. Because we were . . . but lately . . . There's a disconnect there that I can't quite put my finger on.

The coffee I've been drinking tastes bitter. Of bile. Just like everything else tastes off that I've had to eat or drink over the last seven months. Just like everything in my life feels off.

We'd tried so hard to have this baby. Months of disappointment and finally tests. Then 'There's nothing we can find, just give it time,' and more disappointment until, finally, two lines.

It should be the happiest time of our lives. Certainly the happiest time of my life; nurturing a new human life deep within me, bonding with this kicking, wriggling person made of love about to become our baby.

I expected to love every moment of pregnancy, but I realise now I'd been naïve. This kicking, wriggling person who seems to be made of right angles, jabs and pokes at my stomach muscles, which are permanently aching from the daily retching. It makes me feel sorry for myself. I feel angry that I've been robbed of a positive pregnancy experience that most women get. And I feel guilty that I resent this pregnancy not being what I wanted it to be. Sure, won't the end result be the same? Isn't that what's important?

And Martin, try as he might, can't understand how I feel. I suppose I've been taking that anger and frustration out on him a little.

I feel tears prick at my eyes. Swear at myself. I can't cry again today.

'Eli.' Rachel's voice cuts through my thoughts.

I look up at her, her eyes filled with concern. Her hand reaches across the table and takes mine.

'Eli, you do know Martin would never, ever cheat on you. This isn't about Martin. This is somebody's idea of a stupid joke, or it's about something else we've just not figured out yet. But we will.'

I nod, two fat tears rolling down my cheeks. My nose running, I sniff loudly, grab a tissue from the box on the table and roughly rub at my eyes.

'You're right,' I say. 'Of course you're right.'

I look at the letter again. It doesn't reveal anything new, so in a rage I crumple it up and throw it into the bin beside the fridge.

Rachel smiles. Tells me I've done the right thing and gives my hand a rub before her pager calls her back to a patient.

When she's gone, I take it back out and thrust it deep into the bottom of my handbag.

CHAPTER TWO

Eli

By the time my shift is done, I'm exhausted and I'm pretty sure my ankles have doubled in size. I can't wait to get home, kick off my shoes and feel the cool marble floors of our living space under my tired feet.

But my car's in the garage and I have to wait for Martin to collect me. As usual, he's late. Probably stuck on a work call he can't get out of.

I'm standing with my coat on, looking out at the rain falling onto the hospice car park, when Rachel asks if I need a lift.

'It's not on your way home,' I tell her. 'I couldn't ask you to do that.'

'You didn't. I offered,' she says with a smile. 'It'll save that husband of yours coming out on a night like this and sure, it's not that far out of my way. The kids are at their dad's, so it's not like I'm in a rush to get home anyway. You've had a long day,' she says, and I want to hug her.

'If you're sure?' I ask. 'I'll just check Martin hasn't left.'

'I'm sure,' she smiles.

I dial my husband, who answers after two rings, apologises

and says he'll be with me shortly. I can hear from the background noises that he's still at home.

'Rachel's going to drop me over. You've no need to come out,' I tell him.

He sounds relieved. 'That's great,' he says. 'I can get on with some work while dinner's cooking. It's been a mad day, so busy. But look, I'll talk to you about it when you get home.'

Work has been 'mad' for months now. Longer hours. More trips away. A big project that could bring a lot more work his way. When he wants to talk about it, it generally means he'll tell me about another 'vital' trip away. It's a good thing I'm not the suspicious type.

Or wasn't.

I end the call and tell Rachel I'll take her up on her offer.

'Are you okay?' she asks as she leads the way to her car. 'You're not still mulling over that silly note, are you?'

I force a smile. Shake my head. Lie and say I'm fine and that I'm just tired. Change the conversation to something less likely to make me feel tightness in my chest. We talk about who we're rooting for in *Strictly Come Dancing* until we pull up outside my house.

I feel as if I should invite her in, but I'm too tired to play the gracious host.

'We must get you round for dinner some time,' I say to her. 'Have a proper catch-up outside work, when we aren't both so tired.' I hope that makes up for the lack of invite tonight.

'That'd be lovely,' she says with genuine warmth.

I give her a quick hug then climb out of the car and walk to the front door of my dream home, nervous about what my husband will tell me.

When we first moved to this house just over eighteen months ago, after several years of enduring a three-hour commute between Belfast and Derry, I thought I was the luckiest woman alive. There were certain perks to marrying an architect, not that it really mattered to me what Martin did for a living. I'd fallen head over heels in love within weeks of meeting him.

Set on the banks of Enagh Lough, just outside Derry city, Martin had overseen the renovation of the old farmhouse himself. It had taken a year – and lots of blood, sweat and tears – but he'd made our home magnificent.

The rear of the house, which looked out over the lake and the surrounding woods, was mostly glazed. Large plate glass windows set in natural wood frames. Bifold doors onto wooden decking, leading to our own personal jetty – it was stunning in all seasons.

It had felt like our home from the moment we'd walked over the threshold of that ramshackle farmhouse; of course, it felt more so now. It was our bubble in a hectic world that moved at a breakneck speed.

It feels less of a bubble these days. Pregnancy has made me feel vulnerable in a way I never did before. Reliant, not so much on Martin as an individual but on Martin and I as a team. A couple. Ready to work together on this next scary chapter. I'd watched my mother struggle as a single parent. I don't want that struggle. I don't want my child to grow up not knowing their father. I think of the note, that stupid piece of paper, and a shiver runs through me.

Dropping my bag on the marble floor in the hall, I hang up my coat and call out to Martin that I'm home.

He walks out of the kitchen, apron on, wine glass in hand, and says hello with a smile. His smile still has the power to make me feel weak at the knees. Even now, ten years after we first met. I smile back, for a moment feeling comforted by his presence.

But even from several feet way, the smell of wine makes me feel nauseous. I take a deep breath, try to swallow down the sickness. If I just take a few minutes to settle myself, take another anti-sickness pill, I might be okay to sit with him for dinner.

'Did you not invite Rachel in with you?' he asks, looking behind me.

'Erm, no. I thought you wanted to talk, and I'm so tired. I didn't think . . .'

'That's a shame,' he said. 'She's good company.'

I tense. Am I not good company on my own? 'Well, I said we'll have her over for dinner sometime soon.'

'That'll be nice,' Martin says, moving towards me and pulling me into a hug.

'I'm just going to grab a bath,' I say, pulling back a little. The smell of garlic is assailing my nostrils. 'Do I have time?'

'If you're quick. Maybe twenty minutes. Perhaps you'd be better waiting until you've eaten before you have a soak.'

'I really need to freshen up. My stomach's churning, too. Not sure I'll eat much.'

'I've made a pasta bake. It's quite light. Not creamy or cheesy. You should try some at least, Eli,' he says, his face filled with concern. As if he sees me as more vulnerable now, too. No longer an equal partner.

'You're very good to me,' I say.

'Of course I am,' he smiles. 'I even left mushrooms out of the recipe because I know you can't so much as look at them at the moment.'

I smile. 'I'll be as quick as I can,' I say and continue upstairs, where I run the bath and lie in the water, watching my baby wriggle under my skin, feet and elbows pushing outwards.

I wonder how something so small and innocent can make me feel so sick all the time. I stroke my stomach, whispering, 'I love you,' hoping if I say it enough I'll start to really, really feel it.

After climbing out of the bath, I wrap myself in my fluffy

11

dressing gown and I'm just about to get dressed into my pyjamas, when I hear my phone ring. I look at it and see 'Mum' on the screen. I'm so happy to see her name and I wish, not for the first time, that she lived closer.

'Hi, Mum,' I say.

'What's wrong, pet?' Her reply is immediate. She can always read my mood. Name that emotion in one.

'Ah, it's been a long day,' I say, trying my hardest not to cry.

How is it that talking to my mother instantly brings all my emotions to the fore? I want to tell her about the note but decide not to. She'd only worry and one of us worrying is enough.

'And the baby? Everything's okay there?' she asks, her voice soft but thick with concern.

'Still making me throw up on a regular basis,' I say, a hiccup of self-pity ending my sentence for me.

'You poor pet,' she soothes. 'It'll be worth it. And sure, isn't sickness a sign of a healthy pregnancy?'

'This one'll come out like Superman then,' I say, forcing a laugh.

'And Martin? Is everything okay with you both?'

I nod, make some sort of affirmative noise. I don't want to go down that particular conversational route.

'Look, Mum, I've just got out of the bath. I need to get dried off and into my pyjamas. Martin's making dinner. I'm planning to get something to eat and go to bed. Work was so busy.'

'You're doing too much,' she says and I feel myself bristle.

This is something she and Martin agree on. They don't realise that right now, work is the one place I feel in control.

'I can handle it, Mum. It's just been a long day,' I tell her.

'Well, I don't like the sound of you one bit,' she says. 'I'm going to come and visit on Saturday and I'll hear no arguments.'

There's no way I'm going to argue. I could use some maternal

TLC. I tell her I'll look forward to it and that I love her and then I hang up, lie back on the bed and promise myself just five minutes of rest before dinner.

I wake, of course, much later, as Martin comes up to bed. Blinking and stretching, shivering a little, I ask him what time it is.

'It's gone eleven. You should just go back to sleep.'

'I'm sorry,' I say. 'I didn't mean to sleep. I was planning to come down for dinner.'

My stomach grumbles to reinforce my point.

'Don't worry about it,' he says, unbuttoning his shirt and throwing it into the laundry hamper. 'I've plated some up for you. It's in the fridge.'

Is it my imagination or is his tone not as soft as it was? He sits on the edge of the bed, looking out of the window over the blackness of the lake. I feel the need to be close to him.

'C'm'ere,' I say, reaching my arms out to him.

He turns, gives me a soft smile and climbs under the covers, pulling himself across to me and allowing me to hold him. His hand slips under my dressing gown, to my still naked body. I shiver again, only this time in anticipation. But his hand moves directly to my growing stomach.

'All this'll be worth it,' he says. 'I know you're feeling rotten, but this little one's going to bring us so much happiness and I just know you're going to be the best mum in the world.'

With his words, our house feels like our bubble again and I smile at him, place my hand on top of his and feel calm. He kisses the top of my head and squeezes my hand.

Tempted as I am to fall back to sleep there and then beside him, I know I need to eat something or the nausea will be much worse when it swoops in again.

I sit up, tell him I won't be long.

'I just need a bit of toast or something.'

13

'Are you shunning my pasta bake for the second time in one night?' he asks with a crooked smile.

I stick my tongue out at him. 'Might be too much considering it's so late, but it'll do tomorrow night.'

'Ah, that might be good, actually,' he says, sitting up. 'I still need to talk to you about that.'

I pull on my pyjama bottoms and look around to him while putting on my oversized maternity pyjama top.

'Yeah?'

'I need to go to London again.'

My heart sinks. It's been just a week since his last trip. I know it's a big job, but I hadn't expected him to have to travel quite so much.

The note in my bag niggles at me again.

'A snag with the communal play area,' he says. 'And the landscaper wants to discuss the garden plans with me. Boring stuff, but I have to be on site. I need to feel the space to see how it would work. They want doors moved from the original plan – which means moving the storage area and redesigning the mezzanine slightly.'

There's little point in arguing. What would it look like, anyway? I really would be the Wicked Witch of the West if I asked him to pass the work to one of his colleagues at this stage. This project has been his baby, long before we had an actual baby of our own to worry about.

'How long will you be away for?' I ask.

Last time it was just two nights, which wasn't so bad; even if, by the second night, I found myself increasingly anxious without him close by.

'That's the kicker,' he says. 'I need to be there for a meeting on Tuesday and, realistically, to get the plans done and drawn up . . . There's not much point in me coming back until Tuesday night.'

Friday to Tuesday – four nights – over the weekend.

'I know that means the weekend . . .' he says as if reading my thoughts. 'I thought maybe you could go and see your mum.'

'I'm working on Saturday,' I mutter. 'But Mum was planning to come and visit anyway. See how I am.'

'Well that's perfect, then,' he says, smiling widely. 'You'll be well looked after and I won't have to worry about you so much.'

'You don't have to worry about me anyway,' I say, my tone sharper than I'd like. I cringe at how petulant I sound.

'But I do, because I love you,' he enunciates slowly as if to make the point extra clear.

'If you loved me . . .' I start, the words out of my mouth before I've had time to think.

'If I loved you? Really? And what? I'd quit my job? I'm too tired to go over this again, Eli. I know you're pregnant. I know it's tough. I know your hormones are raging, but . . .' He shakes his head. 'No. I'm not doing this. Not now. Goodnight, Eli.'

Our earlier exchange feels soured.

All I can think is how, despite the nice dinner and the hugs and the smiles, things are far from right between us.

CHAPTER THREE

Eli

I leave him to sleep. A couple of slices of toast and a cup of decaf tea later, my brain still doesn't want to switch off. I sit in the living room, trying to distract myself from my thoughts by watching some American TV show in which a bride-to-be has to choose between a brand-new wedding gown or having her mother's wedding dress remade into something more suitable for a modern bride.

But, of course, my mind keeps drifting back to my own wedding and my own marriage. To my husband lying upstairs resting before his next work trip. I know I should trust him. I think I do trust him. Mostly. But I wonder, should I be asking more questions?

Maybe if I have a look at his emails. His phone. His wallet. Would I find something to confirm my worst fears or would finding nothing reassure me?

I've never snooped on Martin before. I've never felt the need and I do feel guilty. I actually feel like an actor in a soap opera as I walk to the dining table, where his suit jacket is draped over the back of a chair. Delving into the pockets, I pull out a receipt for a single cup of coffee and a chicken salad sandwich.

A half-empty packet of chewing gum. Assorted small change amounting to seventy-eight pence and some fluff.

Not even Columbo could find evidence of foul behaviour in that. Chiding myself, I put everything back as I found it, feeling like I'm the one who's betrayed him. I suppose I have. I've doubted him.

I probably still do, a little.

Taking a deep breath, I remind myself to be mindful. To be in the moment. It's a method we use with our patients to help with anxiety. Our patients who have real problems. Mine are nothing in comparison.

I focus on the ticking of the clock. The gentle hum of the fridge freezer. The sound of the rain tapping on the windows. I close my eyes and lie down on the sofa, where I think of everything I can feel and smell, pushing all other thoughts away until my eyes start to droop and I can feel sleep wash over me.

When I wake, the house is silent and there's a blanket draped over me. I blink, look around. The jacket's gone from the back of the dining room chair. I see a note propped on the coffee table beside a fresh glass of water, informing me my husband's left for the airport and didn't want to wake me as I looked so peaceful. He's ordered me a taxi as he had to take his car and mine's still off the road. He loves me, he says. He'll miss me. And the baby. No mention of the exchange we had last night.

I lift my phone, see that I have just thirty minutes until that taxi arrives, when I need to be in full possession of all of my senses and ready for a day at the hospice. Work will distract me, until home time at least. I wonder, would it be pathetic of me to text my mother and ask her to come down today instead of tomorrow? I know she won't mind. In fact, she'll probably jump at the chance to fuss around me more. So I send the text and I breathe a sigh of relief when, just minutes later, she replies that she'll be with me by home time.

★

I never really believed it when people said they 'didn't have a minute to themselves' before I started working in the hospice.

It's not unusual for me to realise I've been trying to find five minutes to nip to the loo for the last few hours and haven't found the chance. Our break room is filled with half-drunk coffee cups, the fridge with half-eaten lunches. We do what we can when we're needed, because that's what you do when you care for the terminally ill.

You don't clock out for lunch while someone breaks down in pain or fear or grief. When they just need to tell you their story. That's not how it works.

I grab a long overdue toilet break mid-shift, no longer able to ignore the baby kicking my bladder. I realise I've been so busy that I've not had time to think about anything but work. And that feels good.

But I'm still curious. I want to know where the note came from, if possible. I figure if anyone has information about the note, it'll be Lorraine, our all-seeing admin officer, so I wash my hands, straighten my uniform and walk to reception, where she holds court.

'A handwritten letter for you?' she asks, gazing over the top of her purple-rimmed glasses at me as she sits sorting through the day's mail. 'I put a couple of things in your pigeonhole yesterday, but no, I don't remember anything standing out from the norm.'

'No one hand-delivered it?'

'Not to my desk, no. There was some post in the box outside when I came in yesterday morning. It was probably among that.'

18

'Right,' I say, feeling disappointed that I've hit a dead end but wondering how many dead ends I need to hit before I accept there's nothing more sinister to find.

'Is it important?' Lorraine asks. 'Have you got the envelope there? Maybe if I saw it, it might trigger a memory.'

'No, no, it's not important. I'm just nosy,' I lie.

'Well, I hope it was something nice for you. A thank-you card or something.'

'Something like that,' I say and smile before excusing myself to get back to work.

Rachel is on shift, too, and we find ourselves together at lunchtime, with her eating my sandwiches while I make a piece of toast. It's an improvement on some dry biscuits anyway.

'I have to say, Eli, these sandwiches aren't up to Martin's usual standards. You must have words,' she jokes.

'Well, that's because I made those. Martin's away for a few days with work.'

'Again?' she asks, eyebrows raised for just a moment before she readjusts her expression. 'I suppose the project will be nearly done now. Best he gets away before this baby comes, I guess.'

'Yes, some last-minute glitches,' I say, the toast losing its appeal.

We fall into an uncomfortable silence.

'I didn't mean anything,' she says. 'With the "again". Me and my big mouth – you know what I'm like.'

'No, it's fine,' I say. 'He's been away a lot.'

I know Rachel isn't trying to be insensitive. I know she's still sore from the break-up of her own marriage, which ended after her husband had an affair. Or, to be more accurate, numerous affairs.

I change the subject. I don't feel comfortable falling down this particular rabbit hole with her.

'I have to nip out to pick up my car from the garage,' I tell her.

19

'Let me run you there in my car,' she offers. 'I'll pick us up something nice for afternoon break.'

I notice the sandwich I made has barely been touched. It would be churlish of me to refuse her offer of a lift, so I smile and thank her, and we grab our things and climb into her car.

'Excuse the mess,' she says as she throws an empty McDonald's paper into the back seat, which is strewn with empty drinks bottles, a dog lead and a pair of rather smelly football boots.

'It's no messier than it was last night, don't be worrying,' I tell her.

'At least last night the darkness hid the worst of it,' she laughs.

As we drive to the garage, I know I'm too quiet. My head's full of words, but I don't know how to say them without sounding like I'm a paranoid wreck. I hate this feeling. Normally, conversation flows really easily between Rachel and me, and we can share each other's worries and concerns.

'He loves you very much, you know,' Rachel says as we drive over the Foyle Bridge towards the garage. 'That's what's on your mind, isn't it? That stupid note. But you really shouldn't worry. I don't think I've ever seen a more devoted husband. I'm sorry if I spoke out of turn yesterday. He's one of the good guys.'

And he is. Without doubt. I remind myself not to make problems where none exist.

★

At 3.43 p.m., we watch a sixty-three-year-old man hold his fifty-nine-year-old wife's hand as her chest stills. The rattle that's come with each breath for the last twelve hours slows then stops, and the grip she's held on his hand releases. I watch a man, still alive in every physical way that matters, die a little in front of me as he kisses his wife of thirty years on her lips before they have the chance to turn cold.

Then, very tenderly, Rachel and I do what we need to with

his wife who we've cared for over the course of the last week. We remove the tubes and wires. We tidy the bed sheets around her. We open the window, an old hospice tradition, believed to let the spirit of the deceased move on. Then we stand back and let her family begin their grieving process.

'Some are tougher than others,' Rachel says as we leave.

'Yes,' I reply. I can't bring myself to say more. I'm afraid I won't be able to keep it together.

'Almost home time,' she says.

'And we get to do it all again tomorrow,' I respond, too worn out to say anything else.

CHAPTER FOUR

Louise

I'd told myself if I saw her again before the end of the week, it'd be a sign from God that I was right. This baby was the one I'd been waiting for.

I'd been on edge since I first saw her. Always looking at the door of the café, watching every person come in, feeling frustrated when it'd been someone else.

But then, I was in the supermarket, half-heartedly throwing a sad selection of meals for one, to be washed down with a bottle of wine, into my basket, when I saw her hovering around the fresh fruit aisle.

She looked more tired than before. The dark circles under her eyes only highlighted her pallor. She probably needed iron, I thought. She had apples and grapes in her basket, but really she should've been stocking up on leafy greens, red meat. That kind of thing. I was tempted to talk to her, but what would I have said?

What would it have looked like? A mad woman in the supermarket telling her that she needs more iron in her diet.

I followed her from a distance. Watched as she put some fresh bread into her basket. Wholemeal. That was good at least.

As was the fresh orange juice she chose. It was good to see she could make some decent choices for her baby. The chocolate biscuits, the tinned soup — neither of those were particularly nutritious. Not for an expectant mother. I shook my head.

Her baby needed to be well. I needed this baby to be well.

I wasn't one of those crazies who thought a woman became nothing more than an incubator when she fell pregnant, but the baby always had to come first. Anything else was selfish. A mother shouldn't just eat what she wanted, do what she wanted without considering the life she was growing inside her.

Every baby deserved the best start in life.

That's how it had been with me. Not that it mattered in the end.

Maybe I knew nothing. Maybe this woman with her tinned soup and her packet of biscuits knew more than I did. It wouldn't matter in a few months' time anyway. I'd be able to feed my baby all the healthy food they needed.

CHAPTER FIVE

Eli

My mother's car is parked outside my house. I smile when I see it, even though I know she'll probably drive me mad within an hour of being in her company.

As I pick up the couple of bags of shopping I'd left on the passenger seat, I watch the rain bounce off the ground outside, remembering how my mother told me that the splashes of water were actually fairies dancing. I believed her for so long. If I'm honest, I think a part of me still believes her now, or chooses to at least. I rub my tummy. I'll tell my baby that story. Create a bit of magic for them just as my mother had for me. Even when we didn't have much, we'd always had some magic.

I'm still watching the fairies dance and jump, when I see the door to my house open and the porch light switch on. My mother stands there, pulling her cardigan tightly around her as she looks out through the rain. She blinks, looks at me and waves, and I wave back.

Suddenly, I'm the overexcited primary school pupil seeing her mother arrive in the playground at the end of a long day of colouring in and learning to write my letters. I just want a hug from her, so I open the car door and trample through the dancing fairies into my mother's now open arms, still holding the shopping bags.

'Sweetheart, I was so worried. Where've you been? I was expecting you home an hour ago.' The genuine concern in her voice warms my heart.

'I just called into town to pick up a few things. I've not had time to do a big shop so our cupboards are bare. It's just some basics.'

She ushers me in through the door and takes the bags from me. Sitting them on the floor, she helps me out of my coat.

'There was no need. I'm sure you're wrecked after your day at work and the last thing you needed to be doing was running round the shops. Besides, you should know by now that I always come prepared.'

The smell of her special chicken soup hits me and I'm shocked to feel hungry.

'Is that your soup? Oh! Mum, it smells delicious. I got some lovely fresh bread that'll go down a treat with it.'

'We make a great pair,' she says. 'Of course, if you moved back to Belfast we could make a great pair all the time.'

'Mum,' I say, teasing. 'Enough. You know we're settled here. Martin's practice is here. My job is here. Our lovely home is here. Martin's family is here. You could always move down, though.'

She bristles. This is a discussion we've had before.

'You know I have my own life in Belfast,' she says. 'I'm too old to start again somewhere new. You and Martin, though, you're young things who could make a go of things anywhere.'

'Shall we stop this conversation before it gets heated?' I ask. 'And can we also get me some of that soup? I'm hungry.'

'I knew my soup would tempt you,' she says, beaming. 'When you were a little girl, chicken soup always brought you round when you were feeling poorly. You could be looked after like this all the time if—'

'Mum!' I fire a warning shot and she shrugs her shoulders. Tells me she was 'just saying' before taking two bowls from the cupboard and ladling the soup into them.

I slice the bread, bring it and butter to the dining table. Sitting down, I look out through the bifold doors at the darkness of the lake. The rain is battering the glass, raindrops chasing raindrops down the windows. It's going to be a rough night. I catch my reflection against the blackness. Mum's right, I do look worn out.

She carries the soup over on a tray along with two glasses of water and when she sits down, she looks me straight in the eyes.

'So, maybe you can tell me all about what's making you so stressed.'

'I'm not stressed,' I lie.

'Eliana Johnston, I know you better than I know myself. You called me and asked me to come down a day early. Now I know you love me dearly, but you never ask me to come down early unless something's nipping at you.'

'Hughes,' I correct her, 'my name is Eliana Hughes now.' I take a spoonful of soup, blow on it gently before bringing the spoon to my mouth. It's delicious. I try to distract my mother by telling her how lovely it is.

'I know it's lovely,' she says with a smile, 'just as you know you will always be Eliana Johnston to me. But that's not what we're talking about just now, is it?'

'Just now I want to eat my soup, Mum. I'm too tired to think straight, you know?'

'Okay,' she says, but I feel her eyes on me as I eat.

She fusses around after, making sure I'm comfortable and relaxed. Only when I'm curled under a throw on the sofa in front of the blazing fire does she ask me again what's wrong.

'You know you can tell me anything,' she says, her blue eyes wide.

My mother has the most beautiful blue eyes in the world, bright aquamarine. So vibrant. I'm incredibly jealous I haven't inherited them and secretly hope my baby will.

I nod, but I feel a little silly and more than a little embarrassed. How can I tell her that her very-much-in-control daughter is struggling with pregnancy and worried the life she loves is about to disappear from under her feet?

'Everything with the baby okay?'

The baby – always her first thought. I feel a pang of irrational something. Jealousy maybe. Whatever it is it's followed immediately by guilt at having a negative feeling towards my own child.

'The baby's fine. Kicking and wriggling as normal. Still making me sick, so I'm pretty sure my hormones are still doing exactly what they should.'

'You'd tell me, wouldn't you? If you were concerned for the baby at all.'

'Of course, Mum,' I say.

And I mean it. My concern isn't so much for the baby but more about how I'll cope as a mother. Especially if I end up on my own. We're not all like my mother. We don't all thrive on our own.

'Have you told Martin yet that you know the baby is a girl?'

I blush. I'm not at all comfortable with the fact that I know the sex of our baby and he doesn't. But he wants it to be a surprise. I did too, until I started to feel so terribly ill and so worried that it'd affect how I bonded with her. So I'd figured that if I knew, it'd make her more real to me. That it might help.

I'm not in the habit of keeping things from my husband.

Or I hadn't been, but things had been different recently. I suppose I've been trying to justify it to myself, telling myself it doesn't really matter. It'll still be a surprise for him when she's born, but I know that I've broken his trust. Maybe that's part of the reason I'm even entertaining the notion he could be breaking mine, too. I know first-hand how easy it is to lie by omission, to hide what I know. I've even hidden a set of three pink onesies in a drawer upstairs.

'No, Mum, and I don't think I will. We're close now anyway. I don't think it'd do any good to anyone to cause upset now.'

'Well, I can't wait until it's all out in the open. Then I can go legitimately mad in the shops and buy up all the pink in the world.'

'You don't have to go mad in the shops, Mum,' I said. 'You keep your money for yourself.'

'Nonsense! I know I don't have to spend my money on the baby, but I want to, and more than that, I'm going to. I've been saving up.'

'Mum, you need your money. Save it up if you want but keep it for yourself. This baby'll be fine. I promise.'

'I've worked hard all my life, Eli, and if I want to spend my money on my grandchild, I will. And that's the end of it. Sure, what else would I spend my money on? This is something happy! My first grandchild.'

'And probably your last,' I say with a grimace. 'I can't imagine ever going through this again.'

'Everyone feels like that during your stage of pregnancy,' my mother soothes. 'You don't know how you'll feel after the birth, but I can tell you that even if you only have the one child, she'll be more than enough.'

'Did you always feel that way, Mum? Always feel I was enough?' I ask.

She tilts her head to one side and those sparkling blue eyes look at me again. 'From the moment I first held you, my darling, I knew that I'd never need or want anyone else in my life but you. If life had given me more children I'd have loved them too, of course I would. But I never felt anything but complete with you in my life.'

It's too much emotion for pregnant me. I feel my chest tighten and I hug her. 'I love you, Mum,' I whisper into the soft curls of her hair on her cheek, the familiar smell of her Chanel No. 5 perfume comforting me.

'You'll be a great mother, Eliana. Don't doubt yourself. Not even for a second. And I'll be here for you, whenever you need me.'

'I know,' I whisper.

'And you can tell me anything.'

'I know that, too,' I say.

'Like if there was any reason you asked me to come down a day earlier than planned.' She raises one eyebrow.

She's not one to give up easily.

'I told you, Mum, it's nothing. Martin was just going away for work and, well, it's getting closer to the baby coming and all . . .'

'If you're sure that's all?' she asks.

I nod. Thinking that yes, it is indeed easy to lie or just not tell the whole truth. Much too easy.

CHAPTER SIX

Eli

It's just after 9.30 p.m. when my mother, seeing how hard I've been trying to stifle my yawns, orders me off to bed. I don't argue. I'm bone tired but thankful that I'm also feeling soothed by my chat with Mum.

I plug my phone in to charge, rest it on the bedside table and climb under the covers. I'm just about to close my eyes, when it rings.

I see Martin's name on the screen and, suddenly, I desperately want to talk to him. I want to hear his voice. I even think, maybe, just maybe, my mother's right and I should tell him I know about the sex of the baby.

I don't have to tell him she's a girl. I can leave that surprise for him for the big day, but I shouldn't keep from him the fact that I know. Not when I know how much of a spin it's put me in to think he could be keeping something from me.

Answering the call, I do my best to sound jolly, to sound just like the Eli he fell in love with and not the grumpy wife he'd had words with last night.

'Hi, baby, how's your day been?' I say.

He sighs, or maybe it's a yawn. 'Long and busy, but I wanted to check in with you before I settle down for the night. I didn't like how we left things last night.'

'We were both tired, let's just file it under a "bad day" and let it go,' I say.

'How's everything?' he asks.

'It's fine, Martin. Mum came down early and made a big pot of her famous chicken soup. She insisted on doing the washing-up herself and packing me off to bed. I was just settling down. I'm in bed already.'

'I wish I was there with you,' he says softly.

Something in me, the part of me that needs this man always, tightens. I wish I could see his face, feel his breath on my face, his skin touching my skin.

'I wish you were here, too,' I tell him. 'I really do.'

'I'll be home in a few days,' he says. 'We can make up for it then. At least you've got your mother there for company while I'm gone.'

'That's true, but she's not as good at spooning me as you are,' I say.

'Well, I do make for a very good big spoon,' he says and I hear the longing in his voice.

It makes me feel loved. It makes me feel love for him. It makes wonder how I could ever doubt him.

He yawns and I know he's too tired to launch into any deep conversation, so I tell him I love him and promise to talk to him tomorrow. Maybe I'll tell him about the baby's gender then.

I also make a promise to myself to take the stupid note out of my bag in the morning and throw it in the bin where it belongs. And to leave it there this time.

CHAPTER SEVEN

Louise

It couldn't be that hard to follow someone, I figured. Especially at night-time when the roads are quieter. So I did. I walked behind her out of the supermarket. Left my basket abandoned in one of the aisles. Didn't pay. I'd make do with toast for dinner.

Fate smiled kindly on me. The woman had parked her car close to the supermarket exit and I got a full look at the make and model. I knew my own car was parked just two minutes away on the main road, and if I hurried I'd still be able to follow her.

I got to my car as quickly as I could and switched on the engine, cursing that the windows of the old rust bucket I'd the misfortune to drive were so badly steamed up. I stuck the blowers on full. I didn't have time to wait. I couldn't let her get out of my sight and away. I grabbed the old chamois leather I kept in the glovebox and wiped the inside of the windscreen furiously. Just as I looked up, I saw the flash of headlights from the car park exit. Her car emerged and turned left towards the Foyle Bridge.

I swore under my breath. My visibility was still shocking and

I was pointing in the wrong direction. I needed to do a U-turn, but with my rear windows still clouded over I couldn't see clearly enough to do it safely.

I could take a chance, I supposed. I wound down my window and stuck my head out, tried to gauge what else was on the road. She was getting away, so I slammed my car into first and turned the steering wheel. The road was clear and I could make a go for it.

But just as I moved off, the car juddered, stalling with a thud. And the road was no longer clear, and my engine wasn't catching when I turned the key in the ignition. Her rear lights were moving further and further into the distance, blurring with the rain and the condensation and actually, my tears, too.

I slammed my fist on the steering wheel in frustration, the horn blaring loudly.

Kneading my forehead with the heels of my hands, I tried to regain my composure. This was just a setback. This wasn't defeat. I'd still do this. Nothing of worth in this world was ever easily achieved. I reminded myself that I'd asked God to send me a sign and He had. He'd brought her to me and I had to keep faith that He would bring her, and her baby – my baby – to me again.

CHAPTER EIGHT

Eli

The screech of the security alarm wakes me. Did I hear glass breaking? My heart's thumping and I sit up in the darkness, afraid to turn on the light, trying to figure out what's happening as my body adjusts to the rude awakening. I can't think. The noise is too loud.

I put my hand to my stomach – a protective instinct, maybe. It's what a mother should do. Mother. I think of my mum. She's two doors away down the hall. Is she awake? Is she safe? I want to call out, but what if someone's near? An intruder. What if I'm drawing attention to us? My bedroom door's closed but not locked. Why would it be?

I curse the alarm. It's so loud I can't hear if anyone's approaching, climbing the stairs, rattling the door handles.

The security company will call, I remind myself. If I don't answer, they'll send the police. Or at least, I think that's what they'll do. I've never really checked; never felt like we'd really need the system. It was just one of those things.

I try to place the breaking glass – had it happened or had I dreamed it? It has to be real. The alarms only go off if there's a breach into the house.

Climbing out of bed, I lift my phone, switch it to silent mode, creep to the en suite and lock myself in, keeping the lights out. I'm shaking. Adrenaline, I tell myself. A hormone. Just like all the other hormones. It won't kill me. I'll be fine. I hope my mother is. I need her to be okay. I need her to be here with me. And God, I wish Martin were here, too. And where are the police? The call from the security firm? I glance at my phone. They'll call him first, I curse, if no one taps in the security code.

I think of how isolated I am. Here in this beautiful home, which is to all intents and purposes in the middle of nowhere. People don't just walk past. Most people don't even know this house exists, closeted away as it is by the surrounding trees. No one outside these four walls will hear the alarms. No one else'll come running to help us.

I search my phone, fat fingers mistyping as I try to see if I have a number for the security firm saved. I should just call the police. I can't think. The noise of the bloody alarm's starting to hurt my ears and my stomach's swirling, with both fear and pregnancy sickness. I realise that I'm going to throw up. I clamber to the toilet, try to be as quiet as I can.

My mother's still two rooms away. Or I hope she is. What if she's hurt? I grab a towel, wipe my mouth, try to orientate myself after the sickness has made me dizzy. My phone lights up with the sight of an incoming call notification from a private number and I answer, trying to keep my voice low, which is ridiculous given the screeching of the alarms.

A calm voice speaks, asks me for our password and asks if I'm safe.

'I've locked myself in the bathroom,' I whisper. 'I can't hear anything over the noise of the alarm. But I think, I think there was broken glass before. I think I heard a smash.'

'Okay. We've notified the police of a potential break-in.

We can deactivate the alarm if you wish,' the calm voice says.

'Yes, yes, do that,' I say, thinking it might give me a chance to think.

'Okay, Mrs Hughes. We'll do that. The police should be with you soon. If you're in a secure place, we'd recommend you stay there.'

'Okay,' I whisper, trying not to think about my mother. What must she be thinking? Is she scared?

The alarm falls silent. I can still hear buzzing in my ears. A rattle at the bathroom door makes me jump.

'Eli, it's me.' My mother's voice. I hear it and feel it at the same time.

Tears spring to my eyes. I reach for the door and unlock it, pulling her into a hug.

'Mum, you're okay. Thank God. The police are coming.'

She holds me. I allow myself to nestle against the soft fabric of her dressing gown.

'I'm fine,' she says, kissing the top of my head. 'Whoever it was ran away as quickly as they arrived. I was downstairs, couldn't sleep. Heard the crash — it was the glass beside the door. I ran from the kitchen, but they were driving off. I'm sorry I didn't get a look at the vehicle. I don't have my glasses on.'

I can feel her trembling and cold as I hug her.

'Oh, God, no, I'm glad you didn't get near them. And they didn't see you. Mum, you could've been hurt!'

'I didn't think,' she says. 'I just, well, I didn't know what to do. They threw something in. I didn't see what it was, but it looked like it was wrapped in paper.'

I stand up, start to walk towards the stairs.

'Don't you think we should wait? For the police. You don't know what it might be.'

I switch on the landing light and look down into the hall. My mother's right, of course, to be cautious. This is still Northern Ireland. Security alerts aren't a thing of the past. You never know why someone might target you.

But it doesn't look like a device of any sort. It's more rudimentary than that. Solid. I can see the rough edges of a rock, wrapped in what looks like paper. A brown elastic band wrapped around both.

'I think it's just a rock,' I call to her.

'But better to be safe,' she says.

She looks pale in the light. Shaken. She must have had such a fright.

I feel a chill run up my spine. This could've been worse. If they'd seen her, would they have hurt her, or did they see her and that scared them away? I walk down the stairs, get closer to the rock. No signs of wires or tubing. I know I should leave it for the police but I'm curious. I can't understand why anyone would do this.

'Wait there,' I call to my mother.

I open the door of the hall cupboard, dig into a bag filled with other plastic carrier bags and pull two out. Wrapping them around my hands, I walk back to where the rock lies.

'Eliana, you're not going to lift that, are you?' My mother looks horrified.

'It's just a rock. I'll be careful. Look, I'm covering my hands, making sure I don't disturb evidence.'

I can't believe I'm even having this conversation. Evidence? When did my life become an episode of *CSI*? I chide myself for being too flippant. I carefully lift the rock, pull the elastic from it and unwrap the paper. I turn it towards me and staring back at me, I see the same neatly printed writing that I saw on the note in the bottom of my bag.

My stomach drops. I feel my legs start to shake. I can't ignore this. I can't see this as anything more than what it is. A threat. A revelation. An accusation.

SO MUCH TO DO IN LONDON AT THIS TIME
   OF YEAR
ROMANTIC WALKS, PERHAPS?
A DATE AT THE THEATRE?
IF I WERE YOU, I'D WATCH MY HUSBAND
   MORE CLOSELY . . .

I drop the rock. I hear my mother's voice somewhere in the distance just as I hear the siren of an approaching police car.

CHAPTER NINE

Eli

A polite female police officer has made two cups of sweet tea. Mum's sipping gingerly at hers, the rattling of the cup on the saucer showing that she's still on edge. I've put my cup down. I only had to glance at it to know there's no way I'd be able to drink it. My stomach is swirling, my head now sore, adrenaline coursing through my veins. I want to ring Martin. Now. Ask him. Now. Accuse him?

I excuse myself and stand up. I walk to the sink and fill a glass with water so I can wash down one of my anti-sickness pills. Not that I think it'll make any difference just now.

The police officer, Debbie, or Denise, or Dotty or something – I hadn't quite caught it – eyes me sympathetically.

'Sickness tablet,' I tell her. 'It's hyperemesis – morning sickness that doesn't want to go away, essentially. These help.'

'That must be tough,' she says.

'It is. But I'm told it'll be worth it.'

That, of course, was before someone had pointed the finger directly at my husband, telling me he isn't to be trusted. Romantic walks? Theatre dates? Sex? Intimacy? Love? My stomach turns again and I close my eyes, breathe deeply, try to quell the sickness. She must think me such a fool.

'How far gone are you?' she asks.

'Thirty-two weeks. Almost there.'

'Babies have a great way of bringing people together,' she says, and I wonder, is it true? Especially if people don't want to be together to start with. Or at least one of them doesn't appear to.

I shrug my shoulders, walk back to the sofa, where I sit beside my mother. Dotty or Daisy – actually, I think it was Deirdre – sits across from me. Adopts an 'I'm listening' face while her colleague, tall, cropped red hair, eyes bleary with tiredness, continues to make notes.

'So you can't think of who might have done this?' he asks.

William. His name is William. I remember that.

I shake my head.

'Who on earth would want to frighten Eliana?' my mother asks. 'She's a nurse in the hospice, for the love of God. *And* she's pregnant.'

'And your husband's in London, like the note says?'

My face blazes with embarrassment or shame, I can't decide. My name is Eliana and I can't keep my man. I feel my wedding ring pinch at my finger. It's started to get too tight, but that doesn't mean I want to take it off.

'We'll have to talk to him, of course,' William says.

'Of course,' I nod.

'And when is he due back from London?'

'Tuesday,' I reply. 'He's working there.'

William nods, as does Deirdre. I wonder what else they've dealt with tonight. Do they think I'm just some crazy woman with a cheating husband? A waste of police resources.

'If you give me his number, I'll give him a call. Ask a few questions.'

'Of course,' I tell her. 'I imagine he'll be worried. The security company will probably have called him first.'

I rhyme his number off. It's one of only two mobile numbers I remember by heart – his and mine. Deirdre writes it down, stands up, takes her phone from her pocket and taps in the number. She walks out of earshot just after I hear him answer. I'm tempted to follow her . . . I want to hear his reaction. His *first* reaction.

William speaks again. 'We'll investigate all angles,' he says. 'We'll get SOCO out as early as possible in the morning to examine the scene.'

'Can they not come now?' my mother asks, a hint of impatience.

He shakes his head. 'Afraid not. It's more useful if they come when the light's better. They can get a good look at any unusual tyre tracks or the like. We'd ask you not to disturb anything before they get here.'

I feel embarrassed again. I've already lifted the rock, read the note. I did cover my hands, but I probably should've left it where it was.

'It's possible Mr Hughes'll be able to shed some light on everything,' William says, nodding in the direction of his colleague.

'Well, it was hardly him, he's out of the country. I told you that,' my mother fusses.

I say nothing. I know exactly what this policeman isn't saying. This is a domestic. A wronged husband maybe, making sure that his hurt is shared by me, and by default Martin. I think of the note in my bag. The note that just hours ago I was convinced I was going to bin.

'There's something else I need to show you,' I tell him.

I can see my mother's eyes widen. I blush again as I get

up and go to fetch my bag from the hall. She'll be annoyed that I didn't tell her about it when it happened. But it was so vague and I didn't want to believe it. I still don't want to believe it.

It's a bit more crumpled, but it's still there. I pull it out, straighten it and hand it to William. He pauses to put on latex gloves before taking it from me. I suppose it's evidence now. I really must ask his full name again. His rank.

'Sorry, my head's all over the place. Can you tell me your name again?'

'Constable William Dawson,' he replies, not looking up from the note. 'And where did this come from?'

'What is it?' my mother asks impatiently.

'It was delivered to my work. No postmark, so I think hand-delivered. No one saw who left it; I asked our admin officer.'

'And when was this?'

I try to think . . . two days ago, wasn't it?

'The day before yesterday.'

I'm aware of my mother's sharp intake of breath beside me.

'And what actually is it, Eliana?' she says.

I notice William, Constable Dawson, look up at her. Her motherly tone is fierce when in full flow.

'A note, Mum,' I say.

'Well clearly,' she says. 'But what does it say?'

Dawson holds it out in her direction. 'Can you make sure not to touch it? We'll be taking this with us for forensic analysis.'

She nods, and leans towards the note. Her eyes widen and I see her hand go to her chest, to finger the gold crucifix she always wears. I watch as she inhales and turns to me, puts her hand on my knee.

'This doesn't mean anything, Eli. None of this. You're not to be annoying yourself about it.'

I almost laugh. She's trying to tell me this is nothing while we sit in a house that's been broken into, talking to two police officers.

'This puts a different slant on things,' Dawson says. 'Multiple letters.'

'Two is hardly multiple,' I hear my mother interject.

I ignore her, nod to Dawson.

'I don't understand why anyone would do this,' I say.

'Sheer malice,' my mother says. 'Some people have so little to bother them that they put a pregnant woman through this ordeal.'

'We'll see what we can find out. Check for any CCTV close by, see if we can pick up the car on it. There are a number of avenues we can look at,' Dawson says, his expression sympathetic.

Deirdre walks back in. 'I've spoken to your husband. He's obviously concerned about you.'

'I'll call him soon,' I say, thinking there are one or two questions I need to ask him myself.

She looks at her colleague. 'Mr Hughes says he can't think of anyone who may hold a grudge and says there is no truth at all to the allegations in the note. I've asked him to come and see us on Tuesday when he arrives home.'

'There's a second note,' Dawson says. 'Similar kind of thing. I'll just bag it here for evidence.' He takes a small plastic bag from his pocket and slips the note in, sealing it afterwards and handing it Deirdre. She reads it through the clear plastic and looks back at me, sympathy written all over her face. I imagine she thinks I'm deluded too.

'That's your crime reference number. You'll need that when

you contact your insurance company. My number's there, but obviously I'm on night shifts at the moment, so you won't be able to reach me during the day. I'll get a colleague to call you in the morning, or they might come out with SOCO,' Dawson says.

I nod.

'It's entirely up to you if you want to stay here tonight,' he said. 'But obviously we'd advise you to make sure the property's as secure as possible.'

I glance down at my swollen stomach and to my mother, who looks stunned by everything. I wonder how exactly we're supposed to 'secure the property'.

'Maybe we should go to a hotel,' I say to my mother.

'And leave the house open to anyone?' she says. 'No, Eliana. We'll stay here and we'll not let whoever this spiteful creature is win.'

'We can help secure the property for you,' Dawson says. 'It'll be a bit of a make-shift job but it will do until morning?'

'That would be great,' my mother says.

'Good, if you have some bin bags or an old sheet, and some masking tape or something similar?' he asks. My mother nods and sets about gathering what he has asked for. It all still seems very surreal to me.

'If you can think of anything at all that might help, or of anyone who we should talk to, please don't hesitate to call. I'm very sorry you've had this upset,' he says, as he waits. 'And it probably goes without saying that if you receive any more notes from this person, or if you feel in danger at all, that you contact us immediately. Use 999 if necessary, we'll have this address flagged with first responders so that any call from here will be prioritised.'

I nod. By this stage I'm exhausted. I just want them to go. I want to sit down. Close my eyes. Pretend none of this is happening. I want to speak to Martin, but what do I say? Do I ask him outright if he's having an affair? Do I go in all guns blazing? Do I start packing his bags, throw them out into the drive to languish in the rain until he returns? Do I leave? Do I stay and believe him and live in fear of the next note, or the next rock through a window, or the next whatever? Martin, my Martin – romantic walks. Dates. With someone else. I want to scream. This must be what it feels like to have the rug pulled out from under you.

My mother arrives back with a roll of bin bags, some masking tape and a dustpan and brush to lift the broken glass. I offer to help, but both police officers insist that my mother and I sit down. They can manage. I can only imagine they feel sorry for us – this heavily pregnant woman whose husband might be cheating, and this older lady wandering about in her nightie and dressing gown.

I'm relieved when they finally finish their task and leave, sympathetic smiles on their faces, and I finally give in to the tears that have been threatening for the last hour.

'Eliana, why on earth did you not tell me about this note?' Mum's voice cuts through my thoughts, jolts me into the now. 'I knew there was something you weren't telling me – some reason you'd asked me to come down early.'

'There wasn't really anything to tell,' I say. 'I didn't know it was about Martin. I didn't think it *could* be about Martin. Oh! Mum, what am I going to do?'

'You're going to talk to him. You're going to ask him to come home and you're going to talk about this face-to-face.'

I nod. I start to cry and she's beside me, hugging me.

'Wait until you talk to him, Eli,' she soothes. 'He's a good man. Now, how about we try to get some sleep? This will all seem less insurmountable in the morning. Go to bed, darling. Call Martin just to let him hear your voice and just for you to hear his, but then tell him you need him home. You need to talk. I'm sure he'll come.'

'But his work . . .' I say, even though at this moment I don't care about his work.

'His work will still be there the day after tomorrow,' she says and kisses my head. 'Now, young lady,' she adds softly, 'go to bed.'

CHAPTER TEN

Louise

The next time I saw her she looked like a ghost. Her skin was so pale. Her hair lank. I was sure she'd lost weight. She didn't seem to want to eat. She wasn't even making an effort with the cup of tea in front of her.

I remember that feeling. After.

I felt as if I were see-through. As if I were floating and no one else could see me. Because if they did, they wouldn't have laughed and joked with each other. They wouldn't have huddled together to gossip. They wouldn't have smiled at me and wished me good morning.

That man? Well, he wouldn't have said 'Cheer up, love. It might never happen.'

I wasn't one for violence, but I relished the feeling of the bare skin of my palm as it struck his face, the bristles of his beard stinging. The look of shock in his eyes. I'll remember that, just as I'm sure he'll remember the look of anger in mine.

'What would you know?' I asked him before walking off.

He could've come after me, of course. He could've hit me back. He could've called the police. To be completely honest, I didn't care. Nothing was right or fair in the world any more and I didn't give a damn about whether or not I hurt other people.

They didn't care that I was hurting.

That woman, sitting with her moping face over the cup of weak tea she had yet to touch, didn't care that I was hurting. She wouldn't want to think about what had happened to me. Even if I sat down opposite her and opened my heart to her, she would've backed away. She would've covered her ears.

I wanted to scream at her. I wanted to ask her, why wasn't she happy? Why didn't she understand how lucky she was? She was going to be a mother. I wonder, has she ever considered what it would've been like to have been told that was something she'd never be?

'Everything okay for you?' I asked instead with false smile.

She looked at me and offered me a weak smile back. 'Yes, thank you.' Her eyes were drawn back to the tea. I wondered what she saw reflected in it that made it so interesting.

'Is this your first?' I asked.

She blinked back at me. I nodded towards her stomach.

'Yes. My first.'

'Can be a wee bit scary, can't it?' I asked, hoping she'd engage. Open up a bit.

'I suppose,' she answered, her eyes darting back to the magic teacup in front of her once more. Clearly, she wasn't the chatty type.

I wished her well but stayed close by. Cleaning the tables around her even though they were already clean. I made a mental note of her shopping, her handbag, the keys sitting at the top of it – anything that would help me to find out more about her.

I could hardly believe my luck when I heard a voice call to her. A man, tall, handsome. Her husband, maybe. He was as handsome as I'd hoped he'd be. Well dressed. Groomed. A hint of a tan. Healthy. A good genetic gene pool. He looked tired but he wore it well.

'Here you are,' I heard him say. 'I was worried.'

I watched as he moved towards her, hugged her. I noted she didn't hug him back. Just leaned her head in his direction.

I stayed close and Lady Luck rewarded me a second time. Her full name. He used her full name. A jokey comment about her giving him a heart attack. She addressed him by name in return – a jokey exchange despite how tired they both looked. I made a mental note of both and moved on to clean the other tables.

I knew who she was then. I knew who he was. It was all coming together perfectly.

More signs. More prayers being answered.

I knew this was His way of telling me I was on the right track. That if I just kept my faith in God, I'd get what I wanted. As the Bible promised, if I asked, I'd receive.

CHAPTER ELEVEN

Eli

I press the call button and wait for him to answer. It doesn't take long. He sounds concerned, or is it guilty? I want to scream at him. I wish he was here so I could do just that.

'You have to know I have nothing to do with any of this,' he says. 'I've no idea what that note is about. I swear, Eli, I'm not cheating. I've never cheated. You know that. This is someone trying to mess with us.'

I'm almost too tired to speak. 'Martin, I think we need to talk about it. I think you need to come home. Please, come home.'

He doesn't hesitate. 'I'll book flights as soon as we're done talking. Get back as soon as I can. I swear, Eli, you *have* to believe me.'

I imagine he wants me to say that I do believe him. That's it's all laughable that my husband would ever cheat, and any time before the last seven months I would probably have said so. But things are different now. I'm different.

'Look, I'm really tired. Just get home. We'll talk about it then.'

'Okay,' he says. He sounds subdued. Then again, he would be, if he'd been caught. 'I love you, Eliana,' he says.

I tell him I love him, too, and saying the words almost breaks me. Might I have to stop loving him? I can't even think of that.

★

'You're not seriously going to work today?' My mother fusses around me, trying to persuade me just to eat *something*. So far, I've refused a cooked breakfast, porridge and a croissant. She's now making some toast, which she's told me I must eat at least half a slice of, dry if necessary.

'Yes, Mum, I'm seriously going to work. I have to go to work. I don't work somewhere where they can just call in someone else at half an hour's notice.'

'But don't they have bank nurses they can call in?'

I shake my head. While of course they do, it'd be an increased cost to our already stretched budget and we've one patient at least on the ward who's unlikely to make it through the day. I've been caring for him since his admission ten days before and I don't want to cause a big upheaval for his family by suddenly adding someone new to the equation.

'I'll be fine. If it's quiet, I'll even grab an hour's rest in the on-call room. The other staff will look after me.'

I take a bite out of the slice of toast she hands me as if to make a point. The truth is, I desperately want to go back to bed and wake up to find Martin home so we can talk. He's texted to say he's secured a flight into Belfast shortly after lunch. He should be home before dinner. He emphasised his innocence. Told me he loved me. I'd replied with a 'See you then.' I couldn't bring myself to type more.

My mother doesn't look happy at my decision. Nor is she happy that Martin isn't already at our front door.

'Surely there's an earlier flight than lunchtime?' she says before apologising. 'Sorry, Eli, me getting cross won't help. I just worry about you. I worry about you both. This is very upsetting.'

She says it like it should be news to me, even though I'm painfully aware of just how upsetting it is.

'He'll be here soon enough,' I tell her. 'I'll be at work anyway.'

'I can't say I approve, but you always were a stubborn one, Eliana Johnston.'

'Hughes,' I remind her. 'Eliana Hughes.'

'You'll always be Eliana Johnston to me, my darling,' she says.

She tells me she'll stay, not go back to Belfast. She'll deal with the SOCO people. I tell her to call the hospice directly if the police need more information. I'll call back as soon as I get a minute.

'I'll call a glazier and get someone out to fix that window,' she says. 'It shouldn't be too expensive. You don't want to lose your good record with your insurance company.'

Ever practical, my mother. And good in a crisis – much better than I am, anyway.

My head is already thumping when I reach work. I'm rubbing my temples when Rachel walks into the nurses' station and sits down beside me.

'Tough night?' she asks.

'You've no idea. We had someone peg a rock through the window.'

Her eyes widen.

'Seriously? At your house? Jesus, Eli, are you okay?'

I know I can tell Rachel everything if I want to. All about the rock, and the note and what the note said. She'll be there for me. But for some reason I can't face it. Not today. Maybe it's just that I don't want her looking at me with her sad eyes and inwardly welcoming me to her ditched wives' club. Martin isn't like her ex. Martin and I aren't like they were.

So I nod. 'I am, apart from this headache. But I'll take a few paracetamol and get on with things. Can you give me fifteen minutes to pull myself together and I'll get stuck in? Mr Connors, is he still . . . ?'

'With us? Yes, but his resps are slowing. The family are here. I think we need to make sure we've a nurse near them at all times. I sense of a bit of tension between two of the sons.'

Losing a parent is always tough, and we're used to seeing emotions overspill, so I nod to Rachel. 'I'll keep a special eye.'

'That'd be good,' she says as I fish in my bag and pull out a packet of paracetamol. 'Eli,' she says as she makes to leave. 'Are you sure it's just a headache? I mean, with the stress and all? Do you want me to check your blood pressure? Have you any swelling in your feet or fingers?'

'Rachel, I love you but it's just a headache and I'm going to say this as nicely as I can. Can you stop fussing around me? I've had enough fuss for one day from my mother.'

I'm snappy and I can hear it in my voice. I don't like it.

Rachel looks put out. She mutters something about only wanting to help and says she'll leave me to it before turning on her heel and leaving. I swear under my breath and wish I'd started the whole day differently.

I fill a glass with water and take my tablets. Decide I need to get on with my work, where I'll probably watch someone else die. That'll be the least distressing part of my day.

CHAPTER TWELVE

Eli

Work always has the ability to take me away from everything. Even on days like today, when I'm existing after just a few hours' sleep and trying to wrap my head around the notion that my husband might be cheating on me.

And that someone out there seems intent on doing whatever it takes to let me know about it.

I'm too busy to allow it anything more than fleeting space in my head. I have other people to care for. People to keep comfortable. An emergency respite admission for a young woman who has stage four breast cancer and can't get any relief from her pain. Emotional support to offer to Mr Connor's family to keep them from hitting out at one another as their grief rages.

I know how to do this job well.

There's a comfort in that. There's stress involved, of course, but it's a good stress – an adrenaline buzz, but of the good kind.

There's a huge sense of achievement that comes with making sure someone suffers as little as possible in their last hours and moments. It's always sad, yes. Don't get me wrong. I have cried and will cry for many of our patients and for their families, but I feel proud that I can make a horrific experience less so.

So, although I'm dead on my feet and my head's still aching, I'm almost sorry when my shift ends. I'd happily have stayed on at work for another few hours if they'd let me, but Rachel is ushering me towards the door as soon as staff changeover is done.

'I'll be following you out of the door, so on you go. You're exhausted and I can't have you taking ill on my conscience. Try, if you can, to relax on your days off.'

I shrug and she gives me a sympathetic look. 'You know where I am if you need me. The kids are still with their dad, so I'm a free agent.'

'Well in that case, I'm sure you'll have much more you could be doing than being bothered with my worries,' I tell her.

'You're my friend, Eli. You and Martin both. I care about you.'

I feel bad for being snappy with her earlier, so I reach out for a hug. 'I don't know what I've done to deserve you, but thanks for listening.'

'You'd do the same for me in return,' she says before opening the door and giving me a gentle push outwards.

When I get into the car, I take my phone from my bag and see a series of messages from Martin, the last of which says his flight was delayed and is now due to land at Belfast just before six. He hopes to be able to make it home before 8.30 p.m. He's going to call into the police station on his way home and speak to Constable Dawson.

For a moment or two I wonder whether we can just forget it all. Brush it all under the carpet. Can I live with knowing what I know?

I'm afraid to ask him about the allegations. I'm afraid of the argument we'll have. If he continues to deny it, should I believe him? If he admits it, should I leave?

The thought hits me in the stomach with the force of the kick from my baby that follows. This is not how we planned it. This is not how it's meant to be.

I know I'll make it home before him by half an hour or so. I wonder whether to stop and pick up a takeaway on the way home, like I often do on a Saturday night. But this is hardly any normal Saturday night. I'm going home to ask him again, only this time directly, if he's having an affair. I need to see his face as he answers me. See if I can tell if he's lying.

I shake my head – I won't pick up a takeaway. I won't act as if everything's normal when it so clearly isn't. Everything feels sullied.

As I pull out of the hospice driveway and turn left towards the Foyle Bridge, I'm glad my mother's at home. I imagine Martin won't feel as glad, even though the pair of them have always got along well. He's been made aware of my mother's interrogation techniques from the stories I've regaled him with about my youth.

We'd rubbed along quite nicely together. I've never given her much trouble, not even as a teenager. But there were a few memorable occasions – some missing vodka from one of the bottles in her drinks' cabinet, to name one where she went full bad cop on me. I wondered, would she go full bad cop on Martin? Or would she play the good cop role while I lost control of my temper?

CHAPTER THIRTEEN

Eli

When I get home I find that my mother's cooked a full roast dinner with all the trimmings and she calls to me that it's almost ready as I walk into the house. The window by the door's been fixed. It's almost as if nothing has happened, but of course it has.

'Mum, I'll not be able to eat this, lovely and all as it is,' I say, trying not to make her feel rejected.

'Just eat what you can, pet,' she soothes. 'You're just skin and bone and that bump. I don't know how that baby can be getting everything she needs with you eating so little.'

'The baby's fine. The baby'll take whatever it needs from me, even if I don't eat much. It leeches it from my system like a little, well, leech, I suppose.'

I watch my mother shudder. 'That's a horrible way to think about your baby,' she scolds.

I don't think so. I'm pragmatic about these things. Logical. Perhaps it's my medical training. I look at things differently sometimes. In a detached fashion. The life inside me *is* a parasite of sorts, after all; not that I'd say that to my mother. She'd be apoplectic with rage at my use of such a word. Even if I qualified it by saying she was a very cute parasite. Even if I don't reveal just how scared I am that I don't feel that all-encompassing motherly love so many women talk about.

'You know I don't mean it in a bad way,' I say, smiling at her. 'Let me go and freshen up. I won't be long.'

Upstairs, I strip off my uniform and throw it in the laundry basket before having a quick shower. I still feel the need to look and feel more presentable for Martin.

I wonder if the police will have had any new information for him. Maybe I should've called myself and checked for updates. Asked if they were looking at any other leads. Mum's told me that the SOCO team were very nice and understanding but not particularly forthcoming with any information about where the investigation was.

I brush my wet hair out and look at it hanging limply around my face. I need a haircut, I know that. I look in the mirror at the tired eyes looking back at me. They've been tired since I became pregnant. I've become pale and uninteresting. Could I blame him for looking elsewhere?

I jump when I hear the front door open and close. Hear his voice, muffled, call out a hello and my mother answer, telling him that I'm upstairs and will be down soon.

I sit for a moment, almost too afraid to move. I'm scared to see him.

Martin's always told me that he knows me like no one else in the world knows me. I like to think I'm the same with him. I can read his facial expressions in seconds. I know the two-second pause that always happens when he's caught out on a lie. Although, admittedly, in the past it's been about trivial things, like spending too much money on some silly gadget we haven't discussed or when some of the Maltesers I keep hidden in the back of the cupboard went missing. It has never before, in the ten-year history of our relationship, been about anything of any great seriousness.

My hand goes to my stomach, instinctively, I suppose. It still shocks me to find a bump there. To feel another being inside me. I glance back into the mirror, start to give myself a little pep talk, and I'm just turning to leave the room, when I hear him bound up the stairs. He always comes up the stairs two at a time like an excited teenager. Even when tired, he still gallops up. Before I know it he's at the door, pushing the handle down and coming in, his face creased with concern.

'Eli . . .' he says as if he doesn't know what to say next. Which he probably doesn't. Life doesn't prepare you for conversations like this.

I see his face and a mixture of every emotion possible rushes through me. Love. Fear. Betrayal.

'You're here,' I state.

'I am,' he says, walking towards me.

I want to hug him. I want him to hold me, but I feel myself holding back.

He senses it. He looks wounded and I feel guilty, but I also feel torn. I shouldn't be feeling guilty. I should be the one feeling wounded.

If it's true.

'I need to ask you to your face and I need you to understand why I'm asking. Are you seeing someone else?' I blurt.

There's no pause. Not even a minute one. The wounded look is multiplied. He sags.

'You shouldn't need to ask me that,' he says.

'I know,' I say, tears pricking at my eyes. 'But I do need to. For me. Are you having an affair, Martin?'

He takes a step back. Or maybe I do. I'm not sure.

'Eli, I've told you, no. I've told you I never would. You

can't have believed it either, or you'd have mentioned that first note to me. It shouldn't have been down to the police to tell me.'

'It seemed so ridiculous at the time,' I tell him, feeling defensive.

'So what's changed, Eli?'

'Martin, someone threw a rock through our window in the middle of the night. They made specific allegations. They seem determined to make sure I know about it.'

He swears under his breath. 'This is bullshit,' he says.

I want so much to say 'I know' and to de-escalate this quickly. But I can't.

'I don't know what to believe,' I say.

'You should. You should know me, Eli. You should trust me and trust us.'

I think back to when Rachel split from Ryan. How he'd told her the same thing. How she'd said she believed him out of a sense of duty until the evidence was so undeniable neither he nor she could deny their marriage was in tatters. She was so angry at herself that she'd let him fool her. Am I letting Martin, and my desire for us to be okay, fool me now?

But Martin isn't Ryan. Martin's one of the good ones – always has been.

He looks so genuinely wounded that I feel my heart lurch. I want to believe him. It's easier to believe him. We're about to have a baby, but I can't ignore what's happened. I doubt the person behind the notes would let me, either.

'I want to believe you. I do . . . but . . . the rock through the window. Who does that, Martin? Who puts a rock through someone's window? Especially ours. In the middle of nowhere. They had to drive down here and go to all that effort to make sure I saw it. Why would anyone do that if there wasn't some truth in it?'

I'm sobbing now. Gulping down mouthfuls of air as my entire body aches with grief at it all.

'And it's not like things have been great between us, is it? Ever since this baby . . .'

'Don't start about the baby. We both wanted a baby, Eli. We tried so hard and so long to conceive this baby and yet, you seem unhappy. As if you regret it. This is our baby, Eli.'

I see tears well in his eyes, too. They look greener than ever. He looks so incredibly handsome in his anger and his grief, it makes it all harder.

'I don't regret it, but you don't understand, Martin. It's been hard. Being so sick all the time. You being away with work every five minutes. This isn't how it's meant to be. And I know, believe me, I know I've not been easy to live with, but that doesn't excuse you having an affair.'

'I've told you, I'm not seeing anyone else!' He's shouting now. Bellowing.

I'm aware of my mother's footsteps on the oak stairs.

'I don't know if I can believe you,' I say, and it's out there in a way that I can't take back. The trust between us dented.

'Don't you shout at my daughter.' My mother's voice cuts through. Steely. Ice-like. The voice she uses when it's clear she'll countenance no nonsense whatsoever. 'She's pregnant and exhausted and all this stress doesn't help.'

He blinks at her. He's not used to my mother telling him what to do.

'I didn't cheat on her, Angela,' he says. 'I don't know how to get that through to her. To you both.'

'You have to understand how this looks,' she says, her voice softer now. 'If it were reversed, wouldn't you feel vulnerable? You weren't here and what happened last night was terrifying.' She shudders.

He sags again. 'You've no idea how much I regret not being

here last night, regret that you both went through that. But I don't know how to prove that I'm telling the truth.' He turns to me. 'You can go through my things if you want, Eli. My phone, my computer, my bank statements and credit card statements. You can do whatever you need to reassure yourself that I'm telling the truth.'

For a moment I contemplate it, but it would just damage us more, wouldn't it? It would show a complete lack of faith in him and us. I shake my head wearily.

I can see the exhaustion on Martin's face, can feel what little energy I have left drain from my body. I sit on the edge of the bed and put my head in my hands. A wave of nausea washes over me.

A hand is on my knee. I'm aware of someone in front of me. I don't know if it's my mum or Martin. I don't know who I want it to be. I just want to get through the next minute without being sick.

'Eli.' His voice. Soft. Breaking. 'I wish I could explain all this to you. But all I can do is tell you, and tell you again and again and as many times as you need to hear it, that this is all some sick fabrication.'

'Are you okay, Eli?' My mother's voice cuts in.

I raise a hand to signal that I am, although of course I'm not. If I just have a little lie-down, maybe I'll feel better. I pull myself back on the bed, rest my head on the pillow.

'Just a moment,' I say, 'until the sickness passes.'

'Have you taken your tablet?' Martin asks.

I nod, my eyes closed. Concentrating on trying to feel well.

'She gets sick if she's stressed,' I hear him say to my mother.

'I know. None of this is good for her,' my mother says as if I'm not in the room.

In that second I wish she wasn't here. I wish that Martin

would lie down on the bed beside me and we could talk about what's really going on.

But maybe it's all gone beyond that now. Things have been said. I've admitted I doubt him. I've admitted I'm struggling with this pregnancy. It's all out of control.

CHAPTER FOURTEEN

Louise

Once I found my focus, it proved relatively easy to track them both down. That was the thing with living in that part of the world. Everyone knows everyone's business and while that had been a curse to me as everything was falling apart, I could see that, as I put everything back together again, it was also a blessing.

It wasn't hard to find out where they worked and, more importantly, where they lived. The leafy suburbs, of course. I should've known. They'd that look about them. Well-groomed, professional people. In a nice house, with loads of greenery nearby. Fields to run through. Streams to wade through. Trees to climb. I was sure they already had plans to build a tree house. I imagined they'd have a swing in that big garden. The perfect childhood awaited their perfect baby.

But money can't buy love. There was nothing to say that just because they had a nice house in a nice area they'd be good parents. I watched them, you see. I saw how early he went to work. How he came back late.

She worked long hours, too. And they weren't swamped with visitors. If I didn't take this baby, who'd end up watching her?

Would she just spend her days amusing herself on her state-of-the-art swing, with no one to push her? No one to feed her imagination. To have teddy bears' picnics in the tree house with.

The house looked too well kept for finger-painting and messy play. Their routine too regimented. I saw it all. I saw her bring home takeaway dinners. Children need fresh, home-prepared food. It didn't have to cost the earth. A lot of people make that mistake.

A child needs love and attention and to be nurtured and nourished. I had all the love in the world to give and so much more. Cruelty would've been leaving this baby with those people who'd never be home for her.

CHAPTER FIFTEEN

Eli

Although the heating is on full blast, the atmosphere downstairs is frosty.

My mother carries a plate of mashed potato and gravy to the dining table, which she's served for me, then she nods to Martin that he can help himself. She looks at me as he retreats to plate up his dinner and tilts her head to one side – international sign language for 'Are you okay?' I nod, shrug my shoulders and look at the food in front of me. I still don't feel like eating.

'Are you not eating, Mum?' I ask as I sit down.

'I'll eat later,' she says. 'I think the stress of the last twenty-four hours is catching up with me. I feel done in.'

She does look tired. Pale even. She's not elderly. She's only sixty-two, but at times her vulnerability shows. I realise it's been exceptionally selfish of me to leave her here all day to deal with SOCO and the glaziers on her own, even if she insisted she was more than okay to do so.

'Oh, Mum, you've gone to all this effort.'

'I can have some tomorrow for sure,' she says. 'Look, I'm going to take a cup of tea up to bed with me, if that's okay. Give you young ones space to talk.'

'You don't have to go on our account,' Martin says. 'Look, Angela, I'm so sorry you've been caught up in all this. And I understand that your loyalty 100 per cent has to be to Eli, but I promised you a long time ago that I'd never hurt her and you have to believe me when I say that's still true. I've decided I won't go away again. Not while this is happening. Someone else can take over at work for a bit.'

I'm taken aback. This project is his. He won the bid, worked on it from the ground up. It's nearly there and I know he wants to see it through to completion.

'I'll do whatever it takes to prove I'm all in,' he says.

My mother nods, pulls her cardigan a little tighter around her.

'This is between you two,' she says. 'I like to think I'm a good judge of character, Martin, and I'd very much like to believe you're telling both of us the truth. Eli deserves only good things, and so does this baby. I know you young ones face different pressures these days, but the key is to keep working at it.'

'We will,' he says earnestly. 'And I'll be on to the police again and again until they find out who's responsible. I won't go away until all this is sorted. I won't leave her vulnerable here alone again.'

She gives him one of her smiles. It's a start.

CHAPTER SIXTEEN

Eli

Sunday brunch is usually a relaxed affair, but there's an awkward silence as we sit around the table picking at the food Martin's made for us. We're all being perfectly polite to each other, but it feels scripted.

We're all wounded and tired.

I sit peeling flaky pastry from a croissant I'm not going to eat while my mother nibbles at a piece of toast. Martin's doing his best to tuck into his eggs and bacon, but everything feels off.

'I've been thinking.' My mother speaks and both Martin and I look at her. 'Somebody somewhere is probably just jealous and trying to throw a spanner in the works. I think you have to trust in each other to put this right.'

Martin and I glance at each other.

'Trust in each other,' she says. 'Listen to each other.'

She smiles and we smile back, tight, forced. It'll take more than words to fix this.

'I was thinking I might head back to Belfast today,' she says. 'Since Martin's here. I'd say you two need your time alone. You certainly don't need an old dear like me getting under your feet.'

68

'Don't feel you have to go,' Martin says, but I know he's already mentally packing her bags.

'I don't feel I have to, but I think it would be right to.'

I don't know how I feel about that. It's been nice to have her here – even if my entire world has been spinning out of control these last few days. I chide myself. I'm a grown woman, for the love of God. I shouldn't be so pathetic. I force a smile onto my face.

'Well, I suppose you want to get back to your evening classes and all and your work.'

'Well, work is a good bit quieter these days. The need for me isn't what it was before all those stupid accounting computer programmes,' she says, 'but I do have some stuff to catch up on. That said, Eli, you know that I'm here for you whenever you need me. And you too, Martin.' That last bit sounds less convincing.

If the truth be told, I could do with them both being out of my hair to give me space to think about everything, but then again, I don't want to be alone. I feel even more vulnerable now, in this house where people can break windows. I've never felt unsafe here before. I've thrived on the seclusion of our home, felt we were untouchable in many ways. Maybe I'm being punished by the karma gods for being smug.

Everything, except for work, is developing rough edges and I want to find and hit a pause button. I put the croissant, still untouched, back on my plate and get up. I need a little air, so I walk out onto our decking. The coldness of the morning forces an intake of breath and I pull my cardigan tightly around myself, over my bump, then cross my arms and walk across the deck to the edge of the lake.

It's a crisp morning. There's a glint of frost where the dew would normally twinkle. There's something almost magical-looking about it. This dream house in a dream location. I let the cool air fill my lungs again and again until I feel two strong hands on my shoulders, the comfort of Martin's presence behind me. I lean back into him.

'What do you need me to do, Eli?' he asks. 'To fix this. Just tell me.'

'If I knew who was behind these notes, I'd feel better. It's the not knowing.'

'I've been racking my brains but I can't think of anyone who'd take against either of us. There are no aggrieved clients in my past as far as I know and you, well . . . it goes without saying, who could be angry enough at you to do something like this? It doesn't make sense. I'm at a loss.'

He pulls me tighter. Kisses the top of my head. I try to react as I normally would, enjoy the intimacy, but something is cracked between us.

'Look, I need to call Jim. Tell him to take over the London job going forwards. He's expecting me back tonight, so I need to warn him to gen up for the presentation. Send him my notes, that kind of thing.'

I feel guilty. And worried. This is his pet project and my distrust is keeping him from seeing it through to the end. Am I being incredibly selfish? Will he end up resenting me over this? It could fracture things between us further. If I let him go, will he believe that I want to trust him, after all? Will it help to fix things between us? I've always been a peacemaker. A people-pleaser. I'll tie myself up into tiny knots so as not to offend anyone.

'Go to London,' I say, my voice not more than a whisper.

'What?'

'Go to London. See this project through. I'll ask Mum to stay.'

'Eli, no. I don't want you here alone until we know who's behind this.'

'I won't be here alone. Mum'll be here.'

'And those notes, you do believe me, don't you? If you need me to stay and work through this with you, I will.'

His green eyes are set on me. I hear his words but I know where his heart lies at the moment.

So I tie myself up into another little knot and I lie. I tell him I believe him. I tell him there will be time to work through it all properly when he gets back.

'I swear, Eli. I swear on my life. I swear on our baby's life, you've no reason not to trust me,' he says.

'Then go,' I say.

A part of me is hoping he says no. Hopes that he'll stay anyway. That part of me is soon disappointed. He kisses the top of my head again, tells me he loves me and darts off across the decking.

'I'll just confirm my travel arrangements then,' he calls to the wind as he goes.

In the silence of the morning at the edge of the lake, not a person around to disturb me, I try not to feel hurt by the speed of his departure. I mentally try not to file it into the big paranoia folder in my head.

CHAPTER SEVENTEEN

Louise

I've thought about her husband a lot. That handsome man who hugged her in the café. Who joked with her and made her smile, even though she'd looked so lost before he arrived.

I knew his name. It ran through my head on a loop. I'd say it just to see how it sounded. I wrote it down then scribbled it out. I couldn't risk leaving any connection, but I did feel a connection. He'd be the father of my child, after all.

I wanted to know as much about him as I could. What he did. What he liked. How he spent his free time. What books he read and what movies he watched. Was he excited about the baby his wife was carrying? The baby who'd be mine. Would he have been a hands-on kind of dad? Was he one of those 'new men' types – not afraid to change a nappy or push a pram?

I thought I might ask her a little about him when I next saw her. Slip it into the conversation casually. 'Your husband must be excited?' I'd ask. It's possible she'd offer me something to go on. A little insight into his life and his personality.

He'd looked like a good man. Peter had been a good man.

He'd been a good husband to me. He'd have made a brilliant father to our children, if life hadn't been so cruel.

God never gives you any more than you can handle, I reminded myself. He must have thought I could handle an awful lot. Peter – he wasn't up to God's test.

CHAPTER EIGHTEEN

Eli

My mother reacts just as I'd expect when I tell her Martin's going back to London. She looks at me as if I've lost the plot, even though all along she's been assuring me she doesn't think there's any truth in those horrible notes.

'Are you sure you don't want him to stay?' she says. 'Did he say something to you to influence you to let him go?'

'No, Mum,' I say. 'I just realise if I trust him I have to prove that I trust him and this is one way to do that.'

'Hmm.' She eyes me. 'He should be the one proving things to you, though.'

'I think we both need to work on that and let the police work on finding out the truth of what's going on.'

'And being here, without him, while all this is going on? Are you not scared?'

I am, of course I am, but I don't want to let whoever's behind this win. I don't want them to know they're scaring me.

'Sure, but I have you,' I say with a forced smile. 'Haven't you always kept me safe? Haven't you always told me that a mama bear protects her baby bears? You'll stay with me, won't you?'

My mother, hearing the phrase she'd quoted to me every time I felt scared as a child, can't help but smile back.

'Of course I'll stay, but I'm not sure how that mama bear story holds up now that I'm older and have a dodgy knee.'

I see it then. A chink in her perfect armour. Fear, perhaps. I suppose fear of what's happened is natural. I'm shaken by it myself. My mother had been downstairs, close to it, when it happened. She'd run out, fearless, I'd thought, to see who was there. Now that the adrenaline had worn off, she was more aware that there could actually have been an intruder inside the house. There would've been little she could've done to defend herself, or me.

'Well, I suppose, then, we're in this together, Mum. There will have to be a bit of mutual protecting.'

I pull her into a hug, allow myself to melt into the soft fabric of her jumper, the scent of her perfume mixed with talcum powder. The scent of home.

'Look,' I say, pulling back, 'why don't we do something nice to distract ourselves? You've been on at me to do some shopping for this baby. Why don't we go together? Today. To Mothercare. You can help me to look at a crib and maybe a pram. I know nothing about this stuff and I'd really value your opinion.'

I force enthusiasm into my voice. I don't really want to go baby shopping. Martin and I have already more or less decided on what pram, sorry, travel system, we're going to get. Well, Martin has. I just nodded when he showed me one he said rated highly in *Which?* magazine that was considered to offer value and style. I hope my mother will jump at the idea of coming with me. That we can share some lovely mother/

daughter time, where we don't have to talk about everything that's happened over the last few days.

'Ah, pet, I don't know,' my mother says. 'I didn't sleep well last night and I might not be the best company.'

Perhaps irrationally, I find myself welling up at her answer. I'd expected her to react with enthusiasm at the notion of going shopping with me. She was always trying to drag me round the shops in Belfast. Admittedly, she normally likes to stay close to home when she comes to visit me – always citing that our house is like a country escape and she'd prefer not to get caught up in the traffic and noise of a city when it was such a big part of her daily landscape at home. But I really thought she'd be itching to get out baby shopping. I was relying on her to be extra excited about it to gee me along.

She must see the disappointment in my face.

'Look,' she says, 'here's an idea. How about you come home with me for a bit? You're off for a couple of days. It might help you to get away from all this for a while. Get your head round it. We can shop tomorrow together. There's a lovely new coffee place close to Victoria Square. And they have the Mamas & Papas store there too, as well as some lovely little baby boutiques. We can sit in front of the fire tonight, with a mug of hot chocolate, made just how you like it, with marshmallows and everything. It'll give us the chance to have a good chat, just like old times.'

There's a certain appeal to it. There is, if I'm honest, a massive appeal to it. To escape back to Belfast where I'd spent my teenage years, to the familiar sounds and smells of home. My old bedroom isn't quite how I left it when I moved out, but my mother's made sure it's still very much my room. Yes, there's a double bed where the single one once was, and the Take That posters aren't on the walls any more, but she's got framed pictures of me, my friends, and Martin and I hung on the wall.

My mother's living room is the perfect haven in a busy city. Even though her house is close to Queen's University, once she pulls the heavy curtains across the bay window in the evening, it feels like a cocoon of safety. I hadn't been a teenager who routinely disappeared up to my room and away from my mother. When my friends went home, I'd often come and sit with her in front of the fire, both of us talking about our days. Those were good times. Innocent times.

And I miss them, want to relive just a little of what that was like, so I find myself nodding to my mother and saying that sounds like a brilliant idea. She rewards me with a broad smile and I leave her in my living room, which suddenly feels sterile in comparison, and go upstairs to pack an overnight bag.

Martin's standing by the bed, looking at his open case.

'I'm going to Mum's for a day or two,' I tell him. 'Just for a change of scenery. After everything . . .'

He looks at me and nods. 'I understand. I feel awful that you've been through this. That I wasn't here when that rock came through the window.'

'It's not your fault,' I tell him, even though I can't say with absolute certainty that it wasn't. 'Did you confirm your travel arrangements?'

'Flying out of Belfast tonight at eight,' he says. 'But only if you're sure?'

I'm as sure as I'm likely to be, so I nod.

'I can be back if you need me, at any time. I can fly back tomorrow if you want. Fly out again on Tuesday. Whatever you need to make this work.'

I know that's not true. After all, he couldn't get an earlier flight back this time and even then he was delayed, but I had to believe his intentions were honest. I had to try and trust him.

'I'll be fine with Mum,' I say and I kiss him lightly on the lips.

He bends down and kisses my stomach, whispers that he loves our baby and that he loves me. I ignore the uneasy feeling in the pit of my stomach and start packing.

CHAPTER NINETEEN

Eli

After I've said goodbye to Martin – a strange goodbye in which we tried to pretend that everything was normal – I send a quick message to Rachel, telling her I'll be in Belfast in case she needs me for anything work-related.

Martin always jokingly says I'm married to the job and not him. I always reply that at least my job involves real people and not just drawings of buildings, and then we pull silly faces at each other until we both admit we're borderline workaholics and unlikely to change.

Until the baby is born, that is.

Then, well, we don't really quite know what 'then' will entail. That's still up for discussion. I've no doubt it'll be hard for me to step away from work for my maternity leave. Dealing with palliative care is much less intimidating to me than dealing with a new baby. Still, I push that thought to the back of my head as I send the message to Rachel. I'll deal with it – we'll deal with it – when the time comes.

It's not long before she messages me back:

Delighted you're getting away, even if only for a day or two. You need to rest up. All will be good here. Xx

I smile at my phone, unplug my charger from beside the bed and toss it into my case. Glancing around my room, I'm happy that I have everything I need. My mother's waiting for me at the bottom of the stairs.

'Are we taking both cars?' I ask. 'That way I can just drive back when I need to come home. I prefer driving now to the bus.'

My mother's face drops. 'Here was me hoping we'd have a girly road trip.'

'Ah, Mum,' I say, 'sure, you'll have me all to yourself, in your own space and everything, when we get to Belfast.'

She smiles weakly. The kind of smile that sends offspring guilt into overdrive.

'Okay,' she says. 'I suppose. But promise me, if you get to Belfast before me, don't go upstairs. I've a surprise for you and I want to see your face when you see it.'

I'm intrigued and although the rebellious part of me is tempted to look anyway, I know I've never been able to bluff my mother. She'll know straight away if I've had a sneak peek. I promise her I'll wait.

'You're a good girl, Eliana Johnston,' she says.

'Hughes,' I remind her. 'Hughes.'

★

I never feel odd letting myself into my mother's house. Martin says he thinks it strange that I still refer to my mother's house as home or 'the house' as if it were a constant anchoring point in my life, which, of course, it totally is.

'This is your home now,' he'd tease, gesturing his arms around the expanse of our kitchen diner. 'We've done a lot to make sure it's your home. Why do you keep harking back to your mum's?'

'This is my home, too,' I'd told him.

It isn't as easy as he thinks to break ties from the house in which I'd spent my formative years. I'd lived here until I was twenty-seven – seeing no reason to add rent bills to the cost of studying. Whereas Martin had flown the family nest at the first chance, moving from Derry to London to study at eighteen. His parents had downsized once it was clear he had no intention of moving back in, so he didn't have a pull to his teenage bedroom, the kitchen he'd learned to cook in or the living room he'd sat in with his friends.

While waiting for my mother, I make the place as cosy as I can. I switch on the Tiffany lamps in the hall and living room. Pull the curtains across to block the cold, wet evening. I switch her heating on to full power and light the fire she's prepared in the hearth. Then I make a pot of tea and am just about to start rifling through the biscuit tin to find something that appeals to my churning stomach, when I hear my mother's key turn in the lock.

'I'm in the kitchen,' I call to her. 'I'll make you a cup of tea.'

'Can I show you my surprise first?' she calls from the hall. 'Come upstairs! I hope you don't mind, but I've done a little something for you and I really hope you'll appreciate it.'

I follow her upstairs, towards what had always been the spare room. Too small to be much of a guest room, it normally holds all the bits and pieces Mum can't really find use for elsewhere. Things like boxes of my old clothes and toys that she can never bring herself to get rid of. I sort of expect that when she opens the door, I'll see that she's sorted through some of my old things and pulled out a few choice items for me to take back to Derry.

What I'm not expecting is that an almost fully decorated nursery will greet me. I gasp as I'm met with a room decorated in neutral hues of cream and beige. A white cot and matching dresser with changing table. A rocking chair padded with soft cream cushions, lined curtains reaching down to the floor. There's a rug in the shape of a teddy bear on the floor and in one corner are at least five boxes of nappies stacked on top of each other. A number of other shopping bags sit around the room. It's too much to take in and if I'm honest, I don't know how to react.

My head's screaming at me to thank my mother. To tell her she's a star and that this is beyond lovely, but my heart? My heart is sore, jealous, angry that someone else has put together a nursery for my baby before I've had the chance to do it myself. I know this makes me an ungrateful brat.

As I try to find the words that won't cut my mother in half with hurt, she starts to speak.

'I probably went overboard, but once I started, well, I got a bit carried away. And I thought it'd be lovely for my grandchild to have a place to stay when you come to visit – a room of her own. It's been so long since you've been up, what with you being so unwell, and I didn't want to trouble you with it. It's mostly second-hand. So don't worry that I spent too much. It's all good quality, though, and I cleaned it all thoroughly.'

I'm still staring, tears now sliding down my face. I wonder if my mother'll equate them with gratitude. She continues to speak.

'You won't remember, but when you were a baby, we had so little. I was never able to decorate a nursery for you. It wasn't quite as bad as having you sleep in a drawer, but it wasn't far off. Just you and me. In a bedsit in Paisley, barely room to walk around the place once the crib and my bed were in the room. Most of your clothes in those early months were from charity shops. I suppose I wanted to do something more for my grand-child, now that I can.'

I look at her face, her expression one of sorrow, and I feel guilty for feeling cross with her. I have to bury these feelings. I smile through my tears, hug her and tell her I love her very much. It's not until I'm alone in my old room that I properly cry over the fact that my mother seems to care about my baby more than I do.

I put my hand to my stomach, which is churning as usual, despite me having taken my anti-sickness tablet, and I will my baby to kick or wriggle or respond to my touch in some way to tell me not to worry. To tell me the love will come later. That it's fine. That we'll work it out. The two of us. Just like we'll work it out, the three of us. The baby, Martin and me.

My baby doesn't move, though. She seems to be sleeping, blissfully unaware of my inner turmoil.

CHAPTER TWENTY

Louise

It was a shame I couldn't have brought my baby back to the house I'd lived in with Peter. Everything had been there and ready for her. But it would've been much, much too risky.

I just knew she was going to be a girl. I could tell by the shape of her mother's bump, sitting high and to the front. I sat with my wedding ring, which I'd put in my jewellery box six months before, on a piece of yarn and I'd let it swing over the palm of my hand. The first time, of course, it had swung back and forth and back and forth, and I'd whispered my baby's name to the wind. My first baby. Who never had a chance. Gone before my stomach had even started swelling.

It was a heartache I'd experience again and again: eleven weeks, six weeks, eight weeks, twenty-one weeks. Thirty-three weeks. The one that broke me. Totally. Twenty-three weeks had been cruel. Thirty-three had been devastating. I'd been so very sure that time. Had felt his kicks. His wriggles. His hiccups. I'd felt as if I knew him. Then he was gone. It had broken both me and everything around me.

The wedding ring I'd been swinging had stilled for just a moment, and I'd closed my eyes and thought of my new baby.

It had started to swirl round and round. A girl. She was going to be a girl, just as I'd thought.

I felt such a wave of joy as I'd sat there in the room I'd prepared for him, my baby boy. A sense that finally, my prayers were being answered. I'd looked at the cot. The cream wallpaper. The matching yellow curtains. The rug on the floor in the shape of a teddy bear. At the Babygros in white and lemon and pale green folded on the chest of drawers. The packets of nappies. The changing mat, still in its wrapper, the breast-feeding pillow behind my back on the rocker. Yes, it was a shame my new baby would never see that room, just as my son hadn't.

But there was no way no hide a baby there. Not in that house. Not in that neighbourhood. Not in that city, where everyone knew everyone else's business and thought nothing of sharing it with every Tom, Dick and Harry they met on the street.

I'd already been the subject of enough gossip. 'Isn't that the poor woman whose baby died?' Their whispers were never quite quiet enough and most of them asked their insensitive questions to their insensitive friends with all the subtlety of a brick hurled through a window.

I'd come to recognise the sad eyes. Heads nodding in my direction. The swivel of eyes towards me before the heads bowed together and the whispering continued. 'That poor woman.'

Those who'd had the guts to speak to me weren't much better. People who barely spoke to me before now came over with their faux sympathy. They weren't really sorry for my troubles, of course. They were just relieved that my troubles weren't theirs. It was evident in the way they held on to the handles of their prams a little tighter.

The unthinkable had happened to me and they thanked God every day that it hadn't happened to them.

And then, to rub salt in the wounds, the one person who could even begin to understand what I was going through, left me. Peter. My husband. The father to the children we'd never hold.

I can't deal with this any more. I've tried to understand. I'm grieving, too, but you're unreachable. You seem to want to make it your life's work to be as miserable as possible.

He'd written that in the note he'd left on the kitchen table. Was it bad to say that when I read it, all I felt was relief? A part of me had come to hate him, you see, for not understanding why I couldn't simply get up and face each day as if my whole world hadn't imploded around me.

When I heard him whistle around the house, I swear to God, I wanted to stab him. I was afraid I might *actually* stab him. I didn't trust myself. I felt calmer after he left. I didn't even try to stop him.

But it was good to find a new energy. A positive energy. To think I was back in His favour. The God who'd forsaken me was making things right. I just had to work with His plan.

The person I was would have to vanish. I'd leave what remnants of this life I still had behind, with that same sense of relief.

A flash of guilt for that woman washed over me as I packed up that room, but it was just that. A flash – gone in a second. It wouldn't be the same for her. She could have another baby – one she actually wanted. She wouldn't have to give birth to a corpse. The baby would breathe. She'd hold her baby, still warm, in her arms. Rock her. And then I'd take her to be mine and give her a brilliant life.

That's what any mother would want for their child, wasn't

it? I mean, it was like the Judgement of Solomon. Surely a mother would want a baby to be loved and cared for rather than be robbed of a life altogether?

She'd move on. She'd get over it. This would be her cross to carry, but it was time for me to put mine down. It had been too heavy for too long.

I'd looked around the nursery again before standing up. All these things would be packaged up, delivered to the charity shop. They'd be grateful for them. People would look at me and then chat among themselves. 'She seems to be getting better. She must be coming to terms with it. She's moving on.'

CHAPTER TWENTY-ONE

Eli

Mum's tidying up, leaving me sitting curled up on the sofa in front of the fire in her living room, a green mohair throw over my legs. A half-drunk mug of tea is sat on the floor beside me. Served with an almost even milk to tea ratio, it's cooled quickly and now the tepid liquid makes me feel queasy, but I'm too tired, and too comfortable, to move. I can feel my eyes drooping already, the lure of my bed growing too strong to ignore.

Stifling a yawn, I climb the stairs and I'm getting ready for bed when I hear a message ping on my phone. The sender is listed simply as 'Anonymous'. Curiosity nipping at me, I click to open it:

I'm surprised you let him go back to London. Even more surprised you left your lovely house without upping those security measures. I thought more of you. But cheers for the drink. I'll never understand why he sleeps in someone else's bed when his own is so comfortable.

There's a picture attached. One of my crystal glasses, a wedding present, sitting on my bedside table. A measure of what looks like whisky in it. My head struggles to process what I'm seeing. I know what it looks like, but it can't be. My house. My life. Someone else in it. It's surreal. Not the kind of thing that actually happens in real life. I hit the message again, look at the information being sent to me. There's no number attached. None. Just that word: anonymous. How is that even possible?

It starts to sink in – quickly, an anchor hauling me down to reality. Someone was in my house. Could be in my house right now. I can't tell from the picture if it's daylight or night-time. They could be, at this moment, in my bedroom. In my bed. Up close and personal, telling me once again that I'm not to trust my husband. The sucker punches come thick and fast. My stomach turns and tightens until I hear myself scream out for my mother, my screams drowning out the thumping of my heart.

CHAPTER TWENTY-TWO

Eli

'Let me call the police,' my mother says, turning and leaving me sitting staring at the message on my phone.

Am I really seeing what I'm seeing? This message. Will it self-destruct? I take a screenshot just in case as I hear my mother on the phone to a 999 operator reporting a possible break-in at my house.

'She's had a text message,' my mother says. 'With a picture from inside her house. Look, get them to check their records. This is the second incident at this address since Friday. No, she's here now. Safe with me. Scared but safe. Yes. Yes.'

I hear her trot out her phone number while I reread the words in front of me again and again. What's most disturbing? Someone in my house? Another allegation that Martin's cheating? The fact someone seems intent on making sure I get the message loud and clear and doesn't seem to want to leave me alone?

I should call Martin, I suppose. But I don't know if I have the emotional strength just now. He'll deny any wrongdoing. Again. He'll only just have arrived in London. Will be preparing for his big meeting. Putting his work first. I realise I have nothing to say to him in this moment that won't just make things worse between us.

It feels as though there's a ticking time bomb in my hand. I should call that policeman who came out to our house. Constable Dawson? I was sure I had his card with his contact details in my purse. He should be on duty now.

He needs to know something else has happened. He needs to work harder to find out what's going on. I can see his tired face in front of me. His questioning expression. Is this just a domestic? Am I wasting police time?

But someone was or is in my house. I'm not making that up. I don't know whether to be relieved I'm not there, or angry that I can't confront whoever this is head on. Such a coward, sending messages this way. Anonymously.

I hear my mother climb the stairs. She's always in her element when she has a purpose, especially when there's an extra layer of drama to things.

'They're sending a car out to your house now,' she says. 'They're going to contact the officers who came out to us on Friday night to let them know about this latest incident but said you might want to follow up with them yourself when you get home. Has that security firm of yours not called? I have to say, I'd be having words. Someone in your house, pet, and not a word to you? What kind of a system is that?'

'No police officer's coming here?' I ask, surprised.

She shrugs her shoulders. 'They said there wasn't much point. You aren't in any immediate danger. They'll call with any news from the house. If there's anything they need to tell you.'

'But someone's targeting me! Targeting us. How do they know I'm not in any danger? Mum, what if I'd been at home? What if whoever this is had come into the house and I'd been there on my own? Having a nap. Resting because of the baby. What might have happened then?'

I shudder. My mother looks at me open-mouthed, sits and takes my hand.

'You can't think like that,' she says.

'I can't not think like that,' I reply. 'It could've happened.'

'But it didn't,' she says. 'Focus on what you actually know.'

I want to scream that I don't know anything at the moment, but I don't. I can't lose my cool. I can't become hysterical. I need to take control.

'I'm going to phone Constable Dawson now,' I tell her.

'That might be an idea,' she says. 'Check where they're at.'

'I'll push them to try harder. They should be able to trace this message, shouldn't they? Police can trace everything these days.'

I feel a kick square in my ribs. It's enough to make me gasp and grab my stomach.

'Is it the baby? Is everything okay?' My mother puts her hand on my stomach.

For a moment I feel a pinch of something like jealousy. It's childish and selfish of me, I know. But I wish she'd asked how *I* feel. If *I'm* okay. Of course the baby is. She's always okay. Through the sickness and the early spotting and the exhaustion, she's been fine. She's a force to be reckoned with. Looking at the determined look on my mother's face as she feels around for a rogue kick or punch, I figure she takes after her grandmother. Made of stern stuff.

'Everything's fine,' I say, although my chest feels tight.

I'm reluctant to admit to my anxiety, even though it's perfectly understandable given that at this moment there could be some weird anonymous stalker in my house.

'Eli?' I hear my mother's voice, hazy as I focus on the sound of my breath, the beating of my heart and my inner monologue.

I want to put my fingers in my ears to make it stop, except there's no way to make it stop. Not the inner monologue. That keeps going all the time. All. The. Time. I could listen to music, or go to work, or walk along the banks of the lake at the back of the house, or wander through the shops at Victoria Square, or sit there vaguely hearing my mother say my name over and over to try to pull me into the here and now. But the inner monologue would still be there, loud and clear:

There's no smoke without fire.
People don't do things like this unless they really dislike you. Really want to hurt you. Really want to destroy what you have.

Everything goes fuzzy around the edges as I suck in air and try to exhale slowly, my breath coming in shuddering spurts, my stomach tightening further, the voice in my head telling me everything's going wrong and there isn't anything I can do about it. I can't deal with his betrayal. I can't deal with knowing someone's stalking us. Stalking me. That's what it is now, isn't it? Three times.

Most of all, and I hate myself for thinking this, I hate myself for thinking I don't want this, any of this – this baby that we wanted together – without him to help me.

I don't think I can do it alone.

I don't *want* to do it alone.

'Breathe.' My mother's voice cuts through the haze and the noise.

'Eli, you have to breathe,' she repeats, but there's no sense of panic in her voice. It's calm. Pulling me back to me. 'In and out,' she says slowly. 'This is a panic attack. This will pass. You can control it.'

Her voice is rhythmic, soft. I allow it lull me. To wash over me. To bring my breathing back to normal. While she can't silence the voices, she manages to quieten them. She makes them secondary to her soothing tone. She always could.

'Everything will be okay, my darling. I promise you, and remember, I'm always here for you. Always. You're never alone. You'll never be alone. Even if this is true – and I'm not saying it is. You're a strong woman, Eliana. You always have been. You've nothing to fear about anything. Not this person trying to threaten you. Not whatever might happen with Martin. Not this baby. I promise.

'Now lie down, I'll stay here with you. I'll stay here until the police call back. I'll stay here until you talk to Martin. I'll stay here as long as you need me.'

CHAPTER TWENTY-THREE

Louise

I needed to prove to people that I was okay.

My parents had made me go to grief counselling. They'd insisted on it after Peter left. They'd escorted me to the doctor, one of them either side of me to make sure I didn't make a run for it, and they'd begged for help. They didn't want to see me 'do anything stupid', they said.

So I knew if I was to put my plan in motion, I had to make sure that it looked as though I wasn't doing anything stupid at all. I had to appear to have started to cope, and cope well, with my loss. I had to show that I was ready to move on with my life. Was keen to make a new start. Which of course was all true – the only problem being that I knew people wouldn't necessarily understand or approve of my method of moving on. They didn't know what I knew – that God had willed this baby to me.

So the next time I visited my grief counsellor, I made sure I made an effort with my appearance. I made sure I didn't look like a broken woman when I walked through her door. I had a bath, washed my hair. I even had it cut to get rid of all the dead ends. It seemed symbolic.

I'd rifled through my drawers until I found clothes in bright colours. A red jumper, my once favourite pair of blue jeans with a pair of brown boots. I even applied some make-up, but not too much. I didn't want it to look too obvious. I kept the locket on, which carried a lock of my baby's hair, but made sure it sat under my jumper – away from view but close to my heart. I spritzed on some perfume from a bottle my now ex-husband bought me when things seemed much more hopeful.

Word had reached me, as it always did in our hometown, that he'd met someone else. A part of me had been happy for him. He hadn't asked for any of our tragedy, either. But it also hurt.

Within a couple of months she'd fallen pregnant with his baby. So quick. So easy. That news had reached me quickly and easily, too. That she'd been able to give him what he wanted all along. She already had two children – had proven herself to be fertile and able to bring babies safely to term. She was a real woman. A proper woman. Unlike me. When they'd taken my womb, they'd also taken the essence of who I was meant to be.

Looking in the mirror that day, the one when I was to see the counsellor, I felt surprised at my reflection. I'd done a good job. Reclaimed just a little of the femininity that had been taken from me.

I'd practised my smile. Soft. Not too manic. Not too cheery. I wouldn't cry at that session, I knew that. There'd be no need for me to twist a tissue around in my hands until it disintegrated into well-worn flakes and carpeted my counsellor's floor.

I was so confident, I'd even risked a slick of mascara.

My grief counsellor was a woman in her fifties, who wore her grey hair in a bob that always seemed impossibly sleek and who wore no make-up except for a trace of the palest pink lipstick, which was much too light for her skin tone. She lived in flowing skirts and oversized jumpers, and was so softly spoken that I couldn't imagine she'd ever have been anything but a grief counsellor.

Victoria. That was her name. 'After the sponge, not the queen,' she'd said with a wink the first time we met. She was a perfectly lovely woman. She rarely stopped me from raging against the unfairness of it all and she listened intently, but after a time I started to notice a change in her. It was almost as if her mind wandered as we spoke. As if she thought she'd already heard this sad story so many times there was no need for her to listen actively any more.

But I needed to tell it, you see. I needed to keep him alive in the only way I could. I needed to atone for my body's epic fuck-up in killing a baby so close to life. I could almost forgive myself for the others. Almost. But not for him.

I was sure she'd be delighted to see me in a better mood. Upbeat, even. Only not too upbeat that she'd think I was being manic and not actually recovering. Because I was recovering. I was getting better, and all it took was for me to take matters into my own hands.

'You look different,' Victoria said as she looked at me. Assessed me from head to toe.

'I feel different,' I'd replied. 'I feel, well, I feel as if maybe I'm ready to move on. Does that make sense? I mean, I won't forget him. I could never in all my years on earth forget him, and I can't imagine a day when I'll wake up and he won't be there scattered among my first thoughts. But I think I'm ready to start living again. I keep thinking, it's what he would've wanted, isn't it? Me to live my life. To make up, even, for the life he didn't get.'

Victoria nodded, her dangling gold earrings rocking back and forth. 'Well, I have to say, that sounds like a very positive way to look at things. Acknowledge your grief. Feel it when you need to but don't let it consume you.'

It was my turn to nod. 'I'm not saying it'll be easy, but I think I have to do it. I was thinking of maybe finding a new job. Something more enjoyable than wiping tables. I thought maybe I'd do a night class, learn a new skill.'

'It's good to hear you talking so positively. I'm really impressed with you, if you don't mind me saying.'

'I'm impressed with myself, too,' I told her, and not a word of it was a lie.

I resolved to see Victoria again for another few weeks, after which she'd hopefully declare me officially fit for a new life again. I decided to flick through the prospectus for the local college when I got home to find a course that appealed to me – find out where else I could study it. After all, I still needed to move.

CHAPTER TWENTY-FOUR

Eli

I'm running through the people we know. The women we know. Is there anyone Martin's been extra friendly with? Or behaved differently around? Would he be as clichéd as to be sleeping with his secretary? His partner's wife? My friends? Rachel? They've always got along so well . . .

But I trust Rachel. I've always trusted Rachel, with everything. Just as I've trusted my husband.

'You should call Martin. He should know what's happened at home.'

My mother's voice cuts through my thoughts, but I shake my head. I can't think straight. If I'm honest with myself, I'm scared, too – scared to call in case some mystery woman answers the phone. Like a reveal in a movie, the unsuspecting wife hears her husband's mistress purr down the phone . . .

I'm too tired to cry, so I lie down and try to shut the world out for a bit. This doesn't feel like my life any more.

My mother strokes my hair, as she did when I was a child. She tells me she loves me. She tells me over and over it'll be okay.

She can't possibly know that, but I allow myself to believe it, as exhaustion overwhelms me and I drift off to sleep.

★

I wake up an hour or so later. Mum's still beside me, a look of concern on her face.

'Did the police call back?'

She looks down, won't meet my gaze.

'There was no sign of anyone in the house,' she says. 'No sign of any break-in, either. All windows and doors closed. They asked, have you considered who else might have access to your house? Have you given a key to anyone?'

'Well you, obviously. Martin's parents. And our cleaner – but I don't think anyone else has access.'

I'm trying to think. Would Martin have given a key to Jim during the restoration work? Not that it could be Jim. He's in London too, or so I've been led to believe. We've a couple of spare keys, but I'm pretty sure they're still in the kitchen drawer where they always are. I'm running all the scenarios through my head, when I realise my mother's wringing her hands, looking as if she might cry.

'What is it, Mum?' I ask, alarmed. My mother isn't normally one for breaking down.

'I'm so sorry, Eli. I think it might be my fault.'

That makes no sense at all. How could it be? I blink at her.

'Don't be silly,' I start.

'The police said the security system hadn't been set.'

'But I was sure . . .' I say as I try to remember.

I can visualise myself picking up my bags, my keys. Stopping to go to the kitchen to grab my pills. Mum saying she needed a last-minute wee, just as I'm tapping in the code. It's raining heavily and my car door's open. Did I wait for Mum before I went out to close the car door? Did I finish the code? Did I shout to her to tap it in and pull the door behind her when she was done?

'It was me,' she says, her face red and her eyes brimming with tears. 'I mustn't have hit the right buttons. I thought I'd set it, but I mustn't have. I'm not used to those things. I'm sorry. It's my fault.'

I want to be cross with her but she looks so pathetic.

'It's okay, Mum,' I say.

She shakes her head. 'No, it isn't. Eli, someone was in your house. After what happened with the broken window, I made it easy for someone to get in. They could've done anything.'

'They didn't though, Mum,' I say, pushing my own fears down. 'They probably saw my car wasn't there and that's why they felt so bold.'

I try not to think again of what might have happened if I had been in. Would they have left a note again? Had a drink in the kitchen? Would they have hurt me? How far would any of this go?

'But what if—' my mother starts.

'Ifs don't matter,' I tell her. 'Isn't that what you said to me? It only matters what actually happened.'

CHAPTER TWENTY-FIVE

Eli

Mum sleeps beside me that night. It feels comforting to have the solid presence of my mother in the bed beside me. There's something familiar and reassuring about it. Just as there's something reassuring about waking up to the familiar sounds of the house I grew up in. The slow hum of the traffic building on the street outside. The rattle and hiss of the old radiators and the way rain beats against the windows.

I know every creak and hiss of this house like the words of a well-loved song. It's safe here. I'm safe here.

My dreams were muddled last night. Confused. I felt as if I were looking for something, but I couldn't find it, or when I did it just led me to something else to look for – just out of reach. I'd woken on and off for the first few hours, the weight of anxiety pressing down on me.

Mum and I are supposed to go shopping today. We've planned it. A walk to Victoria Square and a look around the baby shops before lunch somewhere nice.

It feels soured now. I don't have the energy or inclination to shop for baby things. I can't play at being enthusiastic when my head's still swimming.

I should take this chance to call Martin, but he'll probably be on-site already. Part of me, of course, doesn't give a damn that he'll be on-site. Why should he live in his bubble of security while I'm spiralling?

Then again, I don't want to make a show of myself, shouting and crying down the phone to him. I know I'll shout and I know I'll cry. I can feel the weight of it all sitting on my chest, the rest still to come out.

Maybe I'll ask Mum to phone him when she wakes.

My stomach gurgles and I realise I'm hungry. I need to eat something and I need to move about a bit, so I creep as quietly as I can out of bed and get dressed before going downstairs to the kitchen.

While I'm making tea and nibbling gingerly on a digestive biscuit, I run through the same lists of names and possibilities as last night. Anyone who has access to a key. Or has had access to a key before. Any women in Martin's life of whom I should be suspicious. Not that I know every woman he comes into contact with, of course.

I even consider booking a flight to London and travelling over to confront him. But travelling when I'm so heavily pregnant and feel so rotten doesn't seem like the best idea. I need to get out of the house, I realise. Get some fresh air, maybe some perspective. A quick walk around the block might work.

I grab my coat, purse and keys and slip out into the wet Belfast morning. It's not long before I'm regretting my decision to go for a walk. As the rain runs off the tip of my nose, I think of running for home but see Kitty's Kitchen, a bakery run by one of my old school pals, ahead of me.

In that moment, I realise how much I miss her and how long it's been since we actually saw each other face-to-face. We spent so much time together when we were teenagers, I don't think either of us could've thought we'd ever grow apart. Some people think Facebook helps people to stay in touch – I think maybe it gives us the illusion we're still in touch because we see occasional insights into each other's lives.

I make the decision to call in, not caring that I look like a drowned scarecrow. I just need a friend. Pushing open the door, the heat hits me, as does the smell of freshly baked bread and cakes.

I see Kate at the counter, her dark hair tied up in a ponytail. A bright red apron. A smile for her customers. I know she's a mum herself now. I feel wretched that I've not even seen her baby yet – not that he's a baby any more. He must be two or three by now.

My shame almost gets the better of me and I'm considering leaving, when she calls my name from across the shop, giving me the same wide smile as she gave the customer she'd been serving when I came in.

'Eli! Imagine seeing you here! It's been so long,' she cheers before telling one of her assistants to give her a few minutes.

We're hugging within seconds. I try to warn her that I'm drenched and she'll end up soaked too, but she laughs.

'I'm not made of sugar and I won't melt. It's so nice to see you. You're looking well.'

I accept the compliment, even though I know she's lying.

'Well, for a pregnant lady with no make-up on and her hair like a scarecrow, I suppose I do look well.' I smile.

'You couldn't look bad if you tried. Here,' she says, guiding me to a table and chairs by the window. 'Sit down. Can I get you anything? Tea, coffee, epidural?'

I'm warmed by her humour.

'You know what, Kate? It's just nice to be in your company. I'm up visiting Mum for a bit and needed some fresh air.'

'Well, it's lovely to see you,' Kate says, taking my hands in hers across the table.

Her eyes are bright, her expression warm. I realise just how much I've missed our friendship.

'I'm so sorry I've not called in sooner,' I say. 'How's your little boy?'

She smiles and reaches into her pocket for her phone.

'A complete terrorist but I wouldn't have him any other way. Keeps me on my toes.'

She shows me her phone and the picture of a young child, grinning at the camera, his face covered in ice cream. He looks as happy as Kate looks proud.

'Do you know what you're having?' she asks, nodding towards my tummy.

'A girl,' I tell her, and I find myself smiling. A genuine smile. It surprises me, in a nice way.

'Ah, that'll be lovely. Wee girls are so special,' she says. 'Sure, look how close you and your mum are.'

I smile again. Think of Mum back at her house, still sleeping. I realise I didn't leave a note to tell her where I'd gone and she'll only worry if she wakes to an empty house.

'Actually, I'd better be off,' I say. 'Mum'll be worried.'

Kate reaches across the table again and takes my hands. 'Can I ask you something? Is everything okay, Eli? You seem a bit out of sorts.'

I wish in that moment I could sit there and tell her everything. That someone's stalking us. That Martin might be cheating. That I'm thinking about every woman in our lives and wondering if I know who it is he's seeing. I want to tell her about the whisky glass and the anonymous message – but I can't bring myself to do that.

'I'm fine,' I lie, forcing a smile. 'It's been so lovely to see you.'

'Take my phone number,' she says, 'in case you want to talk any time.'

I nod and take out my phone, tap her number in and give her mine in return.

'I'm here any time you need,' she says with such genuine warmth that I will myself not to cry and look like a total eejit in front of her.

CHAPTER TWENTY-SIX

Louise

I love you. The simplest sentence in the world. I wondered how many times I'd said it in my lifetime. To my parents. My grandparents. To lovers. To my husband. To the cold, silent baby in my arms.

I wondered how many times I'd meant it. Really meant it. Felt each word as if saying them wasn't enough. As if the expression itself was woefully inadequate for how I really felt. So many times it was a rote response. Something to say.

Like a prayer in Mass. Carried along with the rhythm of the words, the pattern they make:

> The Lord be with you
> And with your spirit.

Drummed in from an early age.

> I love you.
> I love you, too.

I knew when I'd first told Peter I loved him, after we'd been dating for three months, I'd been sure I meant it. But it wasn't until a few months later that I felt the full force of the meaning behind those words. It overwhelmed me.

To be in love with someone.

To have my heart want to burst with affection for them.

It was terrifying. To feel that way.

It made me feel vulnerable.

When you tell someone you love them, truly love them, when you feel as if that's the most intense thing you could ever feel – you open yourself up to so much. You make yourself vulnerable.

For me, 'I love you' meant I see the real you. I like what I see. I love spending time with you. You make me happy. I want you in my life.

I need you in my life.

Please don't leave me.

Please don't hurt me.

Please don't trample on my heart.

Peter didn't trample on my heart. He didn't break it. It was broken when my baby didn't breathe. Nothing else mattered then.

Love certainly didn't matter. Love was cruel. Love was fleeting.

I was sure nothing and no one could make me love again.

Except for this baby. My baby. That's why I needed to have her, you see. Because didn't I deserve to believe in love again?

And I felt those first flushes of love as I watched them. It was love that made me stay close to their house, watching and waiting. Hiding in the shadows. It was love, for my baby and for the God who was answering my prayers, that gave me the patience to keep waiting, even if that patience was wearing thin.

It was love that had me standing in a shop, looking at cuddly toys. There was a bear wearing a red scarf, a soft heart embroidered on one end. I looked around me, just to make sure there was no one I knew nearby. I didn't want them to see me buy this. I didn't want them to wonder why. I didn't want them to know it was for my baby. My first gift to her. I hoped she'd keep this bear always. Until its fluff was threadbare, its stuffing flattened. I hoped she'd always look at it and remember that love could be pure. I already knew that I'd never hurt her. And she'd never hurt me. She'd heal me.

I'd picked up the teddy and walked to the till, smiled at the woman serving. Agreed that it was a lovely bear. I took the bag she handed me, with this toy inside, and brought it home, where I packed it in one of the cases I had ready to take to our new home.

I already had one place lined up to look at.

It wasn't fancy. Not like the home I'd lived in with Peter, where I always thought we'd raise our children, but I didn't need fancy to be happy. I just needed a baby.

It wouldn't be long now.

With every day that passed, we were getting closer.

CHAPTER TWENTY-SEVEN

Eli

Martin calls me just after teatime. He sounds stressed. Launches into a monologue about the pressure of the big meeting tomorrow morning to discuss the progress on-site and the potential for another project.

I listen, wait for him to ask me how I am, which he eventually does after several minutes of work talk. I want to tell him I'm not fine. I want to tell him about the latest message. I want to ask him if he's given a key to our house to anyone else, but he sounds so stressed about the meeting that I don't want to add this stress to his plate. Not when I'll see him tomorrow anyway.

After I hang up, my mother gives me a stern look. I knew she wouldn't be happy.

'Why, Eliana, did you not ask him about the message?'

'I'll see him tomorrow,' I tell her. 'We'll talk then. Face-to-face. He has that big meeting in the morning and I don't want to jeopardise it for him.'

'You let him get away with too much. You always have. Is it any wonder he's acting the way he is?'

'We don't know anything for definite,' I say defensively.

I know I'm kidding myself. I know I'm denying all the evidence that's been put in front of me, but I don't care. I'm too tired to care.

'If it looks like a duck, walks like a duck and quacks like a duck, it's most likely a duck,' she continues in her best lecturing voice. 'I'm not trying to be harsh, darling, but maybe you need to start accepting that he's not the man you thought he was.'

It would be churlish of me to scream at her, 'But I don't want to,' but that's how I feel. I just want it all to go away.

★

Mum and I move around each other like chess pieces all evening. She's annoyed at me. On edge. She thinks I'm letting him get away with murder and that I shouldn't give a stuff if he messes up his big meeting. He deserves to have bad things happen to him.

I take myself to bed early at around nine, hope that sleep will come, but instead I toss and turn all night. When morning comes, my head hurts. As much as I love her, I don't want to have another chat with my mother. I just want to get up and dressed and go home.

Martin is due back mid-afternoon. I want to be there before him. I want to speak to Constable Dawson about the break-in and the message I've received. I'll call the police station, see if he's on duty and if I can speak to him. It'll be harder for him to fob me off face-to-face.

I want to possess as much information as possible before I talk to Martin. I want to see if the police can trace the message I was sent. Then I can confront Martin with what I know.

Confront. That word says it all. It *will* be a confrontation. Probably a horrible one. One in which he'll say all the same things he said on Saturday again and try to persuade me I'm the only woman for him.

I'll want to believe him, of course, because it'd be easier to believe him. I'd love to put it all down to some vindictive person doing the rounds, someone who has a grudge against him or me or just has too much time on their hands. Then the pair of us can move on with our lives, ignoring their petty notes and, hopefully, they'll soon get bored. Or they'll slip up and the police will track them down.

The alternative is that Martin might admit there's truth to it all. My life might implode. I may have to make tough decisions. He might tell me he's in love with someone else. The cleaner. His secretary. A client. Rachel, even.

He may take the decision out of my hands.

We'll have to choose who will move out, or if we'll both move out. I mean, I'll probably be the one to move, because it's his house, really. We bought it together but he's sculpted it into what it is now.

Then there'll be hushed tones from friends and colleagues as I walk past – the poor woman whose husband did the dirty on her when she was pregnant. There'll be sneaky glances to my left hand to see if I'm still wearing a wedding ring. Custody battles over who has this weekend or that holiday with the baby we've made together.

Everything about this makes me feel sick to my very stomach.

CHAPTER TWENTY-EIGHT

Eli

The drive back to Derry is arduous. It's frustrating at the best of times – the lack of a decent motorway or even dual carriageway between the North's two leading cities often makes it slow-going. Today, however, it almost tips me over the edge as I find myself caught behind every tractor, extra cautious driver and slow-moving vehicle between Toome and Drumahoe.

And that's without the trauma of extra roadworks and delays.

By the time my car is climbing the hill to the Waterside area of Derry, past Altnagelvin Area Hospital, I'm desperate for the toilet, grumpy and exhausted. All I really want to do is go home and hide under my duvet, but I've phoned the Waterside Police Service of Northern Ireland (PSNI) station on my journey and have arranged to speak to Constable Dawson in person.

A very polite female police officer warned me over the phone that it's unlikely the police will be able to trace the text message I received, but they'll keep it on file.

'There are sites set up specifically to allow people to send untraceable messages. These new technologies, we try our best to keep up with them but we tend to find if people want to be menacing, they find their ways. Why tech companies allow their software to be used in such a way is beyond me,' she'd said, leaving me devoid of hope that any of this would be solved quickly.

I'm almost at the police station, when my phone starts ringing. It's work. There's no way I can ignore it. No one calls staff on their days off without good cause.

'Eli?' Rachel's voice sounds around the car through the Bluetooth system.

'It's me,' I say. 'What can I do for you?'

'I don't suppose there's any chance you can pull a late shift tonight? I hate to ask, but Margaret's come down with the flu. We can get a bank nurse in if you can't, so don't feel under pressure, but, you know, budgets . . . We'll work the rota so you get your time back.'

I think of how tired I am. Of how I need to talk to Martin. Of how my back aches after the long drive. But then I know Rachel wouldn't ask if she wasn't stuck.

Perhaps it'll do me good to go there, feeling rotten and tired as I am. Work has that habit of helping me to put things in perspective.

'I can be in for seven, if that's okay?' I find myself saying.

'You're a lifesaver,' Rachel says. 'Eli, thank you. I'm pulling an extra shift too, so I'll see you when you get in. Hope you've had a good few days off?'

I almost laugh.

★

The visit to the police station proves as frustrating as I thought it might.

'Without any evidence of a break-in, there's not much we can do. Even with this message,' Constable Dawson tells me, his face serious, the bags under his eyes still there, accompanying a look of indifference.

'But this message *is* evidence. I didn't take that picture. My husband's in England.'

'Could it be an old one? A visitor to your house in the past? We tend to find with most things like this it's someone you know, personal grudge going on. A practical joke got out of hand. I'd suggest you talk to any keyholders.'

'I doubt very much that if a keyholder did this, they're going to admit it. And if this is a joke, it's most certainly not my kind of humour.' I feel a band of tension across my head. 'Surely forensics has turned up some information? Fingerprints? Anything?'

'Nothing conclusive at this stage. The only fingerprints we've positively ID'd so far are from yourself, your husband and your mother. There are a few others to check, but they don't show up on our database. They could belong to someone else familiar with your household. You mentioned you had a cleaner.'

We do have a cleaner, once a week. Caroline. I suppose I could ask her to give a fingerprint sample to police. I'm not sure how she'll react to that.

But apart from her, no. We don't have regular company – not recently anyway. It was different before; when I wasn't pregnant, miserable and a party pooper. The only people I know of who've been in our house recently have been Martin's partner, Jim, and Rachel.

I give him Caroline's details anyway but ask him to let me speak to her first. Then I ask what'll happen if they can't find any concrete information.

He shrugs his shoulders. 'We can't do much without evidence,' he says.

'And the CCTV showed nothing?'

'There's no CCTV close enough to your house to show anything that'd be deemed anything other than circumstantial at best. If your mother could remember any details about the car she saw pull off, that would help.'

But I know Mum can't. It was dark, she was panicking and all she saw was a blaze of headlights.

'I know it must appear very threatening and believe me, we'll keep everything on file,' Constable Dawson says.

What would have to happen for them to take further action than just keeping things on file? 'Could you put on extra patrols in this area? Keep an eye on the house?'

He shrugs. 'We can see about sending a car past every now and again but operationally, I don't think this would be a productive use of police resources. We can review that, of course, if anything else happens. But in the meantime, my advice to you would be to talk to your husband again, but of course, if you feel in any danger, you can call 999 at any time. We'll keep your number on our emergency response list,' he says.

It feels like he's reciting a script. He doesn't really care that this is turning my life upside down. In fact, I'm pretty sure he thinks I'm playing the role of hysterical woman beautifully.

'You should try to keep things in perspective,' he says. 'All we know for certain is that someone seems to want you to know that your husband may be playing away. It sounds to me like you've a friend who wants you to know.'

I'm not sure if there's a hint of a smirk in Dawson's tone as he speaks. As if this isn't the first time he's seen some deluded woman try to find an explanation that differed from the obvious for suspect behaviour.

I suppose I could argue with him to do more, but from the way he's looking behind him, eager to get back to his desk, I realise there's probably little point.

Dejected, I bid him goodbye. He tells me he'll be in touch if anything comes to light. I don't imagine I'll hear from him again.

I get home just twenty minutes before Martin's due to arrive.

It no longer feels like the safe place it once was. It looks exactly the same, but it is not the same. It has been violated. Our home, our marriage, everything has been violated. I sit in the car for a few minutes, taking deep breaths to try and calm myself, then I go in. From a glance around the house, there's no sign that anything is amiss. No whisky glass in the bedroom. All glasses accounted for in the cupboard. I don't keep a close enough eye on our alcohol supplies to know if anything has gone from the bottle, but from what I can see, everything in the house is just as I left it.

There isn't even a feeling anyone's been here – you know, an aura. Does that sound a bit hippy? We believe in that, you see, in the hospice, that people alive or dead leave a presence. I suppose it's my form of religion. A belief in spirit.

Maybe Dawson, with his lack of charm and his dark circles under his eyes, is right. Maybe the picture is an old one. I try to think of exactly when someone would've taken it.

Last New Year had been our last big party – pre-pregnancy. Could it have been taken then? Or could it have been taken at another time? When a guest was in our house. In our bedroom. In our bed. Just at a time when, perhaps, I wasn't there.

I make a quick call to Caroline. Tell her the police might be in touch. She sounds aggrieved and I have to reassure her, repeatedly, that neither Martin nor I believe she has anything to do with recent events. Even though we can't say for sure. Everyone's a suspect at the moment. I feel unsettled when I finish the call. I'm sure it will only be a matter of time before she hands in her notice.

Timed to perfection, I hear Martin's car pull up in the gravel driveway. I suddenly feel off-balance, physically and emotionally. Panic starts to swirl again. The fight or flight response telling me to fly.

I perch on the edge of the bed and focus on my breathing,

willing my legs to stay still. Don't run. Don't bolt. Just get through the moment.

I hear the front door open. A happy 'hello' echoes from downstairs, his footsteps approaching as he launches into a monologue about how the meeting couldn't have gone better and that the London partners were delighted with his work. He presents me with a bunch of flowers. Clearly, he's stopped at M&S on the way home and picked up the best bunch he could find. He's in great form. The issue with the redesign of the hospice has been resolved to everyone's satisfaction. They've been invited to make an official bid for the second project.

I plaster a smile on my face. One so fake, I'm sure he'll be able to see right through me.

'That's great news,' I tell him as he walks into the room. 'I'm delighted for you. And Jim, of course. You've worked very hard.'

I will him not to come close. Not yet. There's only so much I can fake and right now I can't fake tenderness with him.

Dawson's cynical face swims before mine. 'I think you should talk to your husband.'

'We should celebrate,' Martin says, pulling off his tie and throwing it on the floor.

Now, he's walking towards me, arms spread. I don't want him to touch me. I don't want to feel his skin on mine. His breath in my ear. His voice in my head. I don't want to smell him.

'We will,' I say, standing up, moving out of his reach and starting to take my uniform out of the wardrobe. 'But, sadly, not tonight. I've been called in for an extra shift. They were really stuck.'

His face drops. 'I was looking forward to some quality time with you. Especially after the weekend, you know.'

'And I was looking forward to some time with you, too,' I lie. 'But I couldn't say no. I'll make it up to you, I promise.'

I angle past him into the en suite, calling behind me that I just need to grab a quick shower. Locking the door in case he gets any notions to come after me, I set the water running so that I can't hear what he's saying over the noise. And he can't hear the crack in my voice as I call that we'll talk later.

CHAPTER TWENTY-NINE

Louise

I wasn't immune to the fact that not everyone would agree with me that what I was doing was the right thing. But those were probably people who'd led perfectly normal lives and who'd never experienced the tragedy I had.

I had that perfect life once. A husband. A house. A belief that my life was going exactly where I wanted it to go. He went out to work and it was my job to make us a home. To make us a family.

It was my body that had let us down.

It was so unfair. Unfair and cruel. Lots of women didn't want a baby in the way I did. Lots of women didn't want a baby at all. I had friends who'd 'gone to England to deal with a tricky situation' in the past. Who'd destroyed perfectly healthy pregnancies because it wasn't something they'd wanted at the time. They were nothing more than cold-blooded, selfish murderers.

I'd tried to find forgiveness and understanding in my heart for them, but couldn't.

I wondered if they'd have thought any differently if they'd known what I'd known. That nothing can be taken for granted.

A happy ending wasn't always promised, and certainly never guaranteed.

Sometimes you have to make your own. Steal your own, even. It didn't make me a bad person.

I'd never hurt anyone in my life. I'd always done the right thing. I'd followed the rules. I still went to Mass every week, even though I couldn't understand how my God could make me endure so much. Before I realised He had a bigger plan for me.

I've lived a good life. I could give this baby a good life. Full of love and happiness and faith. I knew I could do that. It's what I was born to do.

I had to remain careful, though. I had to protect myself from sinful ways and sinful thoughts. God would've punished me. He might have taken her away from me, if I'd given in to my temptations.

This man in front of me was a temptation sent to try me. I couldn't help it. Each time I saw him, I felt more of a pull, but I knew this was the final test. I had to resist.

Yet, still my heart skipped a beat when I saw him. When I sat outside their house and watched him arrive home. He looked so handsome. His tie loosened. His hair messy. For just a second I wondered, would he ever think me attractive? I wished I could be her – and have him come home to me. I wondered what it'd be like to have him hold me in his arms. To kiss me.

I touched my fingers to my lips. It has been so long since I'd been kissed. So long since I'd been held and loved.

It would have been so easy to give into temptation. So easy and so good.

But it would have destroyed everything I had planned.

CHAPTER THIRTY

Eli

I get to work early, leaving Martin bewildered in my wake. Relief washes over me when I walk across the car park and push open the hospice doors. I'm in my comfort zone here. I know what to do and I do it well.

'Eli, I'm so glad to see you,' Rachel says enthusiastically as I walk in.

She has a handful of files and the look of someone near the end of their rope.

'Busy day?'

'Tough day,' she says. 'Two patients passed today, including Nicola Flanagan. Poor thing. It's been tough for the staff, you know.'

I feel winded. Nicola is, was, only twenty-six, had been battling cervical cancer for the last three years. We knew she was very ill, but there was no way anyone was expecting her to go quite so quickly.

'Oh God, that was very sudden.'

'Too sudden. She just deteriorated on Saturday night and didn't come back from it. The family are distraught, as you can imagine. And the staff, too.'

I think of her mother, who'd always tried to keep smiling any time Nicola was in for respite care, and my heart aches for her. It seems so grossly unfair. I feel tears unexpectedly spring to my eyes. You'd think we'd get used to it, but sometimes it just feels all wrong. The cruelty of it seems to get worse.

'That poor girl,' I say, brushing my tears away hastily.

'At least she's not suffering any more. That's all we can take from it,' Rachel says, but she looks bone tired and as if she could break down herself.

I give her a hug, tell her I'll do my best to make sure she gets some quiet time during the night.

'No rest for the wicked,' she replies with a weak smile. 'But sure, we'll get through it. Can I bring you up to speed on everything?'

'Of course,' I say and follow her to the nurse's office.

'You've no idea how much you're pulling us out of a hole tonight,' she says. 'I hated asking you, especially with you being so pregnant.'

'I'll be out of here soon on maternity leave,' I say, 'you might as well make the most of me while you can.'

The thought of maternity leave makes me shudder. Who knows what state the rest of my life will be in by the time this baby arrives.

'I don't know what we'll do without you. What I'll do without you. I'll miss you, Eli.'

'I hope very much you'll come and see me when I'm off. You know much more about this parenting carry-on than I do. And I require gossipy updates, and a shoulder to cry on when I need it.'

'You'll be too busy enjoying that baby of yours to think of me,' she says, sitting down. 'But you know I'll be there for you if you need me.'

'Thank you,' I tell her, thinking myself ridiculous that I've even, so much as for a second, considered that she could be having a fling with my husband.

'Look,' she says. 'I'm not sure if this is the right thing to do or not, Eli. But something arrived in the post for you today.'

She sorts through the pile of paperwork she's been carrying and hands me a crisp white envelope, with my name neatly printed on the front.

'It looks like the same writing as that other letter,' she says, her face filled with concern. 'I wondered whether to keep it from you because of the stress, but then I thought you needed to see it, in case it needs to be brought to the attention of the police.'

I hold it in my hand. But it feels as if it might as well be a ticking time bomb. I sit down.

'I'm sorry,' Rachel says.

'It's hardly your fault,' I tell her, 'it's not like you sent it.'

I open the envelope, take out the single sheet of white paper:

HE'S NOT THE ONLY ONE BETRAYING YOU.
SHE'S LAUGHING AT YOU BEHIND YOUR BACK.
WITH FRIENDS LIKE HER, WHO NEEDS ENEMIES?

'Are you okay? What does it say?'

I hear Rachel speak and look up at her. A face filled with concern. With friends like her . . .

She has to be who this letter's talking about. Who else could it be? She's my closest friend her. My only real friend, who's spent a lot of time with both Martin and me. If she needs anything fixing in her house, I send him over to help. We've had her at our house for Christmas dinner when her kids were with their father. I'd never even once considered that I could've been pushing them together. I feel sick.

I want to scream at her. I want to slap her square across her face. I want to show her the note and tell her to explain it, but I think of the patients who need us. The shift we have to get through. I focus on it. Push down the hurt and the anger and the sense of betrayal.

Again.

It's what I always do.

Bury it. Get on with things. Make for an easy life.

Pretend there's still good in the world.

'It's not from the same person,' I lie, surprising myself at just how steady my voice sounds. 'It's just an invoice for something I ordered for Martin. I ordered it to come here. It's a surprise for him.'

She looks at me as if she knows I'm lying. I don't care. I don't care any more what she thinks of me. I thrust the note into the bottom of my bag, which I put in my locker, and then I ask her to fill me in on our current patients.

CHAPTER THIRTY-ONE

Eli

I do my best to listen and focus on what Rachel's telling me. Remind myself that our patients are my main concern now. We currently have five patients in for respite and four others in the terminal stages of their illnesses. We're waiting to admit another patient.

'Mrs Doherty's in?' I ask.

'Came in last night,' Rachel says. 'She just wasn't able to manage at home any more, so she's on subcutaneous morphine and Levomepromazine. She was very agitated and anxious earlier. So she was given 2 mg of Midazolam SC to help her rest. She'll be due another top-up soon. I see no reason to withdraw it at this stage. I think we're near the end now.'

I know it's likely her medication needs will only increase at this stage.

'Any family or friends with her?' I ask, although I suspect I already know the answer.

'Her son's on his way from England, but he can't get here until the morning,' Rachel says. 'One of her neighbours was in earlier this evening for a bit, but she's mostly been on her own. She's asked us to hold off on too much sedation until she sees her son, but, well, that's something we have to continue to reassess as the night passes.'

I read her notes. She's already on a high dose of morphine and is requiring frequent top-ups. As a woman who'd rarely complained about her pain levels before, I know things must be bad for her.

'You never get used to how cruel this disease can be, do you?' Rachel asks.

'You don't,' I say, thinking there's a lot of cruelty in the world that we can never prepare for or get used to.

I read the rest of the notes and leave the office quickly. I need to be away from Rachel as soon as I can and for as long as I can.

I walk down the corridor to Mrs Doherty's room, peaking in through the glass panel on the door to see she appears to be sleeping, so I gently press down on the handle and creep in, keen not to disturb her unnecessarily.

It's only been a matter of weeks since I last saw her, when she came in for respite care, but the brutal toll of the past three weeks is evident just by looking at her. She's lost a lot of weight and her skin has developed a crepe-like appearance, almost grey in colour, except for some particularly livid bruises on her hands and arms where IV lines have been sited. Her face is already hollowing out, her cheeks sunken into her face. There's no doubt this poor woman is actively dying in front of my eyes.

Her hair, which she'd been delighted to hang on to through the worst of her treatment, lies plastered to the pillow and the top of her head. She's always been so elegant that I feel for her, lying there free of her usual make-up, her usual blow-dry and set, and even the pearly white dentures that made her smile so bright and beautiful.

'Oh, Dotty, you really have been through the wars,' I whisper as I try to check her heart rate and blood pressure as gently as possible.

Her hands are cold and I hold them in my own, try to warm them up but making sure not to squeeze. She's in enough pain without me adding to it. As I care for her I explain everything I'm doing softly as if she were awake and able to hear me. It's important to remember that even when so very ill, a patient retains the right to dignity.

I see her wooden-handled, soft-bristled brush on her bedside locker and begin to brush her hair gently. I'm no hairdresser and how she's lying makes it difficult to style it properly, but I think I make it more presentable. In her sleep, she smacks her lips slightly. Morphine's known for its tendency to cause dry mouths in patients, so I dip an oral sponge swab in water and gently run it inside her mouth, where she sucks on it without waking.

I check when she's last had a top-up of pain relief to give her a break from the pain and note the time when someone should check on her again. I hope I'll be free to do it. I feel the need to be with her.

I tell her I'll see her a little later and leave her sleeping. I head back to the nurse's station, where I immediately send a text to my mother to tell her that I love her. We still hadn't been on the best of terms when I'd left this morning and my guilt at that is multiplied now that I've seen Mrs Doherty.

As usual for my mother, she replies within minutes:

I love you too, Eliana. How are you? How are things with Martin?

I reply I'm fine; I don't mention that I've not really spoken to Martin yet. I certainly don't mention the latest missive from my mystery stalker. She asks if she can call me when *Coronation Street* is over.

I'm pulling an extra shift in work. I'm fine though. Needed a little headspace. Don't worry.

It's only a matter of seconds before the reply 'of course I worry' lands on my phone. Just seconds later, it rings.

'Mum, you know I'm at work,' I say as I pick up. 'I can't really talk.'

'I'm not happy, Eliana,' she says. 'You should be resting, first of all, not jumping at extra shifts, and you should be at home trying to find out just what Martin is at. I know it's hard. I know you love him, sweetheart, but you can't run from it. You have to know where you stand, before this baby arrives.'

I rub my temples and sigh. I want to cry. But I can't allow myself to start to fall apart now. I'd be afraid I'd never be able to put myself back together again.

'Mum, I'm fine with the shift. I wouldn't have agreed if I didn't think I could manage. I'll talk to Martin when I get home. I just needed a little more space to try to get my head round it all. It's a lot, you know.'

'Don't let yourself be taken for a mug, Eli,' she says. 'I love you too much to see you get hurt by him.'

'I love you too, Mum,' I say, and feel tears spring to my eyes – not just for my own situation, but also with love for my mother and with sorrow for poor Mrs Doherty alone in her room.

CHAPTER THIRTY-TWO

Louise

No one was in the least bit surprised when I said I was moving away to start over again. No one tried to talk me out of it. No one, not even my parents, tried to dissuade me.

That hurt, I suppose. Then again, I imagine they were relieved to see me go at that stage. I might have been getting ready for a whole new life, but the truth was, the person they'd known and loved had gone a long time before.

A big part of her was buried in the ground in a plot at the City Cemetery.

They told me a new start would be good for me. That they thought it was 'just what I needed'. That it would 'do me good to get away from all the reminders'.

They didn't know, of course, that when I went, I'd be saying goodbye to them forever. I always wondered if that would've bothered them.

Everything about this new start had to be fresh and clean and properly organised. I'd actually forgotten just how organised I could be.

I took to it all easily. All the planning – sorting out the logistics. New place to live. When to go. How to get there.

How to appear to have gone but to still be here, just close enough. Where to stay when I was in that limbo of waiting for her to be born, but where no-one from my old life would find me.

The loneliness would get to me, I'd imagined.

So I'd had to be clever. I'd staved off my loneliness by allowing myself to watch them more. Always safely. Always from a distance. Always hidden from view. This quiet little mouse watched them lead their lives. I'd pretended that, in some way, I was part of it. Which I suppose I had been.

I sometimes wondered how he'd have reacted if I'd given him a choice. To come with me and raise his baby together, or stay with her knowing he'd never see his child again. Surely any decent man would choose his child over his wife. Blood over lust.

I told myself off for that. It would've been wrong. It would've been a sin.

The Sixth Commandment: Thou shall not commit adultery. Or would it? I wasn't the one who was married, after all. But could I condone it? Would it make me more of a sinner as one who encouraged it?

CHAPTER THIRTY-THREE

Eli

The only thing worse than a busy night shift is a quiet night shift. The minutes feel like hours. I'd hoped that I'd be kept busy enough to be able to avoid bumping into Rachel, or so I didn't have time to think about Rachel, or my husband, or Rachel and my husband. But the night is dragging and every minute feels like an hour.

Our patients are settled. A few family members sit quietly in their rooms, or on chairs in the communal area, blankets over them, trying to catch a little sleep but afraid to sleep too deeply only to be woken with bad news. We have accommodation on site for them, a couple of bedrooms, but we often find people are reluctant to stray too far from loved ones.

The lights are dimmed. The hospice is illuminated by lamp-lit offices and bedside lights. Nurses with pen torches carrying out their observations, speaking only in whispers to patients and other staff. The silence is broken only by the occasional opening and closing of a door, a beep of an infusion pump, a ticking clock in the staff room; one that we only seem to hear at night.

I long for a buzzer to sound, a rap on the door to call for my attention, a phone to ring. I need a distraction from the mess my life is in – a distraction from the tiredness, emotionally and physically, I'm feeling – or I fear I might just sink under it and not surface for a long time.

I get up and stretch and walk the deserted corridors. The hospice is situated far back from the main road running into Derry from Donegal, looking out over the banks of the River Foyle. Staring out of the windows, I can see the lights of the houses across the river, moving cars, street lights, serving as a reminder that whatever goes on in this particular corner of the world, everything continues as it always does elsewhere.

But there's also the blackness of the night and it's hard to escape the darkness in the world, too. Standing at the window, I'm reminded that someone's out there who's determined to get under my skin, to scare me and threaten me. To destroy the life I have now. And I have no clue who that person is.

I shudder, wrap my cardigan a little tighter over my uniform, and set off back up the corridor. I'll go and sit with Mrs Doherty. Keep her company. Check she has everything she needs. It'll do me good to be there, distracted from my own worries.

A tired-looking junior nurse is only too happy to take a break when I arrive at Mrs Doherty's bedside. I tell him to go and grab a quick nap, followed by a coffee. It takes a while to get used to night shifts.

'How's she been?' I ask as he makes to leave.

'A little more unsettled this last half-hour or so,' he says. 'Her breathing's become more laboured, but it seems to have settled again. Do you think she'll be able to hold on until her son arrives?'

I shrug. The truth is, I don't know. Mrs Doherty could pass in a matter of hours or days. Death isn't always as predictable as we all think. There are signs and stages we watch for, of course, but death doesn't always shift through the gears as it should.

That Mrs Doherty had been talking earlier that day, that she was able to speak to her neighbour when she visited is a positive sign, but a change in breathing, the soft gargle I can hear at the back of her throat? Those are signs that her body's giving up where her mind isn't quite ready. She is a fighter, but even the toughest of fighters have to concede at least once in their lifetime.

'Dotty,' I say softly as I check her chart, 'it's Eli. I'm going to work in here for a wee bit tonight, if you don't mind keeping me company.'

I gently brush her hair back from her face again, use a little lip salve to soothe her lips before I sit down and try to catch up on some of my paperwork by the soft light of her bedside lamp.

I try to stay focused on the journey Mrs Doherty's on. To comfort and guide her. It's true what they say that hearing is one of the last things to go. I can't stand the thought of her listening to the ordinary world go about its business around her as if her life, and her contribution to it, doesn't matter.

During her previous visits with us, Mrs Doherty and I had developed a great rapport. What I love most about her is that she's a no-nonsense sort and one of the few people on this planet who I feel understands me and my mixed feelings towards my baby.

While others would tell me I'm blooming, she'd ask how I was coping finding something that made me feel less nauseous. She discussed what she used to use to help with the side effects of her chemo, I discussed what I did to try to lessen the hormonal surges.

'I only did it the once,' she told me. 'Which was almost unheard of in my day. Every one of my friends was firing out babies like they were shelling peas. A baby in their belly, another on their hip and a tribe around their feet. I didn't see the appeal in doing it more than once,' she'd said with a smile. 'Too much pressure on us women to love everything about motherhood. Don't get me wrong, I love my son very much. I'd do anything for him, but motherhood never fulfilled me the way it did my friends.'

Her honesty had been refreshing. An antidote to my mother's well-meaning but guilt-inducing take that there's nothing in this world that could ever come close to the thrill of holding your own child and raising them. My mother would've had a houseful of children if she could have. 'But things just didn't work out that way. I'll have to make up for it with a houseful of grandchildren instead, eh?' she'd said with a wink.

So I chat to Mrs Doherty again. I tell her how the night sky is filled with stars. How a heavy frost is settling on the grass and tomorrow is bound to be another cold one. I tell her how I find the hospice so peaceful. And, sometime around 3 a.m., I find myself crying a little and telling her I wish she was here, properly here, to talk to me with some of her wit and wisdom. I tell her what a friend she's been to me. How she could always make me laugh; because that was one of her greatest gifts, being able to make me laugh even when I was feeling sorry for myself.

I don't realise the tiredness is getting the better of me as we talk. I know my eyes are growing a little heavier, and every now and again I get up to stretch, to ease the ache in my back and wake up a bit. But still, sitting at her bedside and holding her hand, I drift off at some stage.

I wake to her gasping, her body writhing in pain. I try to soothe her. Put an oxygen mask on her face to try to ease her breathing, but her face is contorting in agony. A horror mask of dying, which in the darkness of the room looks haunting. Her hands are fisting at the sheets, her eyes wide with fear.

Sleepily, my hands shaking, my heart thumping, I administer more meds. More sedative. More pain relief. I just want to help. That's my job, to help. I just don't want her to be scared. I don't want the fear to overwhelm her.

I can do this. I've done it many times. But this time, something feels wrong.

She goes quiet. Is still. For the briefest of moments I feel relief, because the awful noise she's been making has stopped, her body relaxed.

But then something changes. Her chest stills. Her eyes droop. Not quite closed but the light has gone out.

I know she's gone. I know it instinctively. I start to shake. Have I done something wrong? I push down the panic as I start to work through my steps. The dose.

Jesus! The dose.

Hastily calculated.

Wrong.

Fatal.

I feel the room start to spin. I just about manage to hit the panic button before I have to sit down to stop myself from falling. I look to Mrs Doherty, her face like a bizarre mask, still not quite hers. Still wearing a gruesome expression of fear.

Was she scared of me? Did I kill her? Did she know I'd kill her? I'd been so distracted with my own life, so caught up in me and my imploding marriage and my pregnancy and my mother, had I not been concentrating? And I'd been asleep. Oh God . . .

Footsteps. I hear footsteps but they sound as if they're getting further away rather than coming closer. The room spins more. The window. The darkness. Is there someone there? Laughing? I try to breathe as the darkness gets darker. I feel myself slipping away.

CHAPTER THIRTY-FOUR

Eli

Things are hazy. People are blurry shapes. Sounds. Questions. Hushed tones. We have to keep quiet. We have to whisper these conversations. Be aware of our other patients. We have to make sure no one hears. No one gets upset. No one loses faith in what we're doing.

We.

But it's me, you see. Not we. I've messed up. I can dress it up whatever way I want, but I've fucked up on an unforgivable scale. I try to block out the noise, try to run what's happened through my head in slow motion. I'd been distracted. Tired.

Should I have buzzed for help sooner? That was protocol, after all – two people. Double-checking. But she was in so much pain. Her face twisted. But I was used to that, wasn't I? I'd seen it before. It was my job to remain calm in these circumstances. To do my job. A job I knew inside and out.

I'd been calm. Hadn't I? Too many thoughts and feelings. A kick in the ribs. A rattle of nausea. A regret for coming into work and not having a good night's sleep. Wanting to turn back the clock. Not just an hour, but days, months even. Before everything started to go wrong. I want to go home.

The realisation that going home isn't the answer either hits me — there's too much to face there. There's too much to face here. Everything's falling apart.

I can't breathe. In the hushed room, with hushed voices and furtive glances. Rachel's beside me — I'm not sure when she got here. She looks at me and I can't meet her eye. I need her — or at least the person I thought she was — to reassure me, but I also need the person I fear she is to stay away. If she's the 'friend' mentioned in the latest note, then surely they'll have so much more to laugh about now. I've really messed it all up.

I'm ashamed and humiliated and so very sorry. Tears flow freely down my cheeks. I want to tell Mrs Doherty how sorry I am. I want her to hear me. I want her to believe me. I want her back.

I rock slightly back and forth. I look unhinged, I imagine, but I have no reputation left to protect at this stage anyway.

What have I done?

'Eli.' I hear Rachel's voice come into focus. 'Eli, breathe,' she says. I feel her hand on my knee, become aware that she's kneeling in front of me. 'It's okay. It'll be okay.'

I look at her, blinking. How could she think it's okay? How could any of it be okay?

'It's not,' I mutter. 'It's not.'

'There's some tea here, sweet, for the shock,' she says.

I can't even think about drinking it. I know I'll throw it back up. I'm aware one of our doctors is having a whispered conversation with our chairman. There's head-shaking. Chin-rubbing. Did I hear someone mention the police? I want to put my hands over my ears to block it all out.

'I'll take you home. You're too distraught right now. You have to think of the baby,' Rachel says.

I want so much to run away, but not home, and I certainly

don't want *her* of all people to take me there. I'll get no relief from this there.

I shake my head, still can't meet her eyes. 'I gave her too much,' I say, panic rising. 'She should still be here. Her son . . . she won't see her son. I know better. I shouldn't have . . .'

She shushes me. 'She was in a lot of pain, Eli. You said she was screaming with pain. She was dying, Eli. She could've passed away at any time.' She's whispering.

She knows as well as I do that officially it's not likely to be seen like that. There will be an investigation. An inquest. Repercussions for my career, but that's not even what hurts the most now.

'She had a chance to see him. I took away her chance. His chance.'

I feel grief buckle me in half. Grief and more. Shame. Embarrassment. Guilt. As I sob, I swear I can feel every ounce of confidence I have in who I think I am, how good I consider myself to be, release itself from my body into the room around me. Until there's nothing left but the shell of who I was – and the galloping heartbeat of a child who's unfortunate enough to have me for a mother.

I watch as Rachel talks to the others in the room. There's talk of a possible autopsy. As if Dotty hasn't been through enough.

I hear Rachel talk. 'She's been under a lot of stress. There's been some trouble at home. Anyone would crack. I probably shouldn't have called her in for the shift.'

I feel gut-punched. 'Some trouble at home.' It would be laughable, really. I look at her as she talks more, dropping her voice to a whisper. I want to tell her to speak up. Ask what she's saying. That my husband is cheating? That I'm not capable? She's supposed to be on my side. Not this. Not hanging out my dirty laundry. Talking about my personal life. Playing the innocent.

I see sympathetic looks in my direction. I don't deserve them. Rachel turns to me, urges me to drink the tea. 'For the shock,' she repeats. There's a confidence about her. Is it superiority? Is it because my life is more of a colossal disaster than she perceives hers to be? She has the upper hand. The impeccable career. Everyone's friend. My husband's lover . . .

I think of the notes, and the faux sympathy, and her face as she tells our colleagues that I'm 'not myself', and I wonder how I ever trusted her in the first place.

CHAPTER THIRTY-FIVE

Louise

Someone once told me the definition of a sin was when you intentionally hurt yourself or other people.

If the intention is not to hurt, then it couldn't be a sin.

I may have been aware that my actions would result in people getting hurt, but my intention was never to hurt them. Hurting people was never my driving factor.

Love was my driving force.

Love was what made me want to give that baby the very best in life.

Love was what made me want to spend hours being the best parent I could.

Love was what made me push my concerns to one side, to encourage the advances of a married man – when they came. I prayed my God would forgive me. Would understand that I'd been a weak and flawed human. Would understand that I'd been blinded by love.

I never wanted to hurt his wife. So it was only a couple of times. I knew I had to let him be with her. I knew I had my own plans in place and I wasn't prepared to let go of them.

And I knew, with the utmost certainty in the world, that he'd never, ever leave her. She was the mother of his unborn child, after all.

CHAPTER THIRTY-SIX

Angela

Eliana's been gone less than twenty-four hours when she calls me to ask if she can come back.

I can barely make out what she's saying. Her voice is little more than a whisper, but I know something is very wrong. A mother knows.

When I hear how upset she is, I expect her to tell me she's finally had it out with Martin. I hope she's told him where to go. I used to like him, love him even, but he's proven in recent times that he doesn't deserve to have her in his life. He's not a man to be trusted.

He's still denying that he's cheating, of course, despite all the allegations that have been made over the last few days. All the evidence that something is up. Poor Eli, too trusting always.

From the moment she told me about the first note, I've been anticipating this phone call. Steeling myself for it. Waiting for the moment I'd be asked to step in and soothe her, offer a listening ear, a warm hug and a big cup of tea by the fire.

I know that when things go wrong, she turns to me. We're so close. We always have been. Of all the relationships in my life, my bond with Eli is the one I value most. I'll do everything

I can to protect her from hurt. Especially now she's pregnant. It's been so difficult to watch her struggle with her pregnancy. I wish she was able to enjoy it a little, enjoy all those kicks and wriggles and having a gorgeous swollen tummy. But she's been so sick and things with Martin have been so strained.

If only they lived closer, I could help her more. Support her more. Give her something to focus on outside work and her designer home and her errant husband.

I've done my best to try to understand her feelings and her struggles to bond with her baby. But the truth is that I don't. She's the greatest gift the world has ever given to me. Even when we struggled, when times were particularly tough, I never once regretted my decision to keep her and raise her.

I pray Eli will find that same love for her child. Once she holds that baby in her arms, she's sure to feel it. Even the coldest of mothers feel it when they meet their babies. An instinctual pull towards them. An urge to protect at all costs. It's the most overwhelming feeling in the world.

I suppose that's why I'm angry with Martin; although I've tried my very best to hide that from Eli. He must see her struggling too, but still he's abandoned her – skipping off to London at a moment's notice, leaving her isolated in that house. I'd never do that.

So as I hear her sobbing down the phone, asking if she can come and stay, just for a bit, I feel relieved. I'll have her close to me. I can look after her. I can protect her, and her baby.

She sounds so very young and vulnerable and my heart lurches. I wonder if it makes me a bad person, but as I listen to just how much she needs me, really needs me, I feel a warm glow. A renewed sense of purpose.

'Of course you can come and stay, darling,' I soothe. 'Are you okay? Is it Martin? Oh, sweetheart, I'm so sorry, but it'll be okay. I promise you.'

I hear her sniff, gulp back a sob. 'I just need to pack a few things . . . I need to find my case.'

'Are you in a fit state to drive?' I ask, alarmed by how distressed she sounds.

The last thing I want on my conscience is her having an accident on the drive to Belfast because she's too distraught to concentrate properly.

'Erm . . . I don't know, Mum. I think so. I'll be fine . . .'

'I'll come and get you,' I say, already kicking off my house slippers and sliding my feet into my shoes, which I'd left beside the hall table. My keys are in the dish on the console. I'll be in my car and on the way to her in less than a minute. I can be with her in ninety minutes and that way I'll be sure she isn't taking any unnecessary risks.

'I'll be okay,' she says, but I can hear it in her voice.

I shudder. Devastated at her pain but thrilled that she needs me. It's a heady mix.

'I'll be with you in an hour and a half,' I tell her. 'I want you to try to breathe and we'll sort it out. I promise. You're more than welcome here for as long as you need. You know that. I'll be with you soon, my darling. Try to stay calm. Think of the baby.'

★

The rain that's been falling all morning has turned to sleet by the time I find myself nearing Derry. Traffic has started to move frustratingly slowly. It's taking me much longer than I'd hoped to reach Eli and my patience is starting to wear thin.

I try my best not to use bad language, although I can't help but swear at the drivers exercising undue caution at roundabouts and traffic lights. If they can't deal with a bit of sleet, they shouldn't be on the roads in the first place.

When the traffic starts to logjam on the Crescent Link, outside one of the city's big out-of-town retail parks, I find myself fighting the growing tension in my neck, shoulders and arms. I can't show up at Eli's stressed. I need to exude calm.

Lord knows what exactly I'll be walking in to. Is Martin there? Is he going to cause a scene? He always has been one to wear his heart on his sleeve and there's little chance he's going to let his pregnant wife leave without putting up some resistance.

I'd had such high hopes for him when I'd first met him. Not only did he treat Eli with respect, but he also treated me with respect. He seemed fully on board with how close our relationship was and when he'd turned up at my door one evening, when Eli was at work on shift at the City Hospital, to ask for her hand in marriage, he'd impressed on me how it was important to him that he had my full support.

'I know this is a little old-fashioned,' he'd said as he'd perched nervously on my armchair, an untouched cup of tea in his hand, the saucer rattling slightly, belying his nerves. 'But I know that you mean the world to Eli and she wouldn't agree to anything without your full approval. You must know how much I love your daughter and I promise you I'll never do anything to hurt her. Ever. No one could mean more to me than she does and I'd really love it if you'd give us your blessing to get married.'

I love that he asked me for my blessing. To be honest, I'd been feeling a little pushed out. A mother's love is one thing. That first full-on in-love feeling and the infatuation that comes with it is something else. At that moment, Martin Hughes was more exciting to my daughter than I ever could be. I was the comfortable and the reliable. He was the fizz in the pit of her stomach. He was the new and I was the old. His asking, and his reassurance that he'd never hurt her, meant a lot. I'd hoped he'd never hurt me, either.

I'd imagined our lives together as a new chapter in the book that had already been Eli and me. They were both career-oriented but I was fine with that. I understood that things were different for young people these days and besides, I was so very proud of Eli and her chosen field. A daughter of mine, a palliative care nurse! She makes a real difference to people's lives. I'd imagined they'd marry, eventually have children and that perhaps I could step in as a grandma on call for all the child-minding duties. I was still young enough. I'd love it. I'd look forward to it, if truth be told.

I believed that she'd always be near me, just as she used to promise me when she was little.

'We'll always live together, won't we, Mummy?' she'd ask.

'Of course, darling.'

'Or I'll get a house next door to you and knock a hole in the wall so we can come in and out of each other's houses any time we want.'

'Sounds just lovely, my darling.'

'Will you look after my babies when I'm a mummy? Just like you look after me.'

I didn't have to think about it.

But things didn't work out that way, did they? Eli and Martin married. It was a great day, even if they'd insisted on a civil wedding and I didn't get my day in church. I'd been so proud to fulfil my mother-of-the-bride role. To walk my daughter, who I'd raised single-handedly, down the aisle. I was set for our new life.

But he took her away from me. Back to his native Derry. Bit by bit. I suppose the wedding being held there should've been a sign.

Within a year of them getting married, he set up his practice there. Then she got the job at the hospice. And, finally, they ploughed all their savings into that house. Keen to make it their 'forever home'.

It hurt me. It still hurts me. That I'm being written out of their lives. That their day-to-day existence doesn't involve me at all.

But maybe she'll come to see all this upset as a blessing in disguise. As we get closer again. It'll be hard, I know, but I can help her through it.

The traffic jolts forwards another few metres. I turn the radio off. The interminable chatter of the hosts, talking of some sort of political stalemate nonsense that seems to have been on repeat for the last two years, has started to annoy me. Just as the sound of my windscreen wipers, rhythmic as they are, starts to grate and the sound of my indicator nips at me. I look at the clock. I'd told Eli I'd be with her in ninety minutes. It's closer to two hours now. I'm angry at myself for not having a hands-free thingummy fitted in the car like Eli'd nagged me to. I could call her if I did, tell her I'm almost there.

I wonder if she's worried about me. She must be, given the weather and the driving conditions. I hope she isn't upsetting herself too much.

I tap my fingers on the steering wheel impatiently, waiting for the traffic to move again. There appears to have been an accident in the oncoming lane, fairly minor but enough to bring everything to a standstill. Someone's probably misjudged the slippery road surface.

There's no way around it, not from here. I offer up a silent prayer for divine intervention and take deep breaths.

With a knot of tension so tight across my shoulder blades that I want little more than to sink into a hot bath, I pull into the driveway of my daughter's dream home on Judges Road twenty-five minutes later.

The sleet is still falling, threatening to turn to snow, and if we're much longer before we set off back for Belfast there's a danger it'll freeze over and the roads will become too treacherous to risk.

Both their cars are parked outside. I gird myself to see Martin. Eli will want me to be polite yet firm. She won't want me making a scene. Eli doesn't do scenes, even when she's sure she's in the right.

I know if I go in there and start launching an attack on Martin, it may start her thinking defensively about him and, God forbid, if she decides to give him a second chance, I'll end up being the worst in the world for speaking up and voicing my opinions.

It's only a few short steps to the front door, so I put my head down and go straight there, reaching out to ring the doorbell just as the door swings open and a haggard-looking Martin stands in front of me.

Although he's clean-shaven, he looks done in. His shirt is crumpled, his tie undone. His sleeves are rolled up and his hair is far from the neat style he normally wears it in. Ruffled. That's how he looked: ruffled.

'Angela,' he says, looking me in the eye. His expression has a pleading quality about it. I guess this is where he'll tell me it's all a mistake. All a lie. How he doesn't know who's behind it and where he'll implore me to talk some sense into his wife.

'Thank God you're here,' he says, throwing me off guard. 'Please, you have to try to get her to calm down. She's making herself sick. I've tried to tell her that they'll know it was a mistake, a simple mistake. Anyone could have made it.' He drops his voice to a whisper. 'I know it's bad, but we have to try to calm her, for the sake of the baby if nothing else. I know they'll look at the bigger picture. She's a good nurse. She wouldn't have intentionally hurt anyone. These things must happen, when the patients are so vulnerable.'

This isn't what I was expecting. Intentionally hurt someone? My Eli? What are 'these things' he's talking about? What vulnerable patient?

This isn't part of my script. I hear a keening sound from the living room and I feel my stomach tighten.

What has she done?

CHAPTER THIRTY-SEVEN

Angela

I don't like this feeling in my stomach. A lead weight, pulling me down.

'I've told her to speak to a solicitor, in case. She should be able to get someone fairly specialised through her union,' Martin says, turning and heading towards the back of the house and his distraught wife.

I want to scream at him. Why does she need a solicitor? In case of what? But it's clear he assumes I'm already in the know.

My heart's beating loudly, blood whooshing in my ears as I see my daughter. My baby. The one person in this world I'd do anything for. There is she is. Curled, almost foetal, her hands to her face. Her chestnut hair messy. Her hands white with tension. Her cries loud. Pitiful. My child.

In front of me now, she's my baby again. Not the thirty-three-year-old, capable woman she's become but scared and vulnerable. Inconsolable, as if she's in the middle of one of the night terrors that used to torment her as a child. It's terrifying. Most of all because I know I can't just hold her until it passes. I can't just wake her out of it and make it all better again.

She sees me; her face contorts further. 'Oh! Mum,' she wails. 'I killed her. I didn't mean to, but I killed her.'

Her words are a like a punch. No! I want to scream that she didn't. I don't need to know the facts to know that my child didn't kill anyone. Never in a million years.

This was supposed to be about Martin. This mercy dash was supposed to be about his cheating. I was prepared for that. I'm not prepared for this. I fight back a wave of nausea as I sit down and pull her to me – her body rigid with fear and grief.

'You didn't. You didn't. It'll be okay, my darling. It'll be okay.'

I hope that it will be. I can't stand this. I look to Martin, back to Eli.

He speaks.

'There was an incident at the hospice. Eli was on night shift and caring for one of her patients, in the very end stages of her illness. The woman became very distressed and, well, Eli administered medication to help her, but the dose was miscalculated and . . .'

And. That word he leaves hanging there. As if he can't say the words.

'She was in so much distress. I just wanted to help her. I was tired but I should've called a colleague for help. I didn't realise I'd drawn up too much until it was too late. She was gone. I swear,' Eli says, her eyes wide, 'I swear on my life, and this baby's life, it wasn't intentional. She was trying to hang on to see her son. We were trying to help her hang on but I took that from her. I've messed up. I've really messed up.'

Martin speaks. 'Her colleague, Rachel, brought her home, in this state. After she'd spoken to the management team and the police.'

'The police? But it wasn't a crime,' I almost scream.

'They have to investigate everything. All the circumstances and all the factors. Eli's been suspended, on full pay, pending a full investigation. I've told her that's a good sign. If they thought a crime had been committed, they wouldn't have suspended her. She'd have been dismissed. I doubt the police would have let her just walk out of there, either.'

'Intentional or not, I robbed her of what was left of her life,' Eli cries.

'A life in which she was in excruciating pain,' Martin says.

He sits down on the opposite side of the sofa to me and reaches out to hold Eli, but she pulls away. Shakes off his touch as if it hurts her.

'We'll face it together,' Martin says. 'Eli, I promise you, we'll face it together.'

She shakes her head and cries more. 'How can we, Martin?' she asks. 'We can't even think about facing it together.'

He looks stung. I watch as she reaches for her handbag and thrusts an envelope at him. Familiar, crisp and white.

'This arrived today,' she says, her voice shaking.

I watch as he opens it, reads what the paper inside says. He stands and throws it across the room.

'For God's sake. Who the *hell* is doing this?'

He's angry and I see tears form in his eyes.

'What does it say?' I ask.

'It doesn't matter what it says, it's all lies,' he says, angry.

Eli simply shakes her head and I get up and lift the note, see the words printed on the sheet. Another allegation.

'Martin, has Eli told you about the text message?'

'What text message?'

He's blinking at me, confused.

'From an anonymous account,' Eli says. 'A picture from this house. From our bedroom. Making the same allegations. Who is it, Martin? Is it Rachel? Is she who you're laughing with behind my back?'

'Rachel?' he says, incredulous. 'Get a grip, Eli.'

'You can't deny it any more,' I tell him. 'Is it any wonder Eli's making these mistakes in work – when you're putting her through this unbelievable level of stress?'

'But I'm not,' he says, exasperated. 'Someone else is doing this. I've not lied. And I've not been having an affair with Rachel or anyone else. Eli, come on – you really think I'd have a fling with Rachel?'

Eli just looks at him as if she can't process what he's saying.

'Can we go, Mum? I think I need to get away from here.'

'Of course, darling,' I tell her. 'Anything you want.'

CHAPTER THIRTY-EIGHT

Angela

'She's staying here,' Martin says, flashing me an angry look.

I should've known he wouldn't let her go without a fight.

'I can make my own decisions,' she says, her voice shaky but firm. 'Right now, Martin, I don't know who I am any more, or what to believe or what to do. I can't just dismiss these messages because you tell me to.'

'I'm telling you the truth,' he shouts, now standing and pacing back to the kitchen. 'You just want to think the worst of me, just like you want to think the worst of everything and everyone at the moment.'

'That's not true,' Eli says, sitting up straight, squaring up to him.

I sit back in my chair. This is a conversation they need to have between them.

'Why would I want to think the worst of you? That's insane.'

'Yes,' he says. 'It is insane. So much about your behaviour over the last few weeks has bordered on the insane, if you want me to be honest. Moping about feeling sorry for yourself while carrying our baby . . . How do you think that makes me feel? You say you don't know who you are any more, well I don't know who you are any more, either. I can't get through to you. No matter how hard I try. And if you don't trust me, then I don't know what else I can do. I've told you the truth.'

'But the notes . . .' Eli said.

'Fuck the notes and whatever sick bastard is behind them. I don't know how you can't see how ridiculous all this is. It's not like you to be so . . . so . . . blind to the truth. I'm tired of trying to make you believe in me. Believe in us. So why don't you just go! Run to your mother. You're clearly miserable here, so just leave.'

He's crying and Eli's crying. I sit. I say nothing. I need to let them work this out between them.

'I can't talk to you any more,' Eli says. 'We're just pulling each other apart.' She stands up, roughly brushes at her cheeks with the sleeves of her cardigan. Taking a deep breath, her voice shaking, she says, 'I have some bags packed here, Mum.' She gestures to two purple wheeled weekend cases behind the front door. 'They should do for now.'

'Do you have your notes with you?' I ask, ignoring the miserable picture of Martin, standing, head bowed, watching his perfect life disintegrate.

She looks at me blankly. I can see grief and pain and exhaustion all over her face. In that second I feel such a deep love and sadness for her that I almost break down. But I have to stay calm. It's my job to be in control now.

'Your maternity notes, pet. Just in case.'

We have to be prepared for everything. Even the birth of her baby.

'Okay, okay. I'll get them.'

She walks back down the hall to the console and opens a drawer, pulling a green folder out, then she looks at it for just a second before walking back to me.

I don't know if I expect Martin to follow us out. To make

a last-ditch attempt to ask her not to go. But it seems his male pride gets the better of him. He lets us leave.

Side by side, in my car, the sleet still falling, the sound of the windscreen wipers only broken by the occasional sniff from my poor, broken girl, we drive towards Belfast. Her cases are in the boot. Her notes are on the back seat and her hand is clutching mine.

'Let's go home,' I say.

CHAPTER THIRTY-NINE

Louise

He had been easy to talk to. I'm not sure what I expected, but when I saw him sitting at a table in the café across from his office, I knew I had to talk to him.

'Is this seat taken?' I'd asked.

He'd looked at me and smiled, and I was dazzled by his soulful brown eyes. I'm not a vain woman. I don't court the attention of men, but I noticed that he looked me up and down, and I could tell that he liked what he saw.

I'd made more of an effort that day.

I'm not saying I'd intentionally chosen to visit the café closest to his work, but I'm not saying it wasn't intentional, either.

I knew I wanted to talk to him. I knew I couldn't just walk up to his front door and ask to speak to him. That would look insane. This was my best, and safest, option.

He'd gestured at me to sit down, and I did, ordering a cup of tea from the waitress who'd walked past. He took that as an opportunity to ask for a refill of his coffee. He told me he was on his tea break – needed to get out of the office to clear his head. I told him I was going shopping – picking up some pieces for a forthcoming trip away.

I could feel the connection between us, immediately. How it felt comfortable to be with him. How his smile made me feel funny inside.

I never in a million years thought that he'd end up in my bed that afternoon, but at the time it felt so right. We needed each other. It was more than lust. More than a physical act. More than body parts and gasps and moans.

I knew it was wrong. Of course I did. But I think maybe that was part of what made it feel so good. But still, I vowed that I'd never do it again. I couldn't do it again. It complicated everything. It took my focus from what really mattered.

I prayed that night, harder than I'd prayed in months:

Lead me not into temptation
And deliver me from all evil.

CHAPTER FORTY

Angela

Eli is quiet throughout the journey. Occasionally, I notice her wipe away a tear, or I hear a prolonged sigh, but when I ask her how she is, she simply replies that she's 'okay', which of course she isn't. She looks wretched, but I know I can make it better now, you see. I have experience of dealing with some of life's curveballs, after all.

I'd never planned to be a single mother. Always thought I'd live in a lovely semi-detached house with a well-manicured lawn front and back and a swing for the children. I'd dreamed of cooking our dinner just in time for my hard-working, handsome husband to arrive home. And that we'd sit, him and me, with whatever children we were blessed with, around the table and talk about our day.

I never thought I'd end up doing it alone. Without the only man I'd ever loved. With no army of children around my feet. But you make do, don't you? You adapt. You roll with the punches and you don't ever let the hurt and the bitterness in.

Eliana would come to see that. Life might be taking her in a completely new direction, but that didn't mean it was a bad direction.

As long as the powers that be had a bit of sense about them. I hear myself sigh as it crosses my mind that what happened in the hospice could have devastating consequences for Eli. Her career. Her freedom.

We'd call her union. Speak to a rep. See where she stood. We'd take control. Surely accidents happened. It was terribly sad for the poor lady in question, of course, but she had been dying. She was going to die anyway. There was no need for anyone to get hysterical about it.

'Are you okay, Mum?' Eli asks.

I reply that I am. Which isn't exactly true, but I'll be strong for her.

'We've come through worse than this, Eliana. I know how hard this is, but you're a strong woman. I raised you well. We raised each other well, didn't we?'

She nods.

'You must be exhausted,' I say. 'I doubt you've had much sleep.'

She shakes her head.

'Well, we'll deal with things one at a time – one hour at a time and one day at a time. The first thing we'll do is make sure you get a good night's sleep.'

'I'm not sure I'll be able to. My mind's racing,' she says quietly. 'Poor Mrs Doherty. I wonder, maybe, should I go back? Talk to her son. Explain what happened.'

No, I think. That wouldn't be the right thing to do. At all.

'I don't think that'd be a good idea, pet. He'll be very upset. He needs time to think it all through and I really don't think your management would want you to talk to him, either.'

'But I need to tell him I'm sorry,' she says.

'You *never* say sorry,' I say, and I know that sounds cold, but I have to be practical. 'Sorry is an admission of guilt.'

'But I *am* guilty,' she says.

'Look, why don't you wait to see what the investigation throws up.'

Eli goes back to looking out of the window. I can see her breath steam against the car window. I'm transported back to when she was little, when we'd huff and puff on the cold glass of the single glazing in our flat in Paisley and draw stick figures in the condensation. Huddled close. Laughing. Our breath mingling into one exhalation.

'I'll make some warm milk when we get home. We'll get you a warm bath. I'll light the fire in your room if you want, make it nice and cosy for you. I'll even sit in your room with you, sleep beside you if you need me to. I'll do whatever you want me to do. Because you're my child and you mean the world to me. I'm so sorry the world is hurting you just now, but we'll make this right, darling. I promise.'

I hear her sniff but I keep my eyes on the road and focus on moving ever forwards.

When we arrive home, I carry in Eli's cases for her, even though she insists that she's okay to carry them herself. The sleet has turned to snow and the house is cold when we walk in, so I switch on the heating, light the fire that I'd set in the hearth earlier, then carry some logs and firelighters upstairs to light the one in Eli's room. Hopefully, the flicker of the flames and the warmth will soothe Eli to sleep.

Taking one of my fluffiest towels from the airing cupboard, I go into the bathroom and hang it over the towel rail, which is heating nicely. After lighting scented candles, I switch on the taps and run a bath for her, adding some of my expensive oils. No Mr Matey bubble bath any more. No giggles while pulling her shampooed hair into a Mohican. Those days are long gone, but maybe we'll have them again when my granddaughter's born.

I smile. Memories come flooding back of Eli as a little girl and her Sunday night baths before school. I'd sit on the closed toilet seat while she played with her dolls in the bath, chatting nineteen to the dozen to me about her day, her hopes, her dreams, what she wanted for her birthday – even though it was months away. Talking about nothing and everything. It was the nicest ritual of parenthood, lifting her from the bath and wrapping her in a giant towel, dressing her in fresh pyjamas and sitting in front of the fire, brushing her hair out with a large wooden-handled brush.

I'm not sure when that stopped exactly. But it had; her need for help had waned. She'd become this fiercely independent young woman and while I'm so very proud of her, my heart still aches for those precious days.

Now, watching the bubbles foam and rise in the bath, feeling warmth spread through my home, looking at the candles flickering on the windowsill, I feel something else rise and spread within me. No heartache. No loneliness.

Only hope.

Hope that she'll realise that she still needs me in her life.

I call her name and watch as she climbs the stairs, tired and broken-looking.

'This is where it starts to get better,' I assure her.

She blinks at me, her eyes red-rimmed, but no tears fall. She reaches her arms out to me and I pull her into a hug so tight that I can feel her trembling.

'I promise you it'll be okay.'

'I love you, Mum,' she said. 'What would I do without you?'

While Eli soaks in the bath, I do what I said I would. I carry her cases upstairs and unpack them for her, leaving out some pyjamas, her dressing gown and a pair of fluffy bed socks. I fill a hot-water bottle and slip it under the covers of her bed before going into my room and changing into my own pyjamas.

Shrugging my dressing gown on, I pad across the landing

163

and stand at the bathroom door for a moment, just listening to the sound of my child as she bathes. Smiling, I walk downstairs and start preparing some supper. My phone beeps as I cut thick slices of bread ready to toast under the gas grill.

I pick it up to see Martin's name. Rolling my eyes, I open the message:

> Angela, I know I'm public enemy number one just now but you must believe me. I'm telling the truth. I've never cheated on Eli. I never would. I don't know who's behind all this, but there's no truth in it. Can you please help me to help her see sense? I don't feel I can reach her any more. I swear to you, I'd never hurt her.

I can't and won't believe him any more. He's proven himself to be unreliable when it comes to keeping promises. I type:

> The best thing you can do now is give her space.

I hit send and then switch my phone to silent.

I resume preparing our supper, but it strikes me that if Martin's texted me, he most likely will have texted Eli as well. I know her handbag is still in the living room, so I go in and have a look through it. Sure enough, the notification light is flashing on her phone and I can see that the message is from Martin. She'd told me her PIN code before – their wedding anniversary – so I type it in and delete the message from Martin without even reading it.

I don't want him upsetting her any further.

When Eli comes back downstairs, her face scrubbed of all make-up, her hair damp and brushed straight, she looks younger than her years, but there's no denying the tension she's carrying.

'Go and sit down,' I call to her as I load a tray with our

toast and warm milk. 'I'll be in now.'

'I'm not sure I can eat,' she says, but I hope the smell of the buttered toast will whet her appetite.

'You have to try something,' I say. 'Just a little, for me.'

I decide not to mention how much her baby needs the nourishment. I know right now that I need to focus on her, solely on her.

I smile as she nibbles, albeit slowly, on a piece of toast. I encourage her to drink some warm milk.

'I think I'd really just like a cup of tea instead,' she says.

And of course I jump up and make it, coming back to find she's abandoned any attempts at eating. She does, however, sip from her mug. I'll take the victory.

'Shall we watch a movie or something?' I ask, hoping the distraction might help her.

'I'm not sure I've the energy or concentration for it,' Eli says. 'I might just go to bed, if you don't mind. I didn't sleep last night.'

I can tell that each time she thinks about what's happened 'last night', it's like another slap in the face for her. Sleep may be just what she needs – to escape her own thoughts for a while. I should've slipped a sleeping tablet into her tea. The ones I have are safe for use in pregnancy.

'A sleep will do you wonders,' I say.

She pauses for a moment. I expect her to get up and go to bed straight away but she speaks, her voice quiet, small.

'Mum, I'm scared.'

'What of?' I ask.

'Everything. What's going to happen. My marriage, my career – they're both in a mess. And I don't know how to fix it.'

'You don't have to fix it. Not tonight anyway, sweetheart. And it's not all down to you. There are other people who can fix things, you know.'

She starts to cry and I pull her into my arms, relishing the smell of her freshly washed hair, the feel of the weight of her head on my shoulder. I rock and shush, and when she stops sobbing, I lead her up to her room and pull back the duvet on her bed. She climbs in and I pull the cover over her. Her eyes are already drooping as I switch off the light.

'Don't go,' she whispers.

So by the light of the flames flickering in the fireplace, I climb onto the bed beside her and lie down. Holding her hand, I listen as her breathing settles and she falls asleep.

I know it's wrong of me to say this but, as I allow myself to drift off beside her, I feel more content than I have done in a long time.

CHAPTER FORTY-ONE

Angela

I wake early. Sneaking out of Eli's room and into my own. Dawn is just breaking, frost glistening on the pavements outside. I open my bedroom window and fill my lungs with fresh morning air. Soon the street will be busy, but for now it's just me, the fresh new start of a new day, the distant hum of car engines turning over and coming to life. I can't help but smile.

Eli barely stirred during the night and I decide it's best to let her sleep as long as possible, then we can have a lazy breakfast together. We'll speak to her union rep after breakfast, I decide. And then I might encourage her to come for a walk with me. Put some colour in her cheeks. Maybe take a walk around the Botanic Gardens. Lunch in the museum. We'll deal with whatever challenges the day brings in bite-size pieces.

I go downstairs, slip on my coat and set off towards the bakery at the top of the street. I want to try to encourage Eli to eat and I wonder if some of her favourite buns might be enough to tempt her appetite. I know she has a fondness for the iced turnovers from Kitty's Kitchen. It'll also give me a chance to talk to 'Kitty' herself. I'd always thought her a nice girl. Clean-living. A positive influence on Eli when they went to school together.

I'm sure my daughter could do with a friend just now, and it's not like she can pick up the phone to that Rachel one. It mightn't hurt if I can rekindle the friendship she used to have with Kate. It might help her start to see this place as home again. She might even realise it wouldn't be the worst thing in the world if she did end up staying in Belfast.

The bell over the door tinkles as I walk in. Kate's chatting to one of my neighbours, laughing with him while filling a white paper bag with a selection of buns.

It strikes me that she looks so much more carefree than Eli. Much more carefree than Eli's looked in a long time. Kate has the same relaxed look I remember from her teenage years when they both spent time together.

'Mrs Johnston.' I hear Kate speak. 'Good morning to you, what can I get you today?'

'Morning, Kate,' I say. 'Could I have two of your finest turnovers, please, and one of those large treacle scones.'

I know Eli's usually a sucker for a thickly buttered slice of treacle scone.

'Treating yourself today?' Kate asks with a smile that I return.

'Eli's staying with me for a bit. I thought I'd treat us both.'

'Ah, yes. I saw her a few days ago,' Kate tells me. 'She called in briefly. How is she? If you don't mind me saying, she looked worn out.'

'Well, she's been going through a tough time,' I confide before moving closer. 'Maybe you could call in and see her. I know you girls used to be very close and well, I think she could do with a friend right now. One she can trust.'

Kate's eyebrows rise. I know I've said enough to get her concerned – to want to know more. To want to help. But I don't want to be sharing all of our worries with the neighbours, so I say no more.

'I'll do that, then. How long's she here for?'

'I'm not sure yet. It could be a long time . . .'

I dare not hope that this, horrible as it is, could end with my daughter back on my doorstep.

'Oh, okay. Well give her my love,' Kate says as she hands me my change. 'If it's okay, I'll call in after work. I'll just arrange someone to pick Liam up from nursery so he's not running amok in your house.'

'Your wee boy's always welcome in my house, Kate,' I smile. 'Sure, he's a dote.'

Finish with a compliment.

She rewards me with a broad smile. 'We'll see you both later, then,' she says.

I feel so much lighter as I walk back to my house. As if things are finally starting to go right again.

The last few weeks have been so tough. I've been living on my nerves. Afraid to be alone, if I'm honest. I feel as if I'm being watched.

Hunted.

Eli isn't the only person who's been receiving unwanted messages.

CHAPTER FORTY-TWO

Louise

The time had come. I knew I'd have to say goodbye to him.

It was something that had to be done and still, I felt sick at the thought. Then I felt angry with myself for allowing him any space in my heart.

For allowing myself to be weak.

For allowing myself to sin.

I went to church each morning, sat through morning Mass and then, when it was quiet – the daily worshippers gone home to their mid-morning cup of tea and their families – I'd kneeled below the statue of Our Lady and begged her for guidance and forgiveness.

Surely she understood more than anyone what it was like to lose a child. I wondered, had she gone mad afterwards? How could she not have? How could she have watched her only son being subjected to such horror and not question the power of the Devil over the power of her God? But she'd remained steadfast, and I knew I wanted her strength on my side now. I had to believe that she was with me, if I was to take the final few steps – and those final few steps couldn't wait any longer. If I'd stalled any more, I'd have risked everything.

It wouldn't have taken much for people to make the connection — and then I could have lost my baby. I couldn't allow myself to lose another baby. No matter how hard the next step would be, it had to happen.

I kneeled before Our Lady and bowed my head, then I muttered the words to the prayer Memorare over and over again:

> To thee do I come, before thee I stand,
>   sinful and sorrowful.
> O Mother of the Word Incarnate,
> despise not my petitions,
> but in thy mercy hear and answer me.
> Amen.

CHAPTER FORTY-THREE

Angela

There are three emails sitting unopened in my email folder. The first arrived two and a half weeks ago. The second about ten days ago. The third on Thursday last. All of them from the same person.

Part of me wants to look at the emails, of course. As soon as I saw his name, I wanted to look at them. I wanted to see what he had to say for himself. To see why he's come looking for us now, of all times.

I wonder, should I just reply? Tell him to leave me alone. Tell him he has the wrong Angela. Surely there are hundreds of Angela Johnston's in the world. He can't possibly know it's me. Not for definite.

But I don't want any contact with him. None.

I switch off my computer. Unplug it. I'm almost tempted to smash the damn thing. To hell with keeping in touch with people. What I can't see can't hurt me. The world was a better place before computers allowed people to meddle in things that they simply shouldn't.

I go to the kitchen, switch on the radio and sing along to some soul classics from the Seventies. Usually this is enough to make me feel brighter, but today I'm rattled. I feel on edge. My chest tight. The music is too loud. Too intrusive. I switch off the radio. I'm tempted to take a nip of whisky from the bottle in the cupboard, just to take off the edge.

But I don't. I decide I have to keep my focus. Eliana's needs are so much more important than mine now. I'll treat her to breakfast in bed.

I'm not sure if she'll have thought to pack everything yesterday. So I reach into the cupboard over the microwave and take out the bottle of prenatal vitamins I'd bought 'just in case'. I wonder if she's left her notes in the hall. I must have a little look at them, see that she's completely up to date with all of her checks. Actually, it mightn't be a bad idea to get her to see a doctor up here, especially given the stress she's been through over the last few days. I pick up the phone and dial my doctor's surgery to ask for an urgent appointment.

'I know she's not a regular patient, but she's seven and a half months pregnant and has been under a lot of stress. I'm worried about the impact it might have on the baby.'

The receptionist sighs but takes Eli's details anyway, says she'll see what she can do and that she'll call me back. I'd have preferred it if she'd offered me an appointment there and then but I'll take what I can.

I carry the tray of breakfast upstairs, hear Eli call, 'I'm up, Mum,' as I climb.

Putting my elbow to the door, I push my way in.

'Just a small breakfast. From Kitty's. She sends her love, by the way. Said she might call in sometime.'

'I'm not sure I'm in the mood for company,' she says.

'Kate's not company, she's a friend, and she's a lovely girl. It might do you the power of good. She said you called in a few days ago.'

Eli blushes. 'I was just passing, it was raining,' she says. 'But

173

that was before everything at the hospice. She *is* lovely but, Mum, I can't. I just want to hide. I'm too embarrassed to talk to people.'

'You've nothing to hide from,' I tell her. 'You have to stop beating yourself up.'

'I called the RCN,' she tells me.

I sit down, take a breath, wait for her to speak.

'The union say they'll support me, but we all just have to wait until the hospice itself completes their investigation.'

I almost don't want to ask the question but I have to. 'And the police investigation?'

'That's all dependant on what they find. They may decide no crime was committed. They have to look at all the evidence. Even if they decide not to prosecute, I could still be struck off.'

I feel my stomach lurch, but I do what any good mother would do in the situation – I reassure her that it won't come to that. Even though I have no idea if it will or not.

'Best to distract yourself, then,' I say, 'seeing as it's all out of your hands anyway. And there's no better way than to see Kate. She's going to bring her little boy with her, so won't that be nice?'

Eli doesn't look convinced.

★

By eleven thirty, I've persuaded Eli to come out for a walk with me. We have our big coats, gloves and hats on and are walking past The Palm House, the stunning cast-iron glasshouse that provides a focal point to the Botanic Gardens all year round. We've linked arms and Eli's mood has brightened a little.

Mine has, too. I've reassured myself the emails I've received needn't mean anything if I just ignore them.

'You were right, Mum,' she says. 'It was the right idea to get

174

out of the house for a bit. Clear my head. It's been years since I've been here.'

'You always overlook the things that are on your own doorstep,' I tell her.

'I suppose. We all take things for granted, don't we? Even me.' She pauses. 'Mum, do you think maybe I've taken Martin for granted, too?'

I stop and look at her. Her pale face is even whiter in the winter sun.

'You're not to think that way,' I tell her, shaking my head.

'Why not? Maybe it's true, Mum. I know you don't want to think the worst of me, but maybe this is all my fault. I've been hard to live with. Maybe I've pushed him away or not appreciated him and how hard he works because I've been feeling so sorry for myself. It would hardly be any big surprise that he went looking elsewhere.'

I hear her voice break and at any other time I'm sure a part of my heart would break with hers, but not this time. This time I'm angry with her. Actually disappointed in her. It's not an emotion I'm used to experiencing when it comes to my daughter. I find myself unlinking arms with her, breaking away. How can she think that? How can she think anything she could have done can justify her husband having an affair?

'Oh, Eli, you can't think that way.'

'But what if what he said yesterday is right, Mum? That it's me who's changed. You know I've not felt like myself since I've been pregnant. Probably even from before then, when we were trying. I feel everything's been a bit out of my control. And this damned feeling sick all the time. So much for blooming – all I've done is wilt.'

I don't speak, still reeling that she can see fault in herself. That she can turn her anger against Martin inwards and pit it against herself. That's not how I raised her. I raised her to be strong. I raised her to believe she didn't need a man in her life. I'd managed perfectly well without one in mine.

As I feel her arm hook in mine, I resist the urge to pull away.

'Was it like this for you, Mum? Did you bloom when you were carrying me? Or is it all a big pregnancy myth?'

I push down my anger and my fear.

'I enjoyed being pregnant,' I tell her. 'I felt a bit sick at the start but not so much, really. But I wasn't trying to do everything back then. All I really had to concentrate on was being pregnant and having a baby. I wasn't juggling everything the way you young ones do now.'

'But you were on your own. That must have been hard in itself.'

I think back to how it really had been when I was pregnant. It'd been hard. I put my hand to my stomach, trying like the stupid old woman that I am to recall those feelings from all those years ago of a baby, safe and sound, moving inside me.

'Everyone faces their own hardships, sweetheart. Anyone who tells you they have it all sorted is lying. You have to try to hold on to the positives.'

'There doesn't seem to a lot of positives about,' she says.

'This baby's a positive,' I tell her.

She nods, but I know she doesn't realise just how much of a gift her baby is.

'But Martin, Rachel . . . work . . . everything else is . . .' She shakes her head. How can she put it in words?

I hate myself for being twee but I do believe this. 'Things happen for a reason,' I tell her. 'And while it may seem that everything's beyond your control now, that's simply not true. You've taken matters into your own hands about Martin by coming here, giving yourself time to breathe and think properly. With work, I'm sure the investigation will weigh everything up and realise you're a great nurse and you acted with no malice.'

'That doesn't make her any less dead,' Eli says, her face serious.

'She probably would have passed by now anyway. And possibly would've suffered a lot more pain first. It's sad, of course it is, that she didn't get to see her son again, but do you think she'd want his last memory of her to be one where she was in as much pain as she was when you helped her? That would've been horrific for everyone.'

CHAPTER FORTY-FOUR

Angela

Eli is half-heartedly stirring a bowl of vegetable soup when my phone rings. I glance down and see it's a call from my doctors' surgery, so I answer. The still not-very-cheerful receptionist tells me that if Eli wants to call in after three, the doctor will fit her in for a quick check-up. I thank her and hang up.

'Who was that?' Eli asks, putting her spoon down, having apparently given up on her soup.

'My doctors,' I tell her.

'Are you sick?' she asks, and the slight panic in her eyes pleases me in a strange way. It's nice to feel loved.

'No! Lord, no. Nothing like that. Look, I don't want you to be mad, but I figured since you were up here, and you've had some awful shocks recently, it wouldn't do any harm to have a doctor give you the once-over. You're awfully pale-looking and I know I'd rest easier if you had your bloods checked. Especially your iron.'

'Mum, I had my blood checked three weeks ago. I'm fine. And I really don't need to see a doctor.'

'But what if you take another funny turn? Won't you need to have a doctor on your side?'

'It was a panic attack, Mum,' she whispers. 'I just have to work through them.'

'But still, pet. You can't be too cautious with pregnancy. Especially when this one's been giving you so much trouble. And add to that all the stress of the last few days. Wouldn't it be wise to get your blood pressure checked, too?'

'I'm a nurse, you know. I know what warning signs to watch out for.'

'And you're also a nurse under a lot of strain and who hasn't necessarily been on the ball all the time.'

Her face crumples. She sits for a moment or two in silence. I watch the tears pool in her eyes, watch as she tries to blink them away rapidly. I see the almost imperceptible wobble of her bottom lip. The crinkle of her chin. I know the look well. I've seen it often and cut her off at the pass before the tears more times than I can remember.

This time I stay silent, even though a part of me is annoyed at myself for making my daughter cry. I watch as two full, fat tears roll down her cheeks, as her eyes turn red, making her pale skin look even closer to translucent.

'I just worry so much about you, Eli. You're my whole world, you know that, and I want to make sure you're okay. Can you just humour me? You know what I'm like and always have been. I know I'm overprotective, but it was just you and me for so long that I . . . well, I love you, and if you do this for me I'll try to remember to back off. I'm sorry, pet.'

I know I'm hamming up my sadness. My guilt at being too overprotective. Using the 'poor me' routine to get my daughter on side.

'Okay, Mum,' she says. 'And thanks for caring.'

'Darling, that's what I'm here for.'

More tears fall, but I feel the soft squeeze of her hand and I know that we're okay. I squeeze her hand back gently, three short squeezes, which signify 'I love you'. I've done it with her since she was a child, a secret code between us. It was something my own father used to do with me when I was little. It's one of the only things from my own childhood that I've been able to share with Eli.

★

That sound. Rhythmic. Loud. Like a horse galloping. Like a train building up speed. A life preparing to be born. Real. So small, so tiny and so helpless but so very alive. Each beat telling me things are going to change and change for the better. My grandchild. This baby who's going to make my life complete. Our lives complete. This innocent soul who'll probably never realise how much she'll mean to me. How much she's wanted and loved already.

My heart races to try to match the beat of this tiny heart. I think of how I'll hold her, rock her to sleep. Sit in the nursery in the house – a nursery I couldn't provide for Eli when she was little – and sing nursery songs, whisper prayers, give gentle kisses on a soft head that smells of milk and baby powder and innocence.

Innocence. That's what this baby is to me. A chance to start again. To help my daughter be the best mother she can be. To have another little person in my life who loves me dearly.

'Baby sounds perfectly healthy to me,' Dr Laurence declares. 'That's a good, strong heartbeat.'

Eli thanks the doctor as she sits up, wipes the gel from her tummy and pulls her top back down.

'I told you everything would be okay,' she says to me.

I just cry. This is everything I wanted and more.

I can't let anything – not even those stupid emails – stand in my way.

CHAPTER FORTY-FIVE

Louise

I struggled to fight the panic when the pregnant woman disappeared. I wondered if I was being punished. After two nights of waiting for her to come home, I started to get on edge. It wasn't a bad 'on edge' at first. To begin with, I was excited. I wondered if I'd guessed her due date all wrong. Could she have gone to hospital already to have the baby? That wouldn't have been ideal, but I could have worked with it. I supposed. Brought my plans forwards. Or waited until the baby was a bit older. Not ideal, but not awful. As long as the end result was the same.

But then I worried that something might have gone wrong. With her or with the baby. I knew it could happen. God knows I knew it could happen. I had flashbacks to the sombre shaking of heads. The sympathetic looks of medical staff. Me wishing that they'd just let me bleed out and die with him.

But life wouldn't be that cruel to me again. God and the Blessed Virgin wouldn't be that cruel to me again. I'd prayed. I'd petitioned them. I'd lit candles. So many candles. The sacristan had eased me away from them, urged me to leave some for other people's intentions.

I'd called the hospital – both the antenatal ward and the

postnatal ward – and asked to speak to her. Told them I was her sister. I knew they were confused when they told me she wasn't a patient. That they thought a sister should know these things, of course. But I played them off against each other.

'Oh, my mistake. Maybe she's still in antenatal,' I told the gruff-sounding nurse on the postnatal ward.

I told her opposite that perhaps she'd gone straight to delivery.

I didn't care, foolishly, if I sounded mad. I knew I had to control my actions. Not bring attention to myself. But that time was different. Where was she? At least I was reassured that my baby hadn't been born yet, or was on the way, or was in danger.

But I wondered where she was. I thought about asking him, but that would've set alarm bells ringing afterwards, surely. So I said nothing. Decided to try to find out about her family. Find out who they were and where they were. Widen the net, because it simply couldn't go wrong.

I wouldn't allow it to go wrong.

CHAPTER FORTY-SIX

Angela

The doorbell rings shortly after half past five.

Kate. In all the emotion of hearing my granddaughter's heartbeat, I'd forgotten that she was going to call over.

'Oh, Mum,' Eli says. 'Can you tell her I'm sleeping or something? I don't think I've the energy to talk to anyone.'

It's another one of those occasions where I'll have to be cruel to be kind. Sometimes I know her better than she knows herself. Mother always knows best.

'Ah now, Eli. This could be just the thing to lift your spirits. Talking to an old friend. I'm sure you've a lot to catch up on.'

I ignore her protests and walk to the hall, where I see the shadow of Kate and her son through the stained glass of the door.

With a smile on my face, I welcome them both and invite them in.

'I brought some cupcakes from the bakery,' Kate says, handing over a small square-shaped box.

'And my mammy says these flowers are for you,' the little boy standing by her side says, thrusting a bunch of carnations at me with great affection but little grace.

Dark hair, bright blue eyes, a big open smile. What a beautiful little boy he is. I can't wait until there's a child running around this house again. That innocence and cuteness.

I crouch down so that I'm close to his height. 'Well, thank you very much, young man. They're lovely.'

'Mammy, can I have a cupcake?' he asks, taking his gaze from me and staring adoringly up at his mother, who laughs.

'I'm sure you can, Liam. In a moment. Let's go and see my friend first.'

Liam nods and smiles, scuffs his trainer-clad feet together. 'Okay, Mammy.'

'Well you're a very good boy, so I think we can definitely get you a cupcake, and maybe a nice big glass of juice or milk, too.'

'Milk, please,' he says, his big blue eyes staring up at mine once again.

'Oh, Kate, your little boy's a dream.'

She tilts her head and smiles in that way proud parents do when they don't want to appear too boastful.

'You might think differently at bedtime,' she laughs.

'Enjoy the bedtimes, Kate. Soon enough they don't want you near them at bedtime, or any time, really! I used to love reading Eli her bedtime stories. It was such a special time. Now, little man, how about you come with me and I'll get you some milk, then we can make a cup of tea for your mammy and Eli.'

'Is Eli your friend, Mammy?' he asks Kate and she nods.

'She is indeed. We used to go to school together, just like you and Darragh.'

'She's in the living room,' I tell her, adding in a whisper that she's a little out of sorts.

Kate frowns. 'I'll see if I can help.'

'Now, Liam, how about we get these cakes out on a nice plate and, you know what? I think I might have some crayons and paper somewhere. Maybe we could draw some pictures together. I'm not very good though. You might have to help me.'

'My daddy says I'm very good at colouring between the lines,' he says solemnly.

'I bet you are,' I say, leading the way towards the kitchen. 'You look like a very smart boy to me, indeed.'

'I know how to write my own name and everything, and I'm not even at big school yet.'

'Wow!' I say, delighting in spending time with him.

There's nothing I like more than spending time with children. There're so trusting. So innocent. So malleable.

'Why don't you sit up at the table and I'll get these flowers in some water and then we can do some colouring.'

'And eat our cupcakes?'

'Of course,' I laugh. 'You can have first pick!'

I fill a vase with water and put the bunch of carnations inside. I'm not a big fan of carnations. They look cheap. But I remind myself it's the thought that counts and I need to play nice. Then I fill the kettle and take out the tea things.

'Now,' I say, moving around the kitchen and opening a few drawers, 'let me find those crayons.'

I know I have a packet somewhere from when a friend visited with her grandchildren. Finding them, I put them and some paper in front of Liam, pushing his chair closer to the table. Then I take out a glass and pour him some milk.

'Here you go, young man,' I say, allowing him to pick a chocolate-topped cupcake from the box Kate has brought. 'I'll just bring this tea through to your mammy and then we can draw together.'

He looks up at me and smiles, his front teeth already coated in chocolate cream.

I don't spend any real time in the living room. I just put

the tea tray down and notice that the girls are talking. Really talking. Kate is holding Eli's hand in hers. This is all exactly what I'd hoped for. I feel a certain, I don't know, smugness maybe, rise in me as I walk back to the kitchen and sit down opposite Liam.

I pour myself a glass of milk, just like his, and take a big bite of cupcake, making him laugh at the chocolate icing around my mouth.

'What do you think we should draw, Liam?' I ask.

'Hmm,' he says, an exaggerated 'I'm thinking' expression on his face that makes me laugh. 'Well, my mammy and my daddy and my granny all say Santa's coming soon, so maybe we could do a Christmas picture.'

'Ooh, that sounds good,' I say, watching as he picks a red crayon from the box and starts on an outline of a very round Santa tummy. 'Have you written your letter to Santa?' I ask.

'My mammy helped me because I don't know all my letters yet.'

'Your mammy sounds great. And what's Santa going to bring you?'

'Erm . . . a new bike, and a helmet to be safe, and a TV for my bedroom if I'm really good.'

'I'm sure you've been very good, Liam,' I say, watching him colour in Santa, his tongue poking out at the side in concentration.

A TV in a child's bedroom, though? I can't help but judge. So much for spending time on bedtime stories instead.

I start work on a drawing of a Christmas tree, pointy corners, bottle green. I'll draw a star on the top if I can find the yellow crayon.

'What's Santa going to bring you?' Liam asks, blue eyes bright.

'Well, if I'm a really good girl, Santa's going to bring me a new baby to live in this house with me forever,' I tell him.

His eyes widen. 'Like a baby brother or sister? My mammy says I might get one those next Christmas. Do you have a baby in your tummy then? My auntie does and her tummy's all big like Santa's.'

'Well, my wee girl, Eli, who is your mammy's friend, has a baby in her tummy, too. And I'll be this baby's granny.'

'But babies don't live with their grannies,' he says, eyeing me up and down.

He's a smart kid.

'Sometimes they do,' I tell him. 'If their mammies want to come and stay, too. But, Liam, this is a big, big secret, so we must keep it to ourselves or it might not happen.' I put my finger to my lips, mime a 'shh!'.

Liam does the same, a glob of thick chocolate cream sticking to his finger as he does so.

Maybe it's foolish of me to say so much to a three-year-old. I instantly feel guilty. But I couldn't help it. I'm excited now, you see. And it just had to come bubbling out somewhere. I might be getting a brand-new baby to come and live with me . . .

My baby and her baby, under my roof.

CHAPTER FORTY-SEVEN

Angela

I'm flicking through the TV channels trying to find something that Eli and I can watch together, when she appears at the door, ashen-faced.

Immediately, I wonder if everything's okay with the baby, even though it's only been a few hours since we heard that lovely heartbeat.

'Eli, what is it? Is it the baby?' I ask as she walks to the sofa and sits down, looking for all intents and purposes as if she doesn't have the strength to stand any more.

She blinks at me, shakes her head. 'The baby's fine,' she mutters. 'It's not the baby.'

I notice she has her phone in her hands and my heart starts to thump. Has she been speaking to Martin? What has he said?

'Work,' she says, cutting through my thoughts. 'Rachel called when I was upstairs. I've to go to a meeting about what happened with Mrs Doherty tomorrow. Her son'll be there. And the management team. Oh, Mum. I'm going to lose my job, aren't I? And my licence. What if the police are there? And I have to see Rachel. Be professional around her. I can't . . .'

I see her spiral towards another panic attack. She feels out of control. I know that feeling only too well. When everything seems like it's too much. When you want to run and hide.

'We'll get through this, I promise,' I tell her, trying to reassure her the best I can. 'Just keep breathing. Just try to stay calm. Breathe with me.'

Her breath comes in staggered spurts. Shaking, trembling out breaths, a pause, a sucking of air inwards. As if she's forgotten how to do the most natural of all things. I encourage her to count inwardly as she inhales, to let her breath go as if she's whispering. To centre herself.

'No one's infallible, darling,' I soothe. 'No one. They'll see sense. They'll understand. They'll forgive you and move on, because you didn't intend to harm anyone.'

Part of me wonders if I'm trying to reassure myself as much as her.

★

Eli's on edge all evening. Like the proverbial cat on a hot tin roof. She asks if she should phone Martin, tell him about the meeting. He'll be worried, she imagines. Or maybe he'll be too angry to talk to her. She looks distraught at that thought.

I ask her it if it'll make her feel any better. Will he be able to help or will talking to him just remind her of her marital worries? If he's angry, as she fears, could it make everything worse for her?

She eventually agrees it's best to leave it for now. She's tired, her head is sore. So I suggest an early night and I make her a cup of tea, slipping in a sedative pill to get her as good a night's sleep as possible. Once she's asleep, I switch her phone off and unplug the house phone. I don't want anything disturbing her. Tomorrow will be a big enough challenge.

★

As we set off towards Derry shortly after nine, she yawns. I wonder if I gave her too strong a dose. I hope she'll be 'with it' for her meeting. I must stop and make sure she drinks a coffee, even though she's already had one and shouldn't really have another. I want her to put her best foot forward.

Her union rep will meet her at the hospice. Rachel will be there, too. Eli admits she feels sick at the thought of seeing her.

'I don't know how I'll be able to look at her,' she tells me. 'I know it's not definite that she's been seeing him, but . . .'

'I understand,' I say. 'But it's important to keep focus on why you're here today. Don't let her win, Eliana. Don't let her see you crumble.'

'She's always been a good friend to me, or I thought she was. She was my ally and now how am I supposed to trust her to have my back when I can't even trust her with my husband?'

I wish Eli could see that Rachel could never be a real threat to her. Eli outshone her on every level. I remember her at Eli and Martin's wedding. She got sloppy drunk and snivelled all over her slice of wedding cake. Someone took her home early, gently leading her from the restaurant before her mascara ran any further down her cheeks.

Later, Eli told me that Rachel's marriage had recently ended and she was having a hard time. I didn't care. There's no excuse for making a show of yourself in public, and certainly not at your friend's wedding. If you can't behave in public, you belong indoors.

'Let's take it all one thing at a time – one step. Concentrate on work today. Treat Rachel as a colleague and try as hard as you can to block everything else out.'

She gives me a weak smile, goes back to looking out of the window.

CHAPTER FORTY-EIGHT

Louise

Everything was in place. Our new home. Temporary accommodation until the baby was born. I'd even sold my car – got little more than scrap money for it, but when I'd taken my savings out of the credit union, I was able to buy a replacement. It wasn't much better, but it got us to our new home without too much trouble.

I'd already parked that new car outside the flat I'd be staying in until the time was right. It was pretty bleak there. The heating didn't work, for a start, and there was a smell of mould around the place, no matter how often I tried to air it.

The carpet felt damp and sticky under my feet, and the mattress on the single bed in the flat's sole bedroom was heavily soiled. I'd covered it with blankets, then planned to sleep in a sleeping bag on top of those. I'd make do. The main thing was that it was cheap, there'd been no security deposit required and I could leave with little notice. The landlord hadn't even asked for ID. I could've been anyone. Untraceable.

All that was left to do then was to hand the keys to what had been my home over to Peter. He was going to put it up for sale and had given me a lump sum in lieu of my share of the equity. It wasn't a fortune, but it'd pay the rent on my new place for a few months, by which stage I hoped I'd have myself settled with some form of income of my own. I planned to take a book-keeping course. Learn a skill I could use from home so I wouldn't have to leave her.

Still, something inside me held off a little. The pregnant woman still hadn't come home. I couldn't make that final move until I knew where she was.

I followed her husband, hoping for some clues, but his pattern didn't seem to change.

He looked less well-cared-for. Unkempt at times, even. But he came and went as he always did.

All my digging, using all the resources I could find in the local library, including the local love for gossip, only uncovered that she wasn't from here originally. She was 'from upcountry'.

Was it possible she was just away visiting family? Surely her place was at home, with her husband. Waiting for this baby to arrive.

My arms were aching by then. I needed to hold my baby. I needed to feel the warmth of her body against mine. I needed to smell her sweet baby smell. I needed to feel the soft rush of her breath as she exhaled through rosebud lips. I needed to feel the brush of her downy hair against my lips as I kissed the top of her head. Feel her movements. Hear those sweet gurgling noises babies make. Alive babies make.

I needed to know what that was like with my own child. I needed to block out the memory of a kiss that felt all wrong. Of a baby who didn't wriggle or breathe. Whose lips were still like rosebuds but blackened. No pink cheeks. Just a pale grey. Almost blue. No breath. No warmth. Just this awful coldness that felt wrong.

That weight in my arms, that had been in my belly, that was then taken from me. Physically at least. But not emotionally. I carried it with me always. I knew I'd only be able to put it down when I replaced it with the weight of a new baby. My baby.

I prayed that God would send her home soon. And I vowed that I wouldn't let her out of my sight again.

CHAPTER FORTY-NINE

Angela

As we stand outside the hospice, my daughter's hand in mine, I feel my nerves rattle.

My primary fear is for Eli. I'm reminded of her first day at school. The pair of us standing side by side outside a red brick building, holding hands just as we are now. I wore a long beige raincoat that day with black boots and jeans. Sensible. Not quite fashionable. The boots kept the September rain from soaking my feet.

Eli wore a bright pink raincoat, with purple mittens and a purple bobble hat. She looked up at me, her eyes blinking at me from under her fringe, which I'd foolishly cut myself, leaving it slightly longer on one side than the other.

'Do I have to go in, Mummy?' she'd asked me.

My gut response was to scream no. Of course she didn't have to. She didn't have to do anything she didn't want to do. Except that she did have to go to school. She had to leave the safety of our family unit and spend her time with other children, other adults, other influences, and I had to let her. I had to encourage her even. So I put a bright smile on my face and squeezed her hand, those three little squeezes.

'Of course you have to go in, darling. And you have to show them all just how amazing you are. You show them you can write your own name already. And not just Eli. Your full proper Eliana name and your last name. I bet you're the only little girl in your class able to do that.'

She looked at me, her face twisting as she thought about what to say next.

'But can't you teach me everything else? Like you taught me to write my own name.'

'Oh, sweetheart, your teacher will know more things than I could ever know, and she'll make learning lots and lots of fun. And when you come home at the end of each day, we can do all the fun things and not worry about boring old learning. We can even have a hot chocolate today, if you want.'

'With marshmallows?'

'Of course. And cream.'

She didn't look convinced. That was my little girl. Always questioning. Always thinking.

'And you will be here for me at home time?'

'I wouldn't be anywhere else in the world even if I could be,' I told her. 'I will always, always be here for you.'

I watched this little girl, all three foot of her, take a big breath and puff out her chest.

'Okay then, Mummy. We should go in.'

She squeezed my hand and I'm not sure which of us needed the reassurance more.

Standing outside the hospice now, I feel those same emotions. I know in my heart my daughter has to go inside and face whatever will come. I also know there's no way I can face it for her or make it easier for her. I doubt the promise of a hot chocolate will cut it this time.

'I feel sick,' she says, her voice small.

'Whatever happens, we'll cope,' I say. 'Whatever happens, it won't change the fact you're good and kind and wonderful.'

She gives me that same unconvinced look she had when she was four.

'Come on then,' she says. 'I'll get this over and done with.'

She lets go of my hand and walks a few steps in front of me, holding open the large glass-panelled door at the front of the building to allow me in.

I'm not sure what I expect of the hospice itself. A sterile environment. A place with an air of death and dying. Sombre-faced staff. Weeping families in every corridor. It isn't like that at all, of course. It's warm and welcoming. Homely even.

A woman I put in her fifties, with short blonde hair, stands up from behind the reception desk and walks over to us as soon as she sees Eli arrive. She pulls her into a hug and I can hear the pair whisper to each other. Soothing, reassuring noises. They pull apart and the woman looks at me.

'Mrs Johnston, if you come with me I'll get you a tea or coffee. You're in luck today, one of our families brought in some fresh baked scones, too.'

I bristle. 'I was going to go in with Eli, actually,' I say, looking to my daughter for confirmation.

She shakes her head. 'Mum, it's not really the done thing. Lorraine here will look after you.'

'But you can't go in there alone! Not in your condition.'

'I won't be alone. I'll have my union rep. Other staff members.'

I'm not happy. I thought I'd be allowed in with her. That I'd be able fight her corner in the way only a mother can. I don't want to be sidelined to a kitchen with a cup of badly made tea and a home-made scone. Stuff home-made scones.

'Everyone here thinks very highly of Eliana,' Lorraine chimes in.

I want to shout at her to butt out but I can't make a scene.

'I need to do this on my own, Mum. I'll be okay, I promise.'

She looks so brave that I can feel my bruised heart swell with pride.

'Okay,' I concede before giving her a quick hug and allowing Lorraine to lead me to the staff kitchen to make a cup of tea.

'You mustn't worry, Mrs Johnston. People here know what a good nurse Eli is,' she says with her back to me as she lifts a jar down from the cupboard. 'It's a disgrace sometimes the pressure they work under, but everyone knows she wouldn't have done anything to hurt anyone intentionally.'

'No, she wouldn't have.' Terse; I know I sound terse and I have to remind myself to stay calm.

But I'm struggling, I can feel my muscles tense. I'm on edge. I don't want to be here making small talk.

'I mean, I know she's been really unwell with this baby, but even then . . . well, it wouldn't impact on her ability,' Lorraine says, turning round to look at me.

'No it wouldn't. It hasn't.'

'She's very capable,' Lorraine says. 'Can I get you milk and sugar?'

'Just milk, please,' I say, although I don't have much of an appetite for tea or anything else.

'I'm sure they won't be all that long,' she says as she hands me a two-litre carton of milk and sits down opposite me, two cups of tea between us.

I thank her. Succinctly. I don't want to engage in conversation. I look at the clock on the wall. It's been five minutes already.

I sense her looking at me. She's trying to size me up, I imagine. I bow my head. I don't feel comfortable at all.

'I'm sorry,' she begins. 'But do I know you? You're familiar-looking. Did you go to St Mary's?'

'No,' I reply, my heart starting to beat faster. I want to be with Eli. Not here.

'I could swear we've met before. I'm usually very good with

faces. Is it Creggan? Did you grow up there? I grew up in the Heights. I'd say we're not far off the same age. What was your maiden name? Give me a few minutes, I'll be able to place you, I'm sure.'

'We've not met,' I say, annoyed at her persistence. 'I'm not from Derry. I grew up in Belfast, so I think you must have me mixed up with someone else.'

She pulls a face as if she doesn't quite believe what I've told her. I hate her kind. Perpetually nosy.

I look at the clock – how can only ten minutes have passed?

'You must be very excited about the baby?' Lorraine says.

'Of course I am,' I say.

'This is your first grandchild, isn't it?'

'Yes,' I say, wishing she'd stop asking questions.

Why does she think she has the right to ask? I take another breath, although my chest feels tighter. The effort required is something else. Is this what Eli's been feeling over these last few days as her world has fallen in around her ears? Have I done this to my child?

'Eli's an only child,' I tell her. 'So yes.'

'I thought that; about Eli being an only child, that is. Well, a first grandchild is always extra special. I've ruined mine altogether. Well, I love them all, of course, but he'll always have a special place in my heart.'

'I imagine so,' I say.

I know I'm being rude. This Lorraine is perfectly lovely and welcoming, if nosy. She's trying to engage me in conversation, but I want her – no, *need* her – to go.

'This baby will certainly be surrounded by a lot of love. We're all very excited here. It's a long time since we had a baby about the place.'

'Well, I think we should see how things go today. Not get ahead of ourselves.'

If I have my way, this baby will be nowhere near this hospice.

'I'm sure it'll be fine,' Lorraine says again, but her voice is quieter now.

I think she's starting to realise I don't want to talk to her. I don't want her near me. I don't want any of these people near me with their faux concern.

We fall into a not-so-companionable silence. I can't help but look at the clock. Has it slowed? It feels too warm. The heating on full to ward off the wintry weather. I want to push open the window and suck in some fresh air.

A phone rings, breaking the silence with its shrillness. I'm immediately grateful for it.

'Ah, that'll be for me,' Lorraine says. 'No rest for the wicked and all that.'

I give a half-smile.

'There are some magazines here, why don't you distract yourself with a quick read while you wait for Eli?'

She doesn't wait for my response, which I'm exceptionally grateful for.

I glance at the cover of the nearest magazine. 'I thought I could trust my sister, but she tried to ruin my life' the headline screams in red-and-yellow. Cheap and tacky. I wonder what the sister's version of the story is – I know more than most that there's always more to a story than there first appears.

CHAPTER FIFTY

Angela

I'm staring at the cold remnants of my cup of tea, watching little flecks of milk swim to the top of the biscuit-coloured liquid, when I hear the door to the kitchen creak open. I look up immediately and there she is: my daughter – her face pale. Tired-looking. Her eyes red.

'Can we go, Mum? I'm done.'

I want to say yes, grab her and run. But I can't show any panic.

'What did they say?' I ask, standing for a hug.

She sags into my arms.

'They can't link the overdose directly to her death given how critically ill she was anyway. The medication wouldn't have been the primary factor in her passing. The dose was high, but not catastrophic,' she says as she starts to cry. 'I'm not going to lose my licence. There won't be any prosecution or anything like that, but they've started my maternity leave. Want me to take time out.'

Temporary relief floods through me. There will be no prosecution for her to go through. She won't be taken from me.

'That's as good an outcome as you could've hoped for,' I tell her.

'The woman is still dead, Mum. She still didn't get to say goodbye to her son, nor he to her. I'll have to live with that.'

'Did you talk to him?'

She nods. More tears fall.

'He says his mother wouldn't hold anything against me. She spoke so fondly of me to him. He thanked me for helping her to manage her pain.'

I feel tears prick at my eyes. I'm so proud of this woman before me.

'That just makes me feel even guiltier,' she says, pulling away from me. 'Please, Mum, I just need to get out of here. I've a lot of decisions to make. Including whether or not I'll ever be back here.'

'Now's not the time to make hasty decisions,' I tell her, feeling ashamed that my concern for her is dangerously close to being outweighed by the little fizz of excitement in my stomach that comes with the loosening of another string tying my beloved daughter to this city.

We're just leaving, when I hear a voice call to Eli, and she stops and turns around. It's Rachel. She might be in a uniform and not swigging a vodka and Coke, but I recognise her at once. I squeeze Eli's hand. Try to offer some silent reassurance.

Eli walks to her but they're still within earshot, so I can listen in.

'How are things at home?' Rachel asks.

Eli tenses. 'I'm staying in Belfast for a few days,' she says.

A few days? It'll be more than that. I stay quiet, look to the door. I want to leave.

'You know you can talk to me, if you need to,' Rachel says.

She sounds sincere. How Eli keeps her cool is beyond me, but she does. She just nods then turns and walks back towards me. No hugs. No friendly banter. Just her walking towards me and to the door, to my car.

As I switch on the engine, I allow myself to exhale. We got out of there. We've got over this latest hurdle.

But we've a bigger hurdle yet to climb.

'Do you want to go and pick up some more of your things?' I ask her.

'I suppose we should,' Eli says. 'I can't keep wearing this same maternity bra for the foreseeable. Or keep alternating the two tops I packed. I'm not even sure they'll fit me for much longer. I'll have to resort to wearing my nightie over my leggings.'

She gives a weak laugh. It's nice to hear, even if it is strained.

CHAPTER FIFTY-ONE

Angela

My stomach drops when I see Martin's car in the driveway outside their house.

He's home. I'd taken a chance when I messaged him earlier. I'd told him we were coming to pick up some things and maybe it'd be better for both of them if he made sure he was out. In hindsight, it was a stupid move. He hasn't spoken to his wife in a few days. She won't answer his messages – if she even gets them – and he's desperate to see her.

If I'd said nothing, he may well have been at work. We could've been in and out without going anywhere near him.

'We don't have to go in,' I say.

Eli looks at me.

'I mean, if you don't feel comfortable, we can just go. We can shop for the things you need in Belfast. You don't have to put yourself through this. You've had a tough enough day as it is.'

'I have to face him sometime,' she says.

'But it doesn't have to be today.' Am I sounding too controlling? 'Or you can wait in the car. I'll go in for you if you tell me what you need.'

For a second she pauses and I think she's going to agree, but she simply shakes her head.

'I'm almost thirty-four years old, Mum. I need to be able to stand on my own two feet. Even doing the horrible stuff.'

I can't argue with that, even if I'd prefer he doesn't get the chance to try to persuade her of his innocence. So I simply nod and tell her I'll go in with her anyway, just in case she needs me.

The stale air when we walk into the hall is the first thing that greets us. Walking through to the living area, it looks as though a pack of feral students has moved in. Empty takeaway cartons are sitting on the granite worktops, along with a collection of empty beer bottles and a half-drunk bottle of whisky. Eli puts her hand over her nose and mouth and says she feels sick, walking quickly to the bifold doors and pulling them open, letting a gust of freezing air into the room.

The cushions on the sofa are in disarray, a discarded pair jeans and a pair of socks lie on the floor in front of the coffee table, where a pizza sits half eaten in its box, cheese congealing to a dark yellow, tiny pools of oil gathering on the surface.

Paperwork is scattered on the floor, the hearth speckled with chipped pieces of wood and ash where he hasn't brushed up after throwing more logs into the burner. Muddy footprints mark the tiled floors and a cupboard door hangs open. There's no obvious sign of Martin.

'Oh! Mum,' Eli says. 'I wasn't expecting this. He must be struggling.'

'Don't you go feeling sorry for him, Eliana Johnston,' I tell her. 'He's brought this on himself, playing around.'

She sighs. I watch as she rubs her tummy, looks around the room. Does it still feel like her home?

'I really believed he loved me,' she says, walking to the doors and taking a deep breath.

I think I hear a creak on the stairs, which she doesn't seem to notice. I know I have to manipulate this situation to my advantage.

'I've no doubt that he does, Eliana. How could he not? But like many men, he wants his cake and to eat it, too. You deserve more. Your daughter deserves more than a cheating father.'

'Daughter?'

Martin's voice is loud and I swing round to see him walking down the hall. Wretched-looking. A stained T-shirt, pyjama bottoms and an unshaven face.

I fake shock. 'Oh! Martin, I didn't see you . . . I didn't know if you were in. I'm sorry, I shouldn't have said . . .'

Eli's standing there, her face a picture of shock. He'd begged her not to find out the sex of their baby. She knows what his reaction will be.

'Daughter?' he repeats. 'How do you know? Eli?' He looks visibly shaken by her betrayal of his trust.

'Look, Martin, I don't think this is anything to be getting yourself upset about. We're just here to get a few things and we'll be off again.'

He raises a hand to silence me, walks towards Eli. 'How do you know?' he repeats.

'I had to find out,' she says. 'You know I was struggling to bond.'

'You promised,' he says, and I can't tell if he's angry or upset or just a horrible combination of both. 'How could you go behind my back?'

It's just the question I hoped he'd ask.

'You've some nerve talking about going behind people's backs,' I say, walking towards Eli and taking her hand. 'After what you've been at. And with one of your wife's best friends, too. I don't know how the pair of you can hold your heads up at all. You and that hussy should be ashamed of yourselves.'

I feel her squeeze my hand. A silent plea for me not to continue with this. I squeeze her hand back, three times, to try and remind her I love her. I have her back. I'm fighting her corner.

Martin just rolls his eyes. 'This is ridiculous. All of this is so ridiculous.'

He runs his hands through his hair. It looks like it hasn't been washed in a few days so it sits slick against his scalp. I'd always considered my son-in-law to be quite a handsome man, but today? He looks repulsive. In the filth of this living room, I hope that's how my daughter sees him, too.

'I don't want to have this conversation,' Eli says. 'I just want to go home.'

'Home?' He jumps on the word, then lifts one of the empty beer bottles from the coffee tables and throws it at the floor. It smashes, scattering its amber shards across the marble tiles. 'This is your home. Here. With me. With our family. Maybe if you'd put us first, ever, over your mother . . .'

I feel anger start to rise. I want to scream at him that he stole her from me. That from the moment they met she's put him first, but I can't risk that conversation now. My emotions are too raw. I might say something I'll regret. I clasp my hand to my mouth and muffle a fake sob. It has the desired effect.

'Jesus Christ, Martin!' Eli shouts. 'You're the one in the wrong here. You've been cheating, for the love of God. Yes, I found out our baby's sex, but I needed to know to start to fall in love with her. You didn't need to look elsewhere for anything. And you certainly don't need to bring my relationship with my mother into it.'

She pulls my hand and we walk past Martin, who's sat down on the sofa, amid his clutter, and now looks defeated.

'I'm not lying, Eli,' he shouts, but I know she isn't listening.

'Just leave me alone, Martin. Just leave us alone. I'm going to grab a few things and then I'll be gone. I just need you to leave me the hell alone.'

I'm impressed by her determination, but as we reach the top of the stairs, I hear her let out a sob. She stops for just a few seconds, as if the grief has to come out in a short, sharp burst, before she straightens herself.

'Let's get this done, Mum. I just want out of here.'

So I follow her into the bedroom, which is in a similarly unkempt state as the living room. The duvet is crumpled in the middle of the bed. The bed sheets have come away from the mattress. Her scatter cushions are scattered to the four winds. Discarded in piles around the floor are two days of dirty clothes, along with a small mound of damp and smelly towels.

A couple of empty beer bottles sit on the bedside table on Martin's side of the bed, along with some abandoned crisp packets, and beside those sits a saucer with two stubbed-out cigarettes ground into it.

I wrinkle my nose in disgust.

'What do you want me to do, Eli?' I ask her, but she's in a world of her own.

She goes into their walk-in wardrobe and pulls out a mid-size suitcase. I smile inwardly. She means business. She lays it on the floor and starts opening drawers, pulling clothes and underwear from them.

'Shoes,' she says, walking into the wardrobe and bringing out a pair of boots and a pair of trainers, along with a couple of tunic tops still on hangers.

She dumps the lot unceremoniously in her case.

'Should you bring something for the baby?' I ask nervously.

'I've ages to go yet.'

'But surely you have a hospital bag or something like that ready? I know you, Eliana. It won't hurt to bring it, just in case. You don't know how long you'll be in Belfast for.'

She stops then. Stops the hurried throwing of items into her case. Stops the manic way she was moving around the room as if it burned her to be there in the first place. For a second, I fear she'll decide not to go. She'll decide to stay here 'for the sake of the baby'. That the reality of it all has become too much for her.

'Eli?' I say gently. 'I know this is scary, but one thing at a time, eh? Remember.'

Slowly, she turns her head to look at me before pulling herself to standing, wobbling a little as she tries to find a centre of balance she isn't quite used to yet with her expanding tummy.

'You're right. I should. I will. I'll go and get it now from the nursery.'

Breath rushes from me with relief as she leaves the room.

I glance around again until I see them twinkling on the chest of drawers. Cufflinks. The platinum ones, both studded with a single diamond, which Eli had given Martin as a present on their wedding day. I'd helped her choose them. She'd been so happy back then. So full of hope, but then I had been, too. I'd been convinced that we were on our way to a happy ending for us all. Not losing a daughter, gaining a son. All that nonsense. I've been such a fool. Everything gets taken from me in the end. I lose everything I love. But not this time. Not now. I wasn't going to allow it to happen.

Martin doesn't deserve Eli. He never has. He certainly doesn't deserve my granddaughter. I pick the cufflinks up and slip them into my pocket, zipping it closed.

'Do you need any help?' I call to her, but she walks out of the room next to her own, a grey baby-changing bag slung over her shoulder.

'Let's go,' she says and I carry the case downstairs.

Martin's waiting for us. I see his face crumple when he sees the baby bag. I'm not immune to his emotions. I know this is hard for him. But he brought it on himself.

'I spoke out of turn,' he says quietly.

Eli stops, looks at him straight in the face. For a moment I think she's going be swayed by the picture of misery in front of us. That my beautiful people-pleaser of a daughter will decide to put his emotional needs above her own. I hold my breath until she speaks.

'I have to go, Martin,' she says. 'Just let me go.'

He sags but retreats to the living room, and I lift her case and carry it outside again. I'm expecting her to break down but she's stoic. Remarkably calm.

'Mum. I'm thinking, I'm going to drive my own car up to Belfast.'

I don't like that. Not when she's so upset. I want to keep her near me.

'Oh, I'm not sure about that, sweetheart. You were very tired earlier and you've had an awfully stressful day.'

'I want some freedom if I'm to be in Belfast a while. I want to be able to go out and about,' she says.

'You can always borrow my car,' I offer, but she looks determined. I don't want to argue with her. I have to be the hero of the piece today. So, very reluctantly, I agree. 'No, you're right. Take your car. That's very sensible. Just drive safely, okay? I worry about you. I'll stay behind you.'

Maybe if I can see her, I can make sure she's okay.

'I always drive safely,' Eli says, fishing in her handbag for her keys and pointing them at her car to unlock it.

I help her to pack her bags into the boot of her car. Make sure she's checked her fuel levels.

'And you're sure you have everything?' I ask as we stand together on the driveway. I'm reluctant to let her go.

'I've enough anyway,' she says, 'we'll cope.'

She kisses me on the cheek and climbs into the driver's side of her car. I pause for a moment to watch as she turns the key in the ignition and adjusts her seat belt.

In my own car, I take a deep breath and try to centre myself.

I look up to check my mirrors, only to see what looks like a figure in the distance. In the trees. Is someone there? Or are the shadows playing tricks on my mind?

I feel cold, clammy. My skin prickles. I feel as if I'm being watched. My chest tightens. I feel as if I can't breathe.

I look around me. The shadows dance and I can't make out where one shape ends and another begins. We're being watched, I'm sure of it. I can feel eyes on me. I start to feel dizzy. Faint.

I was stupid to ignore those emails.

CHAPTER FIFTY-TWO

Louise

I saw her. She was back. I was so excited, I almost got caught.
   I got too close.
   It was such a stupid mistake to have made.
   Imagine to have gone all that way to mess it up then . . .
   I was feeling more and more on edge as each day passed and sometimes, I swore I was starting to lose my mind.
   Starting to hallucinate. Seeing things that weren't there.
   People who weren't there.
   Hearing voices. Good and evil.
   One telling me I was in God's favour:

> Blessed are those that mourn, for they shall
> be comforted.

One telling me I didn't need to fear the Devil, for I was surely doing His work.
   I had to get a grip. If I didn't get a grip – and quickly – I wouldn't have been well enough to be a mother. I'd had a loose enough grip on my sanity before, so I knew how easy it would have been to let go of it again.

CHAPTER FIFTY-THREE

Angela

'Mum, Jesus, are you okay?'

Eli's voice is there, pulling me back into focus. I feel my chest loosen. I breathe in, almost cry with relief as I exhale.

'You're very pale. And clammy. Mum, let me check you over.'

Her eyes are filled with such concern and such love for me. With her hand on mine, I feel my breathing return to normal. I feel my heartbeat slow. She takes my pulse, puts her hand to my forehead. Soothes me.

'What happened, Mum?' she asks.

'I . . . I thought I saw . . . something. But I'm sure it was just a shadow from the trees.'

The last thing I want is for her to go and look, to put herself in any danger.

She looks past me towards the field to the right of her house. It's still bright; visibility is good despite the rain. I follow her gaze, but no one appears to be there. The branches of the trees are casting shadows, but that's all. I'm sure that's all.

'Maybe I should get Martin,' she says. 'Maybe call the police. What if it's whoever was behind the notes? We could get them, Mum.'

I shake my head. I don't want her to call Martin. I don't want to call the police. I feel silly now. Sure it was just shadows. There's no way he could've traced us here. None. No way he could possibly know.

Eli chews on her lip. A habit she developed in childhood. 'I really think we should.'

'Please, Eli, I just want to go home. I'm sure it was just the stress of the last few days. I've been worried sick about you. I didn't sleep the best last night. The more I think of it, the more I'm sure it was just my imagination running away with me.'

'Oh, Mum,' Eli says, 'I hate that this is causing you so much stress, too.'

'I'll be fine, Eli. Let's just go. I was just being a silly old woman. Get in your car. Let's go. Let's just get out of here.'

'I'll just tell Martin, in case you did see something,' she says and turns to walk to the house.

I call her back.

'I don't want you going in and upsetting yourself again. This has been an ordeal for you as it is. I'll call him. Just to be safe.'

She pauses for a moment then nods. 'Okay. If that's what you want.'

'I'll call him now and I'll be right behind. Go on, get on the road.'

Reluctantly, she leaves as I lift my phone, and I watch her drive off.

As soon as she's out of my sight, I bury it in the bottom of my handbag.

I won't be calling Martin Hughes or anyone else.

★

My head's thumping. It's no wonder after the day I've had. Part of me wants to sit on the sofa and lose myself in a large glass of red wine or two. But I can't. If Eli needs me, I can't risk being drunk.

My anger towards Martin is peaking now. How manipulative he's been – I bet he spent the time between receiving my message telling him to think about staying away to stage the scene of a 'heartbroken husband who can't cope without his wife'.

It's so pathetic. So clichéd. He's using every trick in the book to try to get Eli to feel sorry for him – but this afternoon he'd gone too far. He'd openly criticised her relationship with me. My daughter's as loyal as I am – and she isn't going to let anyone get away with attacking me.

Least of all a man who's been sleeping with her best friend behind her back.

What a stupid, sorry excuse for a man he is.

And to think we'd believed in him for so long. Really thought he'd be able to fit into our family dynamic.

It would've been better for everyone if it had just stayed the two of us.

Men can't be trusted. I know that. Well, I'm not going to let him manipulate her any further.

Eli's in the bath, so I have time to act. I creep upstairs and into my daughter's bedroom, see her handbag hanging on the end of her bed. Very carefully, I peek in until I can see her phone – a blue light flashing to indicate unread notifications. I lift it out, take it into my bedroom and tap in her passcode.

Of course, there's a text message from Martin.

And of course I read it. I click in, feel the pressure in my head get tighter as I look as his needy words:

Please. Eli. I need to speak with you. We need to talk. I'm sorry for how I reacted earlier. I'm just so scared of losing you. I don't know how to prove to you that I'm not a cheat. And Rachel? That's just madness. I love you and our baby. I know things have been tough between us, but if we're to fix things, we need to talk at least. Just the two of us, Eli. I know you love your mum but this has to be about us. You can't just walk away from us. Please call me. You are my person. You will always be my person. All in, remember?

Angry, I type a response, jab the send button:

Martin, leave me alone. Just give me peace. I don't want to fix things any more. Things are broken. They were broken before you cheated.

I pull the back off Eli's phone, remove the SIM card and slip it into the bottom of my jewellery box. The phone itself, I put in a shoebox on top of my wardrobe. She'll never see his message. Never know that I've responded.

Now, I just have to face whatever is in those emails head on. I can't hide from them any more.

CHAPTER FIFTY-FOUR

Eli

Mum seems to be on edge tonight. I suppose I can't blame her. It's been a horrible day all round. I feel guilty for putting her through it. In fact, I feel guilty for *everything* at the moment. Everything I touch seems to be turning to dirt. I feel as if I'm on a roller coaster that I can't get off. I don't know when it'll end – and the safety harnesses seem to be on the blink.

The episode earlier, in the car, had scared me. For a moment I wondered, was she going to have a heart attack? She was so pale and clammy. She looked so frightened. I was terrified that I was going to lose her, too, on top of everything else.

It's clear the stress is getting to her and how could it not? She'd been downstairs when whoever it was had thrown that rock through my window. She'd seen my face when the text message arrived. She'd tried to keep me calm all way to Derry today for the meeting at the hospice.

I feel so ashamed. I'd not only let Mrs Doherty down when it mattered the most, but I'd let myself down, and I'd let my mother down. She's always been so proud of me. How can she be now? Between work and seeing the horror show my marriage is becoming, her rose-tinted glasses must be well and truly shattered.

I know she says I'm welcome to stay with her for as long as I need to, but I'm sure this wasn't in her plan. Having her pregnant daughter back under her roof – her marriage crumbling round her ears. Her pregnant daughter who killed someone – regardless of what any internal inquiry has found.

She's been tetchy with me ever since I came downstairs after my bath. She seems tense.

I ask her if everything's okay and she blinks at me for a second. I half expect her to tell me that of course nothing is okay. Everything is messed up. But she doesn't.

'I think I'm probably just tired, too,' she says, but her eyes don't quite meet mine.

She doesn't seem able to sit still. Keeps getting up to do things. Put a wash on. Brush the floor. Make a cup of tea. Her answer to everything – a cup of tea. When she brings one in to me, I haven't the heart to tell her I really don't think I can face it. So I take it and sip from it gingerly while she sits at the other end of the sofa, seemingly lost in her own thoughts.

'Are you sure you're okay?' I ask. 'You'd tell me, wouldn't you? If something was wrong. Do you feel okay after that funny turn earlier?'

'For goodness' sake, Eli, stop fussing. You'll give me a headache.'

Her tone is so sharp, I feel completely taken aback. I feel tears prick at my eyes, but I hold them in. I won't cry. It's my fault she's wound up.

I just finish my tea, make my excuses and go to bed. She doesn't try to stop me, or ask me to sit with her for just a few more minutes as she normally does. She simply nods, as if she hasn't quite heard me, then goes back to staring at the fire.

By the time I reach the top of the stairs, I start to realise just how very tired I am. I've barely the energy left to brush my teeth.

I'm just about to climb into bed, when I remember I need to charge my phone, so I reach for my bag to find it. Martin always teases me about the weight of my handbag, fakes a pulled muscle if I ask him to hand it to me. I don't think it's that bad but it's bad enough that things often get lost amid the detritus.

I rifle through it. A notebook. My purse. A pocket-sized packet of tissues. Receipts. A half-used box of Rennies. A small hairbrush, pressed powder, two lipsticks. Keys, of course. Some letters from work that I need to file away. An appointment card or two. An empty Polo Mints wrapper. But no phone.

I'm sure I put it in my bag. I try to go over my actions in my head.

I had it before the meeting at the hospice. I'd put it on silent just before we got out of the car. I didn't take it out of my bag while I was inside. I'd brought my bag into my house when I went to pick up my things, but had I taken my phone out then? I can't remember. It's possible I'd got an email, but my brain's increasingly fuzzy and foggy, and I'm not sure even a gun to my head will make me remember with 100 per cent clarity.

I'm too tired to go back downstairs. I'm sure it must have fallen out in the car but it can stay there until morning. My limbs are leaden and I feel my head spin a little. I lie down and let sleep wash over me. I'll worry about everything else tomorrow.

★

I can hear my mother moving about in the kitchen below me when I wake. Silly domestic sounds. Familiar sounds. It sounds different to my home in Derry. My mother's listening to Radio Ulster, a host of Northern Irish voices talking about the news of the day. She's always been a morning person and always hits the ground running. No sitting around in her nightdress. She's up and ready to go within ten minutes of waking. The washing machine will be on. The vacuum will be pulled around the floors whether they need it or not. Windows open to the world. Purse in the pocket of her coat and off she trots to the shops and back again. A newspaper, which she barely looks at these days, and a pint of milk in a bag she pays ten pence for.

There's a comforting routine to it. Or it had been comforting at one stage. As I lie in bed this morning I don't feel comfortable. Yes, I'd slept, but my dreams were strange. Disturbing. In one I could hear a baby cry, a baby I knew was mine, but I couldn't find her, no matter how hard I looked. I feel as if I've spent the night tossing and turning.

I struggle to pull myself away from sleep and sit up. The usual morning bout of nausea washes over me and my need to run and be sick is what gets me out of bed.

I rinse my mouth with mouthwash, not feeling quite brave enough to risk brushing my teeth and sending my gag reflex into overdrive. Then I walk downstairs, where the smell of fresh coffee almost turns my stomach again.

'Mum, have you seen my phone?' I ask, walking into the kitchen.

My mother's sitting at the table, coffee mug cradled in her hands, reading some celebrity gossip in the newspaper. Fully dressed, her greying hair perfectly coiffed, she looks up at me and shakes her head.

'Do you want me to ring it from mine?'

She seems, perhaps, less on edge this morning.

'Could you?' I ask, sitting down at the table and wondering if I dare risk eating anything.

My mother lifts her phone and dials my number. I listen out for my ringtone, but there's only silence.

'It's gone straight to answer. The battery must've died. Where did you last see it?'

'I'm not sure. My head's gone these days,' I tell her, eyeing the slice of wholemeal toast she's eating. 'I might have left it in the car. I'll go and check in a bit.'

I stand up and slip a slice of wholemeal bread into the toaster. 'I hope I didn't leave it at home. I don't think I did, but you know, I wouldn't put it past me at the moment.'

'Wouldn't do you any harm to be without it for a while anyway. Get a proper break. I don't know how you young ones tolerate it, being on call 24/7. Never getting away from those blasted phones. I doubt all those radio waves or whatever can be good for you either. You work with cancer patients, Eli, you should know how dangerous things can be more than most people.'

'Phones are fairly necessary these days, Mum. You know, for work and stuff . . .' I pause.

For work. I feel my stomach sink. There's no work to think of just now. I suppose I don't really have much need for my phone. Who would call me anyway? My estranged husband? The friend he's cheating on me with?

I butter my toast, just a thin skim. Watching it sink into the toasted bread, I pour myself a cup of tea and sit down, but my appetite has left as quickly as it arrived.

'So,' my mother says, closing her paper and declaring there's nothing worth reading in it anyway. 'What shall we do today? Do you fancy going to Victoria Square for a wee run out again? Or there's a lovely new coffee shop opened just down . . .'

'Actually, Mum, I think I might just take it easy. Maybe go and see Kate later. After she's finished at the bakery.'

Mum looks taken aback. She tenses.

'Why not invite her and that lovely wee boy of hers over for tea? I'm sure I could rustle something up. And he's such a dote.'

There's no denying that, Liam's as lovely a little boy as they come, but I feel the need to get out and about. I can't help but feel the growing tension between us is related to just how much time we've spent in close quarters this last week. I think we could both do with a breather from each other.

That's not to mention that it'd be lovely to see Kate again. It had amazed me, really amazed me, how quickly Kate and I had fallen back into old patterns when she visited. When she gave me a big hug and told me everything would be okay, there was something in the timbre of her voice that made me believe her. We'd talked, briefly, about school and about what our old friends were doing, and then she'd asked me, sincerely, her brown eyes fixed on mine, how I really was, and I'd told her.

Kate doesn't know Martin. She doesn't really know the me I've become, if I'm honest, so she's able to look at the situation objectively. Our chat gave me hope that no matter what the outcome, I'll cope.

'You know, Mum, I think it'd be nice just to get out for a bit. Clear my head – besides, you must be getting sick of looking at me by now. You've your own life to lead. Why don't you go and see one of your friends and sure, we can share all the mutual gossip when we get back. I can even message Kate and see if she can save some of her pastries, so we can indulge ourselves at supper.'

I see my mother try her best to hide her upset at my plans not including her, but she's failing miserably. It seems in trying to reduce her stress, I'm only causing her more.

'No,' she says, stone-faced. 'You do your thing and don't worry about me. I've cancelled everything to be here for you, but I'm sure I can find something to do with my time.'

I tell her I love her, try to file her passive-aggressive response in a 'she's stressed and doesn't really mean it' folder in my brain, and offer to go for a walk with her before lunch. It's a half-hearted attempt at appeasement but she seems happier.

First, I just have to call the bakery to see if Kate will be free later. I hate that I can't just text her, which reminds me how much I value having a mobile phone, even if my mother isn't keen on them.

Standing in my mother's hall while she cleans in the kitchen, I think of all the times I called Martin from this spot. All those conversations that went on for hours even though we'd only just left each other a short time before. Things were so much simpler then. We were less complicated. Life was less complicated. We were so in love. I'd have still said we were in love until last week – yes, things were tougher, but we were still in love. Weren't we?

Suddenly, I find myself missing him. Regretting the things I'd done and said yesterday. Maybe I could ring him. Perhaps he'll have found my phone. I could ask him to post it to me. It's a legitimate reason to call him – one not caught up in this mess we've found ourselves in.

I hear my mother call my name and I leave the phone sitting untouched. She'd never understand. She's never had what we have. What we had.

At times, it crosses my mind that she may even be jealous of Martin and of the relationship I had with him.

CHAPTER FIFTY-FIVE

Louise

The day came when I'd finally reached the point of no return. I'd had to make that final leap. So I'd called Peter and told him that I was finally leaving and that if he wanted to call round and pick up my keys, he should do so before lunch. Otherwise, I'd just leave them on the kitchen table for him.

He'd arrived just a little after eleven. Told his boss he needed to nip out for a bit. As if saying goodbye to his ex-wife was a piece of admin that needed to be done. Not the end of everything we had shared.

He'd stood nervously in the hall of the house we'd once shared – the house we'd been so happy to buy. I couldn't help but think it was all just so very sad.

What had happened to those two young people who'd been convinced they'd be together, no matter what?

I know in our marriage vows we'd promised to stay together for better or for worse. But worse didn't really include the horror of what we went through. No couple could survive that. God would understand.

'You're really going?' Peter had said and I'd nodded.

'I need to move on,' I told him. 'I might as well be in the ground with him if I stay here.'

I felt my voice break. Looked at my husband – saw that same pain echoed in his eyes.

'You'll make a good father, Peter,' I told him.

I wished, God, I wished I could tell him not to feel sorry for me. I was going to be a mother. I was going to be okay. I was going to be better than okay. But I couldn't. I couldn't share this part of my journey with anyone, not even him. So I just reached out my hand to him, felt the warmth and strength of his heart beating in his chest.

'A part of me will always love you, Lou,' he said, and I'd nodded.

I couldn't speak because I was afraid of what I might say, or maybe more what I might feel.

Before I knew it, he was bending his head towards mine. Kissing me. Those lips I'd kissed so many times, brushing against mine. I'd gasped in response. Allowed him to kiss me deeper. Even though I'd sworn to Our Lady that I wouldn't commit the sin of adultery again. We may still have been married, not least in the eyes of the Church, but I'd known all along it was wrong. He was in love with someone else. She was carrying his baby. He had to be there for now. I couldn't allow myself to fall back into his arms another time. We should never have given into temptation over these last few weeks. It just made this harder.

I gently pushed him away.

'We can't do this again, Peter. You're too much of a good man for me to allow you to betray her again.'

He looked sad but resigned. 'I understand,' he said.

'And a part of me will always love you, too,' I said.

I owed him that much. I owed the family that we should have had running round our feet in that moment that much.

'Will you give me a forwarding address?' he asked.

'I'm not sure there's any point,' I told him.

'Maybe not,' he said, 'it's just the thought of never being able to contact you again.'

'That's probably for the best,' I told him. 'But look, I'm only going as far as Galway. It's not the end of the world. And I'll be home to visit my family. We may bump into each other again, you never know.'

'You never know,' he repeated, taking the keys from me.

He paused for a moment, looked me up and down and nodded. I knew it was our goodbye.

Just as I knew I'd lied to him.

But this was one sin I had to commit. I simply had no choice.

CHAPTER FIFTY-SIX

Eli

When I arrive at Kate's house, just over two miles away from my mother's home and her overbearing presence, I can't help but feel some sort of relief.

Kate lives in an unassuming semi in the Belfast suburbs. There's a small garden to the front and I can see a trampoline dominating most of the back garden.

Her house looks safe, secure. The kind of family home we'd all dreamed of when we were smaller. It won't win the design awards ours did, but there's an air of homeliness about it that I realise mine, for all its beauty, is lacking.

Her house feels like a proper home. There are pictures of her, her husband and Liam, along with extended family, all over the walls. A large and definitely very shaggy golden retriever, who I've been informed is called Molly, lies snoring under the kitchen table while Kate fusses about making tea. Everything about this home screams 'happy family', from the finger-paintings on the fridge to the holiday snaps Blu-Tacked to the cupboards, to the wedding portraits on the wall in the hall, hanging above three perfectly aligned pairs of wellies. Mummy Bear. Daddy Bear. And, of course, Baby Bear.

I find myself moving my hand to my wriggling tummy. Will my child know the security Liam does? Will she sit kicking her legs while drinking milk at a kitchen table and talking nineteen to the dozen to my friends?

'I'm so glad you called over,' Kate says, pulling me from my thoughts. 'I've been thinking about you a lot.'

She sits down, placing a mug with 'World's Best Daddy' on it in front of me, along with a pint of milk and a sugar bowl.

'Sorry it's not fancy china, but you take us as you find us here,' she says.

'Thanks for having me over. It's great just to get out for a bit. As lovely as Mum is, it can feel a bit claustrophobic at times.'

'I can imagine,' Kate says, sitting down opposite me. 'If I had to live with my mother again, I'm pretty sure one of us would be dead within the first twenty-four hours. She's the best in the world, but wee doses work best for me.'

I laugh. A genuine laugh, and it feels good. I remember Kate's mother well. Lovely but strict. Kate would cringe at her mother's rules when we were younger, but there was always a genuine affection between the two of them.

'Well, I know my mother's heart's in the right place, but she can be a bit overbearing. And well, she seems to be feeling the impact of everything that's been going wrong with me. I thought she might need some space to herself, too.'

'It must be a bit overwhelming for you both,' Kate says.

'Yeah. That's an understatement – it's a wonder the stress hasn't given her a heart attack or put me into early labour. Although Mum would be in her element if I had this baby early. Delighted she gets to be born in Belfast and not in Derry.'

'She does seem really excited about the baby,' Kate says.

'You've got no idea,' I smile. 'She's taking her role as grandmother-to-be very seriously. Did I tell you, she's made her spare room into a fully equipped nursery? Wipes warmer and all. We've not even started back at home. I'm surprised she didn't offer you the guided tour when you came round.'

I laugh again, as does Kate, but there's something hollow about it.

'It's a bit OTT, isn't it?' I ask, and if I'm honest, I hope Kate will tell me that no, it's not over the top at all and it's a lovely gesture.

She gives a half-smile. An awkward shrug. She looks down at her cup of tea.

'You think it is, don't you?' I ask, but I'm not laughing any more. Nor is Kate smiling.

'Biscuits!' she says, jumping to her feet. 'I forgot to get them out.'

She has her back to me and is rifling her cupboards even though her biscuits are in clear view.

'Kate, it might be quite a while since we spent all our time together, but I still know when there's something you're not telling me,' I say.

'I don't want to interfere,' she says, turning back towards me, waving a packet of custard creams in my direction.

'But if there's something I should know . . .'

She looks at me, and then to Liam, who's drawing a car with purple wheels and a bright orange roof.

'Pet,' she says to him, 'why don't you take your biscuits into the living room to eat? In case Molly wakes up and fancies a bite.' She tickles his tummy and he laughs uproariously.

'Can I watch *Toy Story*, Mammy?' he asks.

'Of course you can, my love,' she says, following him into the living room, leaving me feeling uneasy.

I know Kate sees my mother regularly at the bakery. Has something been said? Does she know something I don't?

When she returns, she walks to the fridge and unpins one

of Liam's pictures, handing it to me. It's a Santa with an over-proportioned tummy and a wide smile.

'What's this?' I ask. 'I mean, I guess it's Santa and Liam drew it, but . . .'

'Turn it over,' she says.

I do, and see another drawing. A lady with short, curly brown hair, hands and feet like potatoes, with stick fingers and toes. A small figure, a baby, on her tummy.

I still don't get it. Is it Mary and the baby Jesus? I raise an eyebrow and look at Kate.

'Liam's a very talented artist,' I tell her, 'but I don't think I'm following you.'

'Liam drew that picture when we visited you at your mum's. I asked him about it. He told me that 'Langela' told him Santa was bringing her a baby to live in her house forever.'

The baby, my baby, kicks and my stomach tightens, then sinks.

'Maybe . . . you know, kids get things mixed up.'

'Maybe,' Kate says. 'I told him that it was you who was getting a baby, but he said your mum had said that it was a secret but the baby was definitely going to live with his or her granny.'

I start to feel uneasy.

'Look, I don't know if it's anything more than a feeling. But when she came to the bakery and asked me to visit you, she said you might be staying with her for a 'very long time'. And just, well, from the conversation we had when I was over, I sensed you didn't really know what was happening and, well, it felt to me like you still hope to go back to Derry.'

'Well, my job's there . . . or was there,' I blurt. 'And Martin . . .'

She shifts uncomfortably in her seat. 'Eli, I'm only telling you this because you've been a very good friend to me in the past. I don't want to upset you, but you know, people talk around here. One of my customers was asking after you the other day, asked if you'd got sorted with a solicitor yet.'

My skin prickles. 'What? I don't need a solicitor. What did they mean?'

She takes a deep breath. 'Eli, your mother was looking for recommendations for a good divorce lawyer.'

I shake my head. My mother? My mother has done this?

'When?' I ask her.

Divorce hasn't even been mentioned. It's not on my radar. Not yet, anyway. I don't understand. I know my mother likes to be organised, but this is moving too quickly, even for her.

'Well that's the thing,' Kate says. 'I was talking to him yesterday, but he said it was a fortnight ago that your mother spoke to him. That he'd meant to get back to her sooner but had been really busy. I didn't think there were any problems with you and Martin that long ago. Didn't you tell me, that first note arrived last week?'

'It did,' I say. 'Your customer must be mistaken.' That's the only logical explanation, after all.

'Maybe,' she says, but she doesn't look convinced. 'If I see him again, I'll ask him if he remembers exactly when. Would that help?'

I nod but there's a sinking feeling right in the pit of my stomach and I start to feel shaky. None of this makes sense.

'And how *are* things with Martin?' she asks. 'Is it a matter of divorce lawyers at dawn?'

I shake my head. Then shrug. 'I don't think so. Not yet, anyway,' I explain, telling her how things were left yesterday. That yes, things are very bad, but I wasn't ready to make any big decisions. Not yet. There was so much to consider.

'You've not had a chance to talk to him, just the two of you,' she says. 'Do you think that might be useful?'

'I don't know. Maybe.'

'Do you want to call him while you're here? Away from your mum's listening ear.'

'I lost my phone. I think I might have left it in Derry. I mean, I was sure I had it with me . . .'

'You can use a landline, you know,' Kate says softly.

'I'm not sure my mother would approve,' I say without really thinking, until Kate tilts her head to one side and gives me a sympathetic look.

'Eli, I've no doubt that your mum loves you and that her intentions are from a good place, but I'm not sure she should stand in the way of you trying to sort out your marriage, especially if you still *want* to sort out your marriage, and I sense you do.'

I can't speak. I'm trying to process everything. Her forever baby. The divorce lawyer. Her clinginess. How she's been on edge all day, and last night, too. She's been snapping and it's not like her.

'Call him,' she says. 'Call him from here. I'll bring you the phone. I'll go and watch *Toy Story* with Liam. I'm not saying your mother's a bad person, Eli, but you need to decide what you want to do for your marriage and your baby and yourself.'

CHAPTER FIFTY-SEVEN

Eli

I tap Martin's number into Kate's phone, my heart thumping in my chest. Kate has done what she said she'd do and has left me with my mug of tea, now tepid, in the comfort of her kitchen, sneaking a call to my husband while wondering what the hell is really happening in my life just now.

Kate's words echo in my head as I dial. I remind myself a three-year-old isn't the most reliable witness in the world, but between that and how my mother had spoken at the bakery, and this divorce solicitor talk, none of this is painting a pretty picture.

I wait until I hear the ringing tone on the other end. As soon as I do, I'm overwhelmed by a desire to hear his voice.

'Hello?' he answers, sounding confused.

Of course he is. He won't know the number calling him.

'Martin,' I say, my voice cracking as I do.

'Eli? Eli, is that you? I've been trying to call you. Your phone keeps going straight to your answer service. I thought maybe you'd blocked me. After that last message . . .'

'What? I've not blocked you,' I say. 'I've lost my phone. That's why I'm calling, to see if I left it in Derry. In the house.'

There's a pause. 'No. No . . . sure, were you not in Belfast when you messaged me last night?'

'I didn't message you,' I say, feeling more confused than ever. 'You must be mistaken. But look, Martin, I'm at a friend's house and I don't have long, so please, just let me say this. I just . . . we need to talk. Be honest with each other. I'm so sorry that I went behind your back to find out the sex of the baby. I needed to know but I didn't want to ruin it for you. It was wrong of me. I was going to keep it a surprise for you. I know I should've spoken to you more about it. I realise I've not been myself. I've been pushing you away. It's no wonder you—'

'I never cheated on you,' Martin says, and I hear the pain in his voice. 'Not now, not ever. Certainly not with Rachel. I can't prove it. It's driving me mad that I can't prove it, but I'm being honest with you. Someone is messing with us, Eli. Someone wants to hurt us. Split us up. I don't know who or why but they're winning, aren't they?'

A little voice repeats in my head. Someone wants to hurt us. Someone wants to split us up.

Someone.

I say nothing. I can't speak.

'You do believe me, don't you?' he says.

'I want to . . .' I tell him, and I do.

But I don't even want to contemplate the alternative. My mother's face flashes before me. I feel sick.

'I've got to go, Martin. I can't talk. I'm sorry,' I say and hang up, not waiting to hear his response.

Someone is lying. My husband. My mother. Or both of them. I'm starting to feel as if I'm losing my mind.

CHAPTER FIFTY-EIGHT

Eli

I'm on edge after talking to Martin. Kate joins me again in the kitchen and I tell her how bereft Martin sounded.

'He's so insistent that he hasn't cheated. Either's he's a brilliant liar or . . .'

'Is there anything about him, in the years that you've known him, which has led you to think he's a brilliant liar?'

Despite the seriousness of the question, I laugh. No. Martin Hughes isn't a good liar. He's never been able to keep secrets, either. Martin Hughes has always been an open book to me. I can always tell. It's the way he can't keep eye contact. His voice goes a little funny. He blushes – his high colour roaring against his ginger hair.

I tell her no. Until last week, I'd never doubted him at all. I'd believed in him entirely.

'And can you think of anyone who'd hold a grudge? Or even have anything to gain by the pair of you splitting up.'

My mind keeps coming back to the same person. One person who'd gain what she wanted – having me back in Belfast. Having her grandchild under her roof. But surely not? My mother is many things, but could she be as calculating as that?

She's always been overprotective, clingy even. I think of how she's been pretty much stuck to me like glue all week. Of her reaction at the hospice when I told her she couldn't come into the meeting. I'd tried to be gentle, but really I wanted to ask her whether she genuinely thought it would look professional of me to drag my mum along.

But then again, she'd been so scared when that rock came through the window. Could she have faked that fear? Had tried to reassure me when the first few notes came in. Had been in my corner all of my life. Could she really be behind it all?

I don't speak. I don't want to say it out loud.

'I wish I had the answer for you, Eli,' Kate says. 'You don't need all the worry right now. Being pregnant is tough enough without adding this kind of thing into the mix. You poor thing.'

Her eyes are so filled with real concern that I find myself crying, again, before making my excuses to leave. I need some time to myself before I go back to Mum's.

She hugs me at the door and tells me that she's here for me whenever I need to talk. I'm incredibly grateful.

'Look, I'm sorry if I made things worse, you know, talking about your mum, but given everything . . . Well, I couldn't in good conscience not tell you,' she says. 'But . . . well, just take care.'

I take the long way home, drive out of the city towards the Lough Shore Park at Jordanstown, where I sit and watch the ferry sail into Belfast Harbour. I can't help but hear the desperation in my husband's voice over and over again. Despite everything, my gut tells me to believe him. No doubt my mother will tell me I'm being soft. Being scared even. Because it's easier to believe him and go back to my comfortable life, have our baby and not have to start all over again.

But if he was telling the truth, then I couldn't just walk away. We'd been so happy.

I rest my arms on the steering wheel and put my head on my arms, my tummy digging into the wheel, the baby jabbing me to show her discomfort. I whisper words of comfort to her.

'I know, baby, but believe me. Stay in there. Things are much less complicated in there.'

I replay the rest of my conversation with Martin as I drive home.

Did he say he'd got a message from me? I didn't send one – I know that with 100 per cent clarity and only one person could have. Only one other person knows my passcode.

If my mother could do that behind my back, what else could she be capable of?

I don't want to go home, but I know I have to. As I park outside her house, I see her curtains twitch. I tense up immediately. My mother. My champion. Could she really be trying to destroy my marriage?

It's unthinkable. When I push open the front door, I find her in the hall, where she just happens to be 'dusting the hall table'.

'It's a bit late for housework, isn't it?' I ask.

'Well, it's a bit late to be coming home as well, Eliana. I didn't think you'd be so long. I've been worried sick – you would've thought you and that Kate one would have more consideration for how I might be feeling.'

Her expression is sharp, flint-like. She's wringing the duster through her hands, twisting it tightly.

'I didn't realise I was on a curfew,' I say.

'It's manners to let someone know when you'll be back. You can't just go gallivanting around the place, especially not in your condition.'

'I've done a lot of things in my condition, as have countless women, Mother. And we're all just fine.'

'Yes, but you've extra complications. Your sickness, and

you're under severe emotional stress. You could've been doing anything.'

My shoulders tense further. 'Like what, Mum? Seriously? Doing anything? What did you think I might be doing? Dancing *Swan Lake*? Bungee jumping? Or do you mean you thought I might be topping myself and my baby with me? Do you seriously believe I'd hurt my baby?' I can hardly believe she's asking.

'Well, you've already admitted that you're struggling to bond. God knows what you might do. Would you prefer I didn't give a thought to that poor baby? God knows she'll have a tough enough start. A daddy who's a cheat and a mum who doesn't give two stuffs about her.'

My jaw drops. I can feel a surge of anger, and something else, hurt maybe, build up inside of me. I have to stop myself from picking something up and throwing it across the room. How dare she! How dare she twist my struggle to bond and make it into something so horrible! That I don't 'give two stuffs' about my baby? I may be struggling, but in this moment my mothering instincts are in full flow. I love this baby. I know whatever happens, I'll care for this baby. I'll protect this baby. With every breath in my body.

How dare she!

'It's only because I love you that I say such things,' she says, her voice contrite.

Is it possible she realises she went too far?

'You don't realise how hard this is for me, too. It's not just about you, Eli. You don't realise what you're putting me through!' she says, her voice breaking.

If this was any other occasion, if I wasn't feeling so attacked, so vulnerable, so unsure of who or what to believe, I'd bend myself over backwards to console her and make her feel better, but she doesn't just get to pull the 'poor me' routine after saying what she did and expect me to forgive and forget. Not this time.

As for her tears, I'm not sure any more that they aren't anything more than her own form of manipulation. Thinking of it, it's one of her signature moves. Lay on the guilt. Lay on the tears. Make it about her and everything she does for me.

'You're all I have, Eliana.'

'I've dedicated my whole life to you, Eliana.'

'If you loved me, Eliana.'

I need to get away from her before I say or do anything I regret. I push past her and start on my way up the stairs.

'Since all this is so hard for you, Mother, I'll go in the morning. Go and stay with Kate maybe. Or go home to my husband and our mutual shoddy parenting of our unborn baby.'

'That's not what I meant . . .' she says, her eyes wide.

Is it panic? Is it anger? Right now, I don't know and I don't care.

'I'm going to bed, Mum. I think we've said enough for tonight.'

For good measure, I even slam my bedroom door, my ire only rising further when I notice the lock I put on when I was eighteen is no longer there. If it had been, I'd have pulled it across to ensure she couldn't get under my skin for the rest of the night.

Instead, I throw myself down on my bed, as much as being seven months pregnant will allow me to, and I scream into my pillow.

CHAPTER FIFTY-NINE

Angela

The slam of the bedroom door shocks me. I've gone too far. I lost my cool and what I said to Eliana was unforgivable.

Things are bad when I can't get her onside by crying. Not that my tears are fake. Not this time. They're real. I'm so scared. I feel like I've been playing this game for so long and I'm growing tired just when I need to be at my sharpest.

I know a part of her believes Martin. Probably a big part of her. He's always been good to her. Why would he betray her now? It's not in his nature.

But I thought, you see, if I presented her with enough 'evidence', she'd believe the worst of him. And that she'd be strong enough to walk away.

I know I'm being selfish, but I've the right to be. I've put my daughter at the centre of my world for thirty-three years now and I'm just supposed to give that up? I'm supposed to say: 'There you go, make your own way. Never worry about your poor mother, all alone in Belfast.'

The truth is I'm scared to be alone. I don't know how to be alone; and as soon as this baby's born my alone status will be confirmed. I know how it goes. I see it happen with my friends and their daughters who've moved away. Once a husband and a baby come along, they're too busy going to Music with Mummy classes, or birthday parties, or group excursions to the zoo, or family holidays to bother with those trips back home that used to mean so much.

I'd given up everything for Eli. I didn't regret it for a second, but I'd always assumed that I'd get to play the role of a doting granny as some sort of reward.

If only Martin hadn't insisted on opening his business in Derry.

If only I'd stayed in Scotland and never come back to this stupid country in the first place.

I've been the author of my own undoing.

Those emails have only confirmed that. Soon, someone else will make a claim on Eli and I won't be able to do anything about it.

What I've done, I've done out of love for her. But I'm not sure she'll see that. Not at first, anyway. Maybe she will when she's a mother herself and feels that bond.

But until that point I have to continue to do everything I can to stick to the original plan. Even if she fights it. She has to realise that sometimes tough love is necessary. Sometimes a parent has to be harsh to get the message across.

Until now, it's been easier than I thought it would be. It didn't take much effort to persuade someone, for a small fee, to hand-deliver the first note to the hospice. A niece of an acquaintance. Studying in Derry. I told her it was a thank-you note, a gift voucher. That I was nervous it'd go missing in the post and as she was heading that way anyway, it'd be lovely of her to drop it in for me. I put a fiver in her hand, 'enough for a pint', as a thank you.

It was just glorious timing that Martin'd had to go to London on business just as it arrived. It meant I could move forwards with my plan faster.

Of course, I felt guilty when I saw how hysterical she was at the smashed window. It'd been tricky to time it all right. To make sure the rock was thrown through the window, that I was able to get in as quickly as possible and trigger the alarm.

My guilt hadn't been enough to stop me gleaning some pleasure from knowing my daughter was getting more suspicious of Martin. I could almost see the wedge between them growing.

Taking the picture in their bedroom to stage it as if someone had broken into their home was a stroke of genius, if I say so myself.

Sending another letter – keeping the pressure on – was just, I suppose, an insurance policy.

And I know I still have another trick up my sleeve or, to be more accurate, in my pocket.

Okay, things are tougher now. But it was never going to be easy all the time. But I can still save this. First, I need to try to get Eli back on side. Even just a little. I'll bring her a peace offering. A cup of tea. Laced with a sedative, of course. In case she *really* gets the notion to go elsewhere.

CHAPTER SIXTY

Louise

There was one aspect of leaving that I knew I'd never be able to get over.

Starting again meant walking away from the cemetery. From where I sat most mornings and hugged the blanket we'd wrapped our baby boy in. I'd tried to imagine what it would feel like to have my child, now healthy and growing, in my arms, instead of this horrific nothingness.

It's strange how empty arms can feel heavier than those that are full.

I reminded myself that every day that he wasn't there. In the ground. Not really. The baby who'd kicked and wriggled and turned somersaults in my stomach. That life energy, the one that had got us so close to becoming parents, couldn't possibly be in the ground. His grave was just a focal point for us. A place I could go to to cry. But he was always with me. Always. I carried the other losses, too, of course. But his was the cruellest of all.

Still, the thought of walking away from his resting place. From my child. It pulled at my heart. It pulled at my conscience. I tried not to think about leaving him for the last time too much. I tried not to think about who would look after his little plot of grass. Who'd put fresh flowers beside that little stone that bears my surname and that expression I'd come to hate. 'Born sleeping' – as if it had all been so peaceful. As if it hadn't been brutal and bloody and horrific. Scalpels and stitches. Infusions. Blood. So much blood. As if there hadn't been screaming, even though he never made a noise.

I begged the doctors to save him. Even though by the time I was awake he was already cold. His lips already blackened. I'd hugged him and tried to warm him up. I'd prayed for a miracle. I remember begging God to prove to me that He existed. Prove it by bringing my baby back. He'd done it with Lazarus. Surely if I pleaded and prayed and promised enough, He'd do this for me . . .

I'd have loved my baby so much. I do love him. I'd have given him the world and everything in it, but I never had the chance. And then I had to prepare myself to walk away from him forever without ever looking back. What kind of a mother did that make me?

When I went to the cemetery, I scratched at the ground, dug a little. Filled a little jam jar with soil. Soil that he nourished. I'd slipped it into my handbag, kissed the stone that bore his name. Noah. My beautiful Noah. Even in his silence, it suited him. It was as if it were made just for him. I'd whispered it – my beautiful Noah, that is. Then I'd sat back on the cold ground and tried to consign every detail to memory. No one was around. It was just the two of us. So I said his name out loud.

Then I shouted it to the sky and vowed that I'd never say it again.

The next baby name I'd mutter would be the one I'd raise to adulthood.

CHAPTER SIXTY-ONE

Angela

Eli's asleep. I sit for a few minutes and watch the rise and fall of her chest. I envy her. The sedative in her tea, which she'd reluctantly accepted after I begged her not to stay mad at me, will ensure she gets a long sleep.

We didn't talk much while she drank her tea. I sat on the edge of her bed and told her I knew she'd love her baby very much. That I'd spoken in anger.

That she should know I could never think that of her.

She'd stayed quiet. Nodding occasionally.

I'd told her I loved her. She hadn't replied but she'd thanked for me the tea. It was something to hang on to.

I doubt I'll sleep well myself – and I can't risk taking a sleeping pill. I have to keep my wits about me. Maybe I'll make a coffee. Do what I need to keep alert. We're not safe any more. People are coming at us from all angles. People trying to ruin what we have.

People we thought were friends. People I should've been able to rely on.

I'm starting to realise that any time I reach out to anyone else for help, they end up letting me down.

The only person I can rely on to keep Eli and me together is me.

CHAPTER SIXTY-TWO

Eli

The noise from the street wakes me. I blink, trying to bring myself into full consciousness, and realise it's already light. It must be at least nine, I think, as I try to keep my eyes open. I can't remember the last time I slept so late.

But today my head feels heavy as I turn to check the time on my phone. It takes a moment or two for me to remember that it's missing. Something nags at me through the brain fog, pulling at some invisible strings in my head. I feel a dull throbbing behind my eyes. Even my limbs feel as if they're weighted down. Numb, I suppose, is how I feel. Physically and emotionally. And just so very tired.

My eyes close again despite my best efforts to open them. I wonder if I'm coming down with flu as I drift off.

When I jump awake again later, the same fight to wake up properly begins all over again.

My head's still foggy. As if there's something I've forgotten but it's just out of reach. I feel my baby move, as if nudging me. 'Wake up, Mummy.' But even a well-placed punch to my bladder doesn't wake me enough to pull me fully from my sleep and into consciousness.

Mummy. Mum. A string connected to my mother is pulled. My brain tries to grab onto it. Something has happened. I vaguely remember having words with her last night – her face full of remorse afterwards.

And Martin, have I spoken to him? It all feels blurry. I haul myself to sitting, fighting the urge just to lie down and sleep some more. I'm hungry, I realise. And in need of the loo.

I pull myself to standing, wobbling as the room swims slightly around me. Something isn't right, I can feel it. I put my hand to my forehead, a primitive check for a fever, but it feels cool. The pain behind my eyes is subsiding, but I still feel as if I'm wrapped in cotton wool and I'm trying to fight my way out of it one delicate white fibre at a time.

Opening the bedroom door, I make my way to the bathroom, using the walls to steady myself. The house is so quiet, but then again, all I can really hear is the whoosh of my own blood coursing through my veins. My baby kicks to remind me to keep moving and I do.

In the bathroom, I splash my face with water to shock my body into full awareness.

Looking at myself in the mirror, it feels as if I'm out of focus. I put my hand to the mirror, just to check it's there. To check it's real. That I'm real. I'm starting to feel sick now, hyperemesis, or anxiety, or hunger, or something just beyond my reach.

I call for my mother, my voice weak, reedy. I want to sit down until I fully come round, so I walk back to my bedroom and sit staring at the closed curtains over the window. Pale pink stripes, a thin gold thread running through them. It strikes me that they don't match the colour of the walls any more. They had, once. When I was a little girl and had a room that screamed pink and princess and floral.

I still don't know what time it is.

'Morning, sleepyhead.'

My mother's voice jolts me into the present. I turn to look at her, watch as she comes into focus.

'You've had quite the sleep,' she says as she carries a tray laden with tea, toast and a glass of water.

'What time is it?' I ask.

'Ach, still early enough,' she says. 'You obviously needed that sleep anyway, Eli. But I'm sure you're hungry. I've brought you some toast, and tea and a glass of water to wash down your pills.'

'I think I might have a shower first,' I say, wondering if that'll wake me up.

'Eat something first, love. I don't want you fainting on me while you're in the shower. I'd be no good having to lift you up. Here, sit back and try to eat something.'

I shuffle back on my bed and take the cup of tea my mother offers me.

She sits and watches me eat. I look at her, this person I know but don't know at the same time. I look at her smile. The soft curves of the wrinkles on her face.

I watch as she hands me half a slice of toast, butter and strawberry jam spread on top, just as I'd taken it when I was a child. This woman who's given me everything and most of all has given me herself. Every part of her.

This woman who'd said horrible, hurtful things to me last night. This woman who I'm not sure if I can trust any more. It's starting to come back to me now. Sitting at Kate's table. A picture. A lawyer. My head's starting to hurt with the effort of trying to remember and trying to stay awake. This feels wrong. There's something about this that feels all wrong.

'Now, Eli, don't forget to take your tablets and sure, maybe then you can get a shower and we can plan the rest of the day.'

I nod and sip my tea. Take a bite of toast but it tastes like sawdust. She's still watching me. Her eyes never leaving me. The weight of the cup feels too much. The effort of keeping my eyes open seems insurmountable.

'I'm still so tired,' I mutter.

'I'd say it's just all the stress and strain of the last few days catching up with you. It was bound to happen. You've been living on adrenaline this past week.'

'Maybe,' I say, putting the teacup down and lying back against the pillows.

'And the baby's moving about okay?'

Her voice cuts through my hazy, almost-asleep state. I open my eyes and see her eyes are fixed on my stomach.

'Yes,' I say, putting my hand to my stomach protectively. My baby. The one she said I didn't care about. More is coming back.

'That's good,' my mother says, standing. 'That's perfect. Now, you rest until you feel less tired,' she says as she backs out of the room, pulling the door closed.

As I drift back towards sleep, something more itches at my brain. My mother. A baby forever. In her house. The nursery. The missing phone. Martin. As my eyes flutter shut despite my best efforts to keep them awake, I'm almost sure I hear the sound of a lock turning.

⭑

It's dark when I wake again. My mouth is dry. My bladder full again. Still I blink, trying to focus in the darkness. I reach over and switch on the bedside lamp beside me before pulling myself to sitting. There are still traffic sounds outside – I guess it's maybe teatime. I wish I had my phone to check. Wonder why no one wears a watch any more. The glass of water Mum brought up earlier is still sitting on the bedside table and I gulp down all that's left in it, grateful to quench my thirst.

My dreams had been weird half dreams. Snippets of conversations. Voices that seemed so real. At one stage I was sure I heard Martin ask for me, try to reach me, and I tried to call out to him but I was dragged back under, unable to move. I hate dreams like that. Hate how they make me feel when I wake up, my heart heavy. I miss him. I need him. I need to drive to Derry again. Without my mother.

My mother. There it is again. The nagging. I started. Surely I hadn't heard a door lock earlier? My door lock.

I get out of bed. Rubbing my stomach, I get rewarded with a gentle kick. I welcome it. As I touch my skin where a hand or foot has just prodded, I'm surprised at the affection that washes over me.

I turn the handle of my bedroom door, pull to open it, but it stays put. I rattle it again. But still it doesn't open. I look to where the lock used to be, high up on my side – so I could lock the world out. I sort of expect it to be there still, but of course it isn't.

As far as I've ever been aware there's no other working lock. We'd never had keys for the locks on the bedroom doors. They'd been long gone when we moved in.

Or they had been. It dawns on me as I rattle the handle again that it's been changed. It's new. Shiny. Bright. And no doubt came with a lock.

My baby kicks as my heart thumps. A surge of protective love runs through me. I don't know what's going on, but I know the most important person in the room at that moment is the little girl growing in my womb. This little innocent soul who's somehow managed to find herself in the middle of some sort of war zone.

'It'll be okay,' I say, rubbing my stomach and then trying the door again.

I bang on the door with my fist as hard as I can. Calling for my mother to open the door. *Now.*

'Don't panic!' I remind myself. Keep calm. Don't assume the worst. But what other assumption can I make?

I hear my mother's footsteps on the stairs.

Her voice is calm, cool, normal.

'I'm on my way, sweetheart.'

'I'm locked in, Mum,' I call. 'What's going on?'

I hear a key turn in the lock and she pulls the door open, her face serene.

'Such a racket. You'll give yourself a sore throat, not to mention sore hands.'

'Mum, you locked me in my bedroom. Why? What's going on?'

I push my way past her. I want out of the room.

'I'm sorry, darling. Force of habit. I usually keep my valuables in your room these days, so I always lock the door when I leave.'

She says it as if it's the most reasonable explanation in the world, even though I've never known her to keep her valuables anywhere other than her own room. On top of her wardrobe. In old shoeboxes. Old shoeboxes that still sit on top of her wardrobe.

'You've had new locks fitted,' I say as I start to make my way to the bathroom.

I turn to close the door, see she's right behind me in the doorway.

'Well, the other ones didn't work, did they?' she says as if there's nothing bizarre about the whole situation.

'Well, I know this one works just fine,' I say, nodding towards the bathroom door lock, 'so if you don't mind?'

'It's nothing I've not seen before,' she says, but she does turn and leave, pulling the door behind her.

I pull the lock across.

'What time is it?' I call.

'After six,' she calls back from the landing. It seems she's waiting for me. 'You really were a sleepyhead!'

'I think I'll grab that shower now, Mum. Why don't you go and put the kettle on? I'll be down in ten minutes or so.'

'I think I'll stay here,' she says, her voice light, and I feel myself tense. 'Since you've been feeling a little off balance, I'd rather be close if you need me. Actually, do you really need to keep that door locked?'

My skin prickles. This is overkill on caring, even for my mother.

'I'll be fine, Mum,' I say, even if I do feel wobbly.

I'm sure I've not reached the stage where I need a full-time carer.

'I've brought you some fresh towels,' she calls, knocking at the door moments later.

I make sure to lock the door as soon as I've taken the towels from her. I can hear her tutting.

I wash quickly, rinse my hair and wrap a towel around me, marvelling momentarily at how it pulls around my expanding stomach. Opening the door, I see my mother sitting on the landing floor, reading her Kindle as if doing so is the most normal thing in the world.

'See, I told you I'd be fine,' I tell her. 'There's no need for you to sit here. I'll be down as soon as I'm dressed.'

'I've left some clean things out for you,' she replies.

'Mum, you do know I can pick out my own clothes, don't you?' There's a hint of irritation in my voice that I can't hide.

'You should watch how you speak to me, Eli. You're not too old that you don't still owe me respect.'

Her voice is cold. Her expression flat. I remember how she was last night. What she'd said. How I told her I'd leave today.

I feel uneasy. When I get to my bedroom, I see fresh pyjamas and underwear laid out on my bed.

'I was thinking I'd actually get properly dressed, Mum, thanks,' I call.

'Why? Sure, it's nearly seven. It'll be bedtime soon.'

'I've slept all day. I'm not likely to go to sleep soon. Anyway, I was thinking I might call over and see Kate again.'

If the truth be told, I'm starting to think I *need* to go and see Kate again. Something feels very wrong here.

'I don't think so,' my mother says, appearing at my door. 'It's a bad night out there and you've clearly been out of sorts. I'd only worry. So I really think you should stay here with me. I've been sat in all day waiting for you to wake up. I thought maybe we could watch a movie. Or look over photos from when you were little. You remember that, don't you, Eli? All the fun we had when you were little. You used to tell me I was your best friend.'

There's something about her manner that's making me feel increasingly uncomfortable. I feel my anxiety heighten. Is it possible she really has been behind all these lies about Martin all along? She seems determined to keep me in her company.

'I think some fresh air might help me come round a bit.'

'Well, if you think so, that's fine. But I'll come with you,' she says in a tone I know not to argue with.

If I'm being fully honest with myself, she's starting to scare me.

CHAPTER SIXTY-THREE

Eli

I need to eat something. If I allow myself to get too hungry, my sickness will get worse and there's nothing quite as painful as throwing up on an empty stomach, so I go to the kitchen and start looking through the cupboards.

Of course, Mum follows me. Watches me as I move around the room.

'Why don't you go and sit down in front of the fire. I'll make you scrambled eggs and bring them through,' she says.

I start to protest. To say I can make them myself. But I know by the look on her face to stop. So I agree. Say I'll sit down. If she's sure.

As I turn to leave the room, I spot a box from Kitty's Kitchen on the worktop.

'Did you go and see Kate today?' I ask, my eyebrow raised.

'Ah no,' my mother says as she bustles around cracking eggs and whisking them violently with a fork, which clatters off the edges of the metal bowl she's using. 'She called in earlier, with that wee boy of hers. Was looking to chat to you, it seems. But I told her you were asleep.'

'Maybe I should just give her a quick call then,' I say. 'Since I missed her. See how she is.'

My mother turns her back from her task and waves her fork at me, gloopy, slimy egg white spattering the kitchen floor.

'Eli, I'm not sure how to say this. But I'm thinking, she's a bit much, isn't she?'

'In what way?' I ask, trying to keep my tone flat. I realise I'm choosing my words carefully.

'Calling round all the time. Having you over. You've hardly seen her in years and now she's all I hear about. Kate this and Kate that. I don't know who taught her about manners either, but calling over unannounced when she knows you're not yourself? She's sticking her nose in our business, Eli, and before you know it, the whole street will know what's going on in your marriage.'

'She's just being a friend, Mum. I'm sure she'd have called first if my phone wasn't missing,' I say, wondering if now is the time to ask her if she really did ask one of our neighbours about a good divorce lawyer, since she's so concerned about the whole street knowing my business.

My mother's eyes narrow. I see her lips tighten. Her expression changes just enough that I can see she's getting angry.

'God, can you stop going on about that blasted mobile phone? How did the world survive without mobile phones? We don't all need to be able to check up on each other every hour of the day, you know. Keeping tabs, tracing people, people too afraid of their lives to be without one of those devices. All this modern technology! It just allows people to stalk each other, if you ask me.'

I sigh. 'Look, I'll just go and phone Kate and see what she wanted, then we can eat our tea and get on with our evening.'

'If you must, but I'm telling you now, Eli. I don't think I like that girl. I don't think I want her near this house.'

My head hurts. It was my mother who, just days ago, invited Kate here. Insisted that I talk to her, and now she wants me to stay away. I decide to call Kate anyway. I imagine she's worried about me after our chat last night – and it seems increasingly likely that she has good reason.

I close the kitchen door to provide some privacy, but just as I dial, I hear my mother open it again.

Kate answers within three rings, her bright tone turning more serious as soon as she hears my voice.

'I hear you called over today. I'm sorry, I was sleeping,' I say with a forced jollity that I'm really not feeling.

'I did. Are you okay?'

'Ach, I'm just tired. I slept all day. And Mum's keeping a close eye on me. I can hardly move, she's fussing around. I think she's afraid to let me out of her sight,' I say lightly.

I hope Kate will be perceptive enough to read between the lines and sense something isn't as it should be.

'So this isn't about Martin's visit then?' she asks.

Martin's visit? Martin hasn't visited. Has he? Surely not. Not even my mother would let me sleep through that. Would she?

'I'm not sure I know about that,' I say, trying not to give anything away in my voice, knowing my mother's listening.

'When I called today . . . well, I was sure it was him. I know I've never met him, but I recognised him from pictures on your Facebook. He looked upset, Eli. I thought maybe you'd had words. I wondered if that's why your mum told me you were 'sleeping'. I didn't want to push, I mean we don't know each other that well any more . . .'

'I slept all day, just couldn't keep my eyes open,' I say, my heart thumping now.

Those weird dreams where I was sure I'd heard his voice

– were they more than just weird dreams? Maybe he'd really been here. I look at the kitchen door, towards my mother. My heart beats faster.

'Eli, are you not free to talk just now?' Kate asks and I know she's on the right track.

'That's it exactly,' I say brightly. 'I think Mum would wrap me in cotton wool and lock me away until this baby's born if she could.'

'Jesus, Eli. Can you get away at all? Even over to mine for a bit. We can talk.'

'Ah, she's just making tea now to make sure I eat something decent and then she's going to get some old pictures out for us to look at. Sure, who would go out on a night like this anyway? I wouldn't want to worry her.'

'Right . . .' Kate says and I know she's worried, too. 'Eli, I'm sorry if this sounds overdramatic, but do you think you're in danger?'

Do I? I think my mother is most likely being manipulative. I think she might need help. I suppose I do feel afraid to confront her – but do I think she'd actually harm me?

No. Not mum.

'I think she's just making sure I take good care of myself and the baby. We'll be fine,' I say.

'Try to get away tomorrow. Come to the bakery even. She can't object to you taking a wee walk up the street, can she? We can talk then. And if I don't hear from you I'll call in to check when I'm finished for the day. I'll not leave her door until we've spoken, okay?'

'That sounds lovely, Kate. You're very good to think of me and us like that. I'll keep all that in mind.'

There's a pause on the other end of the line. I can imagine my old school friend, who I hadn't seen in years until this week, wondering what the hell she's landed herself in.

'Eli, if you need me, at any time, day or night, you call me, okay?' she says.

'Will do. You take care, Kate. Thanks,' I say and hang up just as my mother pops her head around the door to tell me my tea is ready.

CHAPTER SIXTY-FOUR

Angela

Eli didn't give me any choice. I had to lock her in her room. I've also had to make sure she slept for as much of the day as possible. I needed the time to think.

But I know I can't keep relying on sedatives for much longer. I've taken chances by giving her such a high dose. All afternoon I've been panicking while she slept, terrified I'd gone too far. Given her too much. Hurt the baby.

If only she hadn't been so aggressive with me last night. Hadn't threatened to leave. If only she realised I have her best interests at heart. Stupid girl, thinking she knows what's good for her better than I do.

I hear her talk to Kate on the phone. I can't stop her from making that call, not without sounding every alarm bell going in her head. But it makes me uneasy.

It feels as if we're both playing a game right now in which we both pretend everything's normal. I can almost convince myself it is and that everything is okay, but then I look at her and I notice how she looks at me.

I notice how she flinches almost imperceptibly when I'm

close to her, that something has shifted between us, and I'm not at all sure how or if I can shift it back.

I have a sinking feeling she knows something, but I don't know what. And there's no way for me to know for definite without asking her.

Of course if I ask her, and she doesn't know what I've done, after all, it'll only alert her to the fact that I've been lying. That I've done some things other people might consider to be bad.

Other people who just don't understand.

It's a no-win situation.

So now, this carefully constructed house of cards, which had been standing for more than thirty years, is in danger of coming crumbling down.

I know that if I lose her now, I'll lose her forever. It's all I can do to keep it together, and not fall to the floor and curl up into a ball to try to escape the voices in my head telling me my time is up.

I butter toast as Eli walks back into the room, call her over. I have to appear normal. Exude calm. She looks flustered as she sits down at the table.

'I've buttered you the heel of the loaf, I know you like that the best,' I say, handing her a plate and sitting opposite her.

'Thanks,' she says before picking at her food, mashing the scrambled egg with her fork, bringing it to her lips but not really eating much.

'Kate sends her love. I'm going to go and see her tomorrow. She has some baby things she says I can have.'

She struggles to meet my eye. I feel myself tighten the grip on my knife and fork as my body tenses.

'Sure, I've got us everything we need here. That room's coming down with things.'

'It's nice of her to offer. I didn't want to be rude and say no.'

'And it's a wee boy she has. What could she give you that would suit? I don't know, Eliana. I'm not sure about her. I've told you. I think she's not to be trusted.'

In fact, I know she's not to be trusted. Hadn't she let Eliana phone Martin from her house last night? He'd told me himself when he called at the door. The cheek of him. I'd been shocked when he showed up, asking to speak to Eli. I didn't think he had it in him.

As if I'd let him over my threshold.

'She's out,' I'd told him.

'But her car's there?' he'd said, nodding towards his wife's Nissan Note.

'She does have legs, you know,' I'd said tersely.

'Well, maybe I could come in and wait for her?' He'd raised his eyebrow hopefully.

'I don't think it's a good idea,' I'd told him, leaning just enough of my weight against the door so that he couldn't push his way in if he tried. 'She doesn't want to talk to you, Martin.'

'But she phoned me last night?' he'd said, and it had clicked. She'd called him from Kate's.

'Well that was last night. She was very clear about her feelings this morning.'

'Still, I'd rather wait,' he'd said, moving to come in.

'Martin, I want you to leave. If you don't, I'll call the police and report that you're harassing both my daughter and me. I'm sure it won't look good along with the allegations that you've been cheating and someone's been threatening Eli over it all.'

'Angela, you know that the allegations are unfounded. I think if you ask Eli, she'll tell you she believes the same now.'

'My daughter's told me she doesn't want you in her life and that's all that matters to me, so why don't you stop upsetting yourself and all of us and just leave.'

'She's my wife and she's carrying my baby!' he'd spat at me, angry.

'And she's my daughter and I swear to you, Martin, nothing in this world will make me allow you to hurt her any more.'

'I've not done anything wrong,' he'd shouted.

But the truth is he *had* done something wrong. He just selfishly didn't realise it was me he'd wronged and not my daughter.

'Just go,' I'd told him, slamming the door and then panicking that the noise might have woken Eli.

I'd stood in silence in the hall for a moment, listening for any sign of movement upstairs. When it stayed quiet, I'd walked to my window and looked out, just in time to see Martin drive off.

But I know it's only a matter of time before he comes back. I have to deal with this once and for all.

'Eli,' I say, adopting my very best concerned-mother tone of voice. 'I don't want to upset you any further, but I can't keep this from you either.'

She looks at me. Probably the first time she's looked directly at me since our argument last night.

'You need to know the truth.'

CHAPTER SIXTY-FIVE

Louise

I'd been watching her house. I saw it empty for a few days and then I saw the lights come on, the car in the driveway, the sight of a tired and pale woman rocking a baby in her arms walking back and forth in front of the window. The ceiling light illuminated the picture of motherhood in front of me.

Advertised it, even.

I saw her handsome husband leave for work each morning just before nine. He didn't return at lunchtime. But he came home just after five – no working late with a newborn. I noticed that she was never dressed in time for him coming home. That she handed the baby to him when he walked in the door and he took up the task of walking in front of the window for a while, until it was time to close the curtains. The show ended for another day.

It had been ten days since I first saw them walking up and down in the living room. It was then I decided it wouldn't be wise to leave it much longer. The day I'd been waiting for, planning for and praying for had come.

I'd stopped and bought a bunch of flowers. I'd coloured my hair red and that day I'd pulled it back into a bun. I'd put on a pair of reading glasses I'd bought in the chemist. It was a weak disguise, admittedly, but I hoped it would be enough to confuse her tired eyes.

I'd slipped into a dress, a coat and a pair of horrible sensible shoes – brown, laced – which I picked up in a charity shop. I could discard them as soon as I got away.

I parked my car two streets away. I had a large bag with me. A blanket in it. A folder. Maternity notes. She'd have had no reason to know or think they were mine and not hers.

I'd seen how tired she was. How her eyes were dead in her head from exhaustion. How she looked ahead, staring into space as she paced up and down and up and down in front of the window.

She was practically begging someone to take her child.

A girl.

My daughter.

I'd seen a pink balloon. Pink cards. Flowers – pink carnations. A pink blanket.

It was meant to be.

I knew it all along.

My Eliana was ready for me to bring her home.

CHAPTER SIXTY-SIX

Eli

Mum leaves the room, leaving me wondering just what she was going to tell me. Will she admit what she's been doing? Apologise even.

Maybe if she apologises I can forgive her. I can try to understand.

She came back downstairs and pushed a white envelope in front of me. Just like the others. The same printed handwriting. A stamp on this one. No postmark. My hands start to shake.

'This came earlier when you were sleeping,' she says. 'I was just going to throw it away. I didn't see any need to annoy you further if you'd left Martin anyway. But then I thought you might need it as evidence, you know, in the divorce hearing.'

I open the envelope. A cufflink falls out. One of the one's I'd bought Martin as a wedding present. The note is three-lines long this time:

Thought you might want this back.
My slut of a girlfriend had it among her things, after your husband's trip to England. Seems he had company for a night or two.

'Oh, Eli,' she says. 'I'm so sorry. So very sorry. He's such a bastard.'

She looks so genuine. So honest. So completely like my mother. Totally believable in every way. Totally normal. And yet this is proof that not only is my husband *not* lying to me, but that *she* is. And she's been lying to me all along.

I can barely look at her, let alone breathe.

'I need some space,' I mutter and, as fast my feet can carry me, I rush to my room, close the door and sit in front of it.

My head's spinning, nausea rising. I swallow it down, try to calm my breathing. I can feel the full force of a panic attack, or something like it, something more visceral, start to descend on me. Fear? Yes, fear is there. That my mother can be so twisted. So messed up. So fully evil. Protecting her 'baby bear'. That childish saying makes me feel sick now. There's nothing about what she's done that can be construed as protecting me. She's betrayed me in the worst way.

The one person who I never thought would hurt me is playing some twisted game — a game in which she seems set on destroying my marriage. Now. Now, when we're having a baby. She's swooped in when I'm at my most vulnerable — when my marriage is at its most vulnerable — and she's created a show of smoke and mirrors so twisted that I've walked out on Martin.

My heart aches for him. I'm trying to breathe. Trying to stay calm for me, and for our baby. This baby I hadn't felt connected to for so long but who I now want to protect more than anything. I want Martin. I'd scream with frustration if I thought it'd do any good. I want to call him, but I'm here with no phone and my mother on red alert for my every move.

And God, I'm angry. Anger is my primary emotion. *She* did it. She's been behind it. No one posted that blasted cufflink. It wasn't among anyone's things when they returned from London. It had been on the chest of drawers in my bedroom just two days before when I'd picked up more clothes. I'd seen the pair there, glinting in the sunlight as I'd packed my case. I'd almost lifted them myself. I'd been so angry at Martin. I'd wanted to take them. A stupid, puerile attempt to wind him up – taking back the wedding present I'd gifted to him. They'd been there and now, here was one of them. In my mother's house. With a note matching the other notes.

I don't know who she is any more and, worse still, what she's capable of. She's unstable. Willing to lie and steal and fake a break-in. To scare me. To make me think I was being hunted in some way. She'd looked so distraught that night, but she'd known all along there was no bogeyman to be afraid of. She was the bogeyman.

I need to get out of this house as quickly as I can, but I'm scared of what she might do. Maybe I should just make a run for it. My car keys are in my handbag on the end of my bed. I could be out and away and . . . as long as she doesn't lock the bedroom door again. That was nothing to do with her 'valuables', I realise, horrified. It was about control. All this has been about control.

I scramble to my knees, crawl to my bag and look for my keys. If I go now, before she has the chance to turn the key in the lock, I might have a chance.

They aren't there. Nor is my purse, my bank cards. I know beyond a shadow of a doubt that's where I'd put them the night before when I'd let myself in from Kate's.

Another gut punch. I know she's taken them just as she took my phone.

'It'll be okay, Eli.'

'Whatever happens, I'm here for you, Eli.'

'Look what I've done for you and the baby, Eli.'

She's deluded. Sick in the head. Dangerous.

I feel my stomach tighten as fear and nausea wash over me

again. I'm going to be sick. There's no way to hold it back. I get to my feet and half run, half stumble to the door, through to the bathroom, where whatever small amount of dinner I managed to eat comes back up. I convulse as my stomach tightens and I retch again and again, desperate to purge myself, even though there's nothing left to purge.

I feel a cold sweat break out at the back of my neck, spreading over my body, down my back, beads of sweat running down between my breasts. I feel my arms and legs shake. The violence of my sickness, coupled with the pressure of the baby, makes me lose control of my bladder. Powerless to stop the indignity of my wetting myself, I sob as I convulse over the toilet bowl, suddenly sure I'll faint. I'm going to lose consciousness. I might bang my head as I fall. Hurt my stomach. Hurt my baby. I want to scream for help, but who will help me? Really help me. My mother?

The blackness creeps over me slowly, starting at the back of my neck, through my head, a mixture of warmth and tingling, until I feel the world start to close in around me. My body becomes weightless and I'm falling, trying to turn to protect my baby. I try to keep my eyes open, but I'm gone.

CHAPTER SIXTY-SEVEN

Louise

My heart was thumping in my chest when I knocked on her door. Not with fear, mind. I wasn't scared. I was just desperate to see my baby. To hold her. I felt as if I'd just given birth and the primal urge for skin-to-skin contact was strong.

Just as it had been with Noah. As soon as I came round from the anaesthetic, I'd begged for him.

'Let me hold him,' I'd screamed, even after they'd taken him away for the last time, leaving me to hug nothing but my empty arms to my chest.

She opened the door with my child in her arms, Eliana. She was the most beautiful baby. So small. So delicate. Rosebud lips. A button nose. Soft lashes gently grazing her cheeks as she slept in her arms. The woman looked at me, examined me, and for a moment I was sure she could place me as 'that woman in the café'.

'I'm here to see you and your baby,' I stuttered, flashing my folder at her. 'I'm from the health visitor team. I'm here to see if we can offer you any support.'

'Support?' she said, blinking into the daylight. 'Like what kind of support?'

I could see she was taking me at my word. Probably too tired, too shell-shocked from the birth to think otherwise.

'We know being a new mum can be a daunting time,' I said, my best sympathetic look on my face. 'A lot of people don't talk about that. How scary it can feel. I'm one of a new team offering a listening ear for mums and, of course, if we can offer any practical support, we will. But it seems as if your little one's doing just fine.'

I nodded towards the baby sleeping in her arms. She looked down and I saw it then, what I never thought I'd see from her. Love. A bond. Despite her tiredness. Despite her difficult pregnancy. I saw she had the desire to be a good mum.

I couldn't waver. I deserved that baby as much as she did, if not more. She can always have another baby. I can't. So I didn't waver, and just as she looked at the baby, I did too. Just as she felt that bond, I felt that bond. Just as she wanted to make things work, I wanted to make things work.

I was a mother as much as she was. In that moment I felt it.

'Maybe I could come in and we could chat over a cup of tea,' I asked. 'Just a friendly chat, nothing to be worried about.'

She nodded, turned and led me into her living room.

'If you want to show me where your tea things are, I'll make us both a cup and we can chat,' I said.

As I'd hoped, she said she'd make the tea and told me to take a seat. She'd only be a minute, she said. She apologised for being in her dressing gown still. I told her not to worry. I don't think I'd dressed for an entire month after my child's birth, I told her.

I watch as she laid the baby oh so tenderly in her crib. She turned to look at me and asked how I took my tea. I told her milk but no sugar. 'I'm sweet enough,' I smiled, and she gave me a warm smile in return.

I could see she trusted me. Liked me, even. I could see she was grateful for someone to talk to. In different circumstances, perhaps we could've been friends.

But we wouldn't ever be friends. As I heard her potter around the kitchen, I crept out of her house, the baby wrapped in a blanket in the large bag I'd brought with me. Lying on top of Noah's notes.

I was sure she'd understand in time, but I couldn't wait around.

I'll never know for sure if it was her wailing that I heard carried on the wind as I turned out of the street and hurried towards my car. I don't want to think about it too much.

I promised my baby as I put her in the car, that I was going to give her the best of everything. My beautiful Eliana would have everything.

In ten minutes we'd be outside Derry on the road to Belfast. In the space of two hours we'd be on the ferry to Scotland. It was the safest way to travel. No searches. No passport control. By dinner time we'd be sitting in a bedsit in Paisley.

I thought maybe they'd be looking for the person I was before. But I doubted it. Louise Barr moved away to Galway weeks before. She'd gone to start again. She wasn't on anyone's radar.

I decided I would change my name. In Scotland, I was able to register Eliana as mine after a few weeks. A home birth, you see, I'd told them. Didn't realise I was pregnant. Had periods the whole way through. Delivered her myself on the bathroom floor. Had been too shocked by it all to come forwards to register you before.

Then we just had to keep our heads down. Live our lives. No one would have any reason to question why.

When she would ask me about her father, I'd tell her she was conceived on a night out that took a nasty turn. I'd say enough to make her think it was too painful for me to talk about, that I might not know his name. I'd say enough to stop her asking me about him again.

No one would suspect what I'd done.

Not even my baby.

Especially not my baby.

Eliana must never know.

CHAPTER SIXTY-EIGHT

Eli

A cool cloth to my forehead. Soft light. A gentle voice. The world starts to come back into focus. Slowly. I start to get a sense of my own body again. A cold floor beneath me. Something under my head. A towel. I'm not ready to open my eyes just yet. Dampness, cool around my legs, reminds me of the indignity that's just passed. I feel tears prick at my still closed eyes. My hand goes to my stomach, willing my baby to move.

'I'm here, Eli,' my mother's voice soothes. 'I'm here, my darling Eliana, and everything's going to be okay. Mum is here.'

Something inside me folds in on itself and cries out. Not her. Not now. But I stay quiet. Just as the world is coming into focus, so is the reality of what my mother has done.

I have to stay calm, or at least appear calm. I feel my mother's hand on my shoulder, feel her breath – smell her breath – as she whispers in my ear. My skin crawls.

'My poor baby. My poor, poor girl. You'll be okay. We'll get you cleaned up and resting. You'll be fine.'

The nausea is still coursing through my body. I still feel sick. Sick and weak.

I think of how I'd slept all day. Maybe I am getting sick. Properly sick. Or maybe . . . No. Not even my mother would go that far. Had she put something in my food or drink?

'Shall we get you up?' my mother says, her voice sounding full of genuine concern. 'Can you strip off and I'll run a shower if you feel well enough? Just a quick wash and I'll get those soiled clothes in the machine.'

'I'm sorry,' I mutter, humiliated despite my fear and my sickness.

'Not at all, darling,' my mother says, helping me to my feet and supporting me while another wave of nausea floods through me and I retch again, dry heaving and feeling my muscles strain.

Maybe this is my way out. I could play to her overprotective nature . . .

'Mum, I really don't feel very well at all. Maybe, I think, maybe you should phone a doctor. Maybe even an ambulance.'

If I can get out of here safely, if I can get away from her . . .

'Nonsense,' she says matter-of-factly. 'It's just those hormones. I'll look after you. Just like I did when you were little. Now, come on. Strip off and we'll get you cleaned up.'

'I'll be okay on my own,' I mutter. I don't want her touching me.

'Now now, Eli, you've just fainted. You're still not well. If you think I'm going to take a risk with you falling again, you're very wrong.'

She pulls off my top and pulls down my pyjama bottoms.

'I'll get some towels,' she says as she puts down the lid of the toilet seat and encourages me to sit down.

I hold my pyjama top to me, offering me some privacy at least, as I strip off my knickers. Shame bubbles up inside of me. Shame at having wet myself. Shame at being so vulnerable in front of my mother and shame, and grief, at not really knowing what kind of person she is. I feel the tears start to slide down my face as my mother walks back in and hands me a bath towel before switching on the shower.

'Just a quick clean. You made a bit of a mess,' she said gently. 'There's no need for tears. These things happen.'

She guides me into the shower cubicle, my face crimson, my legs still shaky.

'Good girl,' she says, lifting a sponge and starting to sponge me down while I shudder.

She's treating me a like a child. Speaking to me in an annoying sing-song voice as if I'm four years old.

'I can do it myself,' I say, my voice a little stronger.

'No need for that tone, Eli,' she says, hurt in her voice. 'I'm only trying to help. I've only ever tried to help.'

I won't cry. I won't give in to the urge to sob. I won't let her see how truly wretched I am. I say nothing.

'Okay, then, I'll clean up this mess and you can clean yourself!' she snaps, pulling back and closing the shower door with a slam.

I watch through the glass as she gets on her knees and uses a towel to mop the floor.

'It's a good thing you didn't go out, sweetheart. Given how sick you are. Was it that letter? The cufflink? I know it must be hugely upsetting, but it's better you know now what he's really like. Before the baby comes. You don't want to have to do a midnight flit with a baby in tow. Now you can just settle yourself to being here, to being a family together. You'll always have me, darling. You and your baby. We'll be good.'

I soap my legs. Try to wash away my shame. Then I soap my tummy, rubbing my bump, thinking of the little creature who's inside, still a couple of months from coming into this world, and I promise even as I stand here unsure of how I'm going to get out of this mess, that no harm is ever going to come to her.

And there's no way in hell I'm letting my mother anywhere near my daughter.

CHAPTER SIXTY-NINE

Angela

I'd never considered Eli the ungrateful type, but she was being cheeky to me. Shunning my help. That tone in her voice when she'd said 'I can do it myself.' She'd practically pushed me away, when I was only trying to look after her.

I know she's upset. I know that cufflink will have knocked her for six, but she doesn't need to take that anger out on me.

I've enough to worry about without becoming her emotional punchbag.

I remind myself she's in shock. She can't deny what he is any more. You only hurt the ones you love, so that's why she's hurting me now. I'm her safe place. Just as I always wanted to be.

I don't like seeing her look so helpless – but I have to break her completely so that I can start to build her up again.

From the strength of her reaction to the cufflink, I think it's safe to say she's broken.

Still, I never want to see her looking so pathetic again. With God's grace, I never will. He will help her through this, just as He helped me in the past. When I asked, I received. It could be the same for Eli. If I could just get her to turn to Him for support. I close my eyes, put my hands to my crucifix, hold it and offer a silent prayer for guidance.

She's vulnerable now. I have to make sure she doesn't slip into self-pity, or self-harm. I have to double my efforts to take care of her and to protect her, and there's no way on this earth I'm going to let her out of my sight any time in the near future.

You know, I might just suggest a weekend break away. Back to Scotland maybe. We can book the ferry and travel over. And sure, who's to say we ever have to come back?

I know hiding her keys might seem a little extreme. As is taking her purse. But it's with her best interests in mind.

I do have one dilemma, though. I've been planning on locking her in her room again, for her own safety, of course, but what if she's sick again? She probably won't be. I mean, there can't be anything left of what I gave her. Maybe I should put a basin on the floor. Some towels. A glass of water.

But if she faints and hurts herself? And I'm asleep and don't hear. I'd never forgive myself if something bad happened to her.

No, the best thing I can do is stay as close to her as I can. I'll sleep beside her. Be there to nurse her, just as I did when she was little. During the happiest years of my life.

My mind goes back to when she was four and had the measles. I'd stayed awake all night just watching her and making sure her temperature didn't rise. She'd been so weak, the rash all over her body. She'd called out for me in her sleep and had clung to me through the day. I hadn't even been able to go to the toilet without carrying her there with me.

I'd been so scared she'd get worse. I'd whispered that I loved her hundreds of times and she'd told me she loved me, too. I'd prayed over her until her fever broke and she started to come back to me and told me I was the best mammy in the world.

I'd give anything to have her look at me with that amount

of love in her eyes again. If I just look after her now the way I looked after her then, maybe she will.

'Come on, darling,' I say, helping her out of the shower and handing her a towel.

I can tell she's embarrassed to be naked in front of me, so I turn my back to her as she dries off and slips on the dry pyjamas I brought her.

'I've thrown your other clothes in the wash,' I tell her. 'We'll get you into bed and comfy. I'll get a basin in case you need to be sick again. Maybe I'll even light the fire for you. We can read something together. Would that be too cheesy? You used to love it when I read to you. Do you remember, Eli?'

'Yes, Mum, of course.'

'Those were happy times. You'd always beg me, 'Just one more chapter, Mum! Then I promise I'll go to sleep.' Except one more chapter was never enough, was it? You'd say, 'I mean it this time. This really will be the last time.' But we kept reading, until you fell asleep, Eli. Do you remember?'

'I do, Mum.'

'And when you were sick. When you were older and you had a cold, I'd curl up beside you and read some more. *Pride and Prejudice*. That was your favourite. "It's a truth universally acknowledged that a single man . . ."'

I wait for her response. Can hear her breath. Shaky. Emotion-filled. Something in my chest tightens. Something isn't right.

I speak again. A little louder. '"It is a truth universally acknowledged that a single man . . ." Oh, Eli, what's the next bit? Help me remember. Surely you know it?'

Her voice meek, subdued, answers me: '". . . in possession of a good fortune must be in want of a wife."'

'That's it!' I say, clapping my hands with glee before turning around to see her standing there in front of me. A grown woman. Pale. Dressed in white cotton pyjamas, more suitable for summer than a wet winter's night in Belfast. Her eyes are red-rimmed and a weak smile plays on her lips. I know instantly it's false. I've seen it before. I know when my child's hiding something. When she's lying. When she's scared.

I see it all there in her now and in that second I know. Whatever's happened in the last few hours, she knows. The cufflink hasn't been enough. I'm losing her.

I can't let go of her. I refuse. I decide to believe that the smile is genuine. I'm not ready to acknowledge the cracks. I keep her gaze.

'I'm sure I still have a copy of it lying around. I'll see if I can find it and we can read together.'

'If you don't mind, Mum, I think I'd like to go back to bed. I'm still feeling queasy and I just want to lie down. There's no need for you to be with me. I'll probably just sleep some more.'

Her gaze slips from mine, just momentarily. The cracks grow wider and deeper. What does she know? How much? What notions has that Kate one planted in her head?

I shake my head. There isn't a chance I'm leaving her alone. No matter what she wants.

'Sweetheart, you've been so ill. There's no way I'm leaving you on your own tonight. I want to make sure you're okay. You've slept all day. I want to make sure it's not something more serious. Go to sleep if you want. I'll read my Kindle or just watch the fire in the hearth. That can be lovely and calming, sweetheart. Maybe you're just getting yourself all worked up and it's making you ill. Hormones can be a curse.'

I wait for her to challenge me but she doesn't. She looks defeated. For the first time, I notice how hollow her cheeks have become. She isn't blooming in pregnancy, she's withering. Just as her mother did.

And she'll grow to hate me, just as her mother did.

Peter was wrong when he'd said all this can be fixed. This

cannot be fixed. I cannot give her back to the Kearneys. I wondered, should I reply to his bloody emails – his incessant 'I need to talk to you' emails – and tell him he's just made everything so much worse?

CHAPTER SEVENTY

Angela

The first email had been short, to the point. He wanted to get in touch with me. Urgently.

> I'm looking to get in touch with Angela Johnston, urgently.
> She was once known as Louise Barr or Louise McLaughlin.
> If you are the same person, can you email me back?
> If not, I apologise for intruding on your time.

I wondered what was so urgent. I opened the second email, hoping it would offer some clue. It was more or less the same as the first.

The third was different, though. It brought all the fears I've been living with over the last thirty-three years into focus.

Reading the words in front of me had made me sick.

> Angela,
> Please excuse the intrusion. I suspect that despite your silence this email is reaching the right person. That it has reached you, Louise.

I need to talk to you. I'm worried about you. Even now. After all these years. I'm so sorry I let you down all those years ago, but please, I need to ask you something.

Maybe you think I've no right to know. You may never reply but I have to ask anyway.

I'm attaching a scan of an article that appeared in the *Derry Journal* a few months back. A feature on the hospice here and the staff.

There's a young woman, Louise. A nurse – thirty-three-years old. Her name is Eliana.

Eliana? Such an unusual name. I'd only heard it once before. When you told me it meant 'God has answered my prayers'. When you told me you'd love to name your daughter Eliana.

In the article this nurse talks of her childhood, her mother – and maybe I'm just an old man and my imagination is running away with me. But I looked her up on Facebook, maybe because of her name, and because she said her mother was called Angela and she was raised in Paisley.

I could see her cover photo. A picture of two women sitting side by side on a blanket on the beach. I'd know you anywhere, Louise. Any time, in any life. You've barely changed. I found your profile, too – no public pictures, but well, it wasn't hard to find what email address it was attached to.

I know you owe me nothing, but I'm pleading with you to come clean now.

I'm right about the Kearney baby, aren't I? She'd be thirty-three, too.

I've always regretted that you and I never worked through the horrible tragedy that befell us. I've had a good life, Louise, but I've carried that pain with me every day. If I could go back and change it, I would. We couldn't fix us, but even now it's not too late to fix this for the Kearney family.

There isn't a happy ending for us, but there can be for them.

I panicked. I'm still panicking now. He knows. He could contact the Kearneys, or the police, or Eli herself. I curse myself for not taking action to get Eli out of Derry sooner. Away from that city where my life had gone so terribly wrong all those years ago. Away from the reality that sooner or later, everything gets found out in that city.

I curse myself for being weak all those years ago. When I'd written to Peter. I just needed to know that Noah was being looked after. The pain of thinking of him lying there all alone nearly ended me. Eli must have been maybe three or four at the time when I gave in to the temptation to contact him. Remembering how he'd loved me, even in those last few weeks.

I told him I'd started again. I was happy. I asked him to please, please let me know that Noah's grave was being looked after. I had to tell him I'd changed my name. I had no choice. We were still in the bedsit and if he'd written to me using my old name I'd never have received it.

I only contacted him the once. I'd been scared after, but we'd moved and I'd not heard from him again. I'd assumed we were safe.

But I was wrong.

About Peter.

About Martin.

About Kate.

About everything.

Well, none of them – not even Eli herself – would get the chance to take my daughter and my grandchild away from me.

Over my dead body.

CHAPTER SEVENTY-ONE

Eli

This is what I've been reduced to. Eliana Hughes, pretending to be asleep while my mother lies on the bed beside me, determined not to leave my side.

She's placed a basin on the floor and a glass of water by my bed. She's pulled the duvet up around me and tucked me in and she's kissed my forehead. She's told me she loves me, and my heart had cracked as I told her I loved her back and realised I was only saying it because I was scared of her.

Just a few weeks ago it had been true. Unquestionable. Unconditional.

Now, I don't even know her.

There's no chance I'm actually going to go to sleep. I need to stay alert. My head is full with so many thoughts. I want so desperately to run to Martin. If I can even get to Kate's house, I can call him and he can come to me.

My mother needs help, that much is sure. Maybe we can help her, maybe. I'm not sure I'll ever be able to forgive her, though.

I listen for hours as my mother reads her Kindle by lamplight, the occasional sigh from her providing my soundscape for the evening while I try to keep my breathing even, keep my body still, close my eyes. Fake a deep sleep. It isn't easy, especially given that adrenaline is coursing through my veins at a rate of knots and the fact that my skin is crawling.

She gets up at one stage to use the bathroom and I contemplate making a run for it there and then. Barefoot if necessary. I could just run out of the door and down the street. I'd maybe be able to flag a taxi down from the end of the road. If a taxi would take a pyjama-wearing, shoeless pregnant woman wandering the streets at the end of November.

Surely they would, though? They wouldn't leave me standing there.

I've just about convinced myself it's worth a try, when I hear the bathroom door open again and the sound of my mother's footsteps on the landing. I fix my eyes closed, try to resume my rhythmic breathing and hope she won't take long to fall asleep. If there's one thing I know about my mother, it's that she sleeps the sleep of the dead and once she's properly out for the count, there's little that can wake her. Especially if I'm quiet. Very quiet.

She switches the lamp off. I wait for the snoring to start. And then a further ten minutes to be sure.

I edge my way so slowly out of bed, slipping my feet into my trainers and lifting my cardigan from the chair by the door. It's chilly outside my room. The heating is turned off and there's no fire to warm me. I'm shaking but I don't think that's just down to the cold.

I tiptoe down the stairs, as delicately as I can at seven and a half months pregnant, and make my way to the front door. I can hear the rain battering at the windows, at the glass panes in the front door. Everything in me screams to get out of here as fast as I can.

I know I have to be careful when opening the door. It's old

and stiff and sometimes creaks loudly. I gently turn the Yale lock and pull, but it won't budge. Swearing internally, I remember that my mother fitted a mortice lock a few months before. But when I look down, I see that, of course, the key isn't there. The door is bolted.

I look around, at the key hooks on the wall over the phone table, on the table, in the plant pot, even reaching in the pockets of the jackets on the coat rack, but the keys are nowhere to be found. My heart rate is rising, along with a sense of panic. I take a couple of deep breaths. I have to stay focused.

Gently opening the living room door, I peek in and look to the sideboard. Damn it! It's too dark to see. I'll have to put a light on. I opt for a small table lamp before pulling out the drawers one by one, one ear trained on the noises around me in case I hear my mother wake and step out of bed.

No keys. No sign of my belongings.

I'm starting to feel increasingly desperate. The windows are small and high – there's no chance I could climb out of them even if I wasn't seven months pregnant. The back door opens onto a small yard with no mews access. It's a dead end. I'm trapped.

I creep through to the kitchen, open the drawers where my mother stores all the detritus that doesn't have a home elsewhere. Hope it'll give me something, maybe even a spare key she's forgotten about hidden in the back of the drawer behind the Blu-Tack and the charger for a mobile phone long since gone. Nothing.

Opening the cupboards, I feel around, right to the back. I pull open the first aid box, just in case. Look in the storage jars, the fridge, on the tops of the cupboards. There's nothing there until my hand brushes against a plastic box – Tupperware. I stand on my tiptoes, my bump hindering my ability to get close to the worktops. I brush the edge of it with my fingers, try to find the corner, to nudge it closer to me, but my hands slip and I manage to push it just a hair's breadth out of reach. I swear – a whispered prayer to someone or something – and stand down, rubbing my stomach where the indentation of the kitchen worktop has pressed into me. My baby kicks in a well-timed response. She's encouraging me to keep going, I know it.

I look around, see the small stepping stool my mother uses when she's cleaning the windows, and I use it to stand up and so that I'm able get a firm hold of the box. It contains a few small cardboard boxes. Some printouts. A few keys – too small to be my house keys.

I look more closely. The boxes are medicines. Medicines my mother has hidden away from her usual medicine store. I look closer, read the labels. Zolpidem. A drug used as a sedative to induce sleep. The prescription just a few days old. I open the box, count the blister pack to see how many tablets are gone. The knot in my stomach tightens. I've been extra sleepy, slept all day. Felt drowsy. Out of it. More than normal pregnancy fatigue, enough to convince me I was coming down with the flu. Have I just been drugged instead?

I pull out the other box. A bottle of Ipecac syrup, designed to induce vomiting. I tug the printed-out pages from below the boxes and see they're full of information downloaded from the Internet on the safe use of sedatives and natural emetics in pregnancy.

I have to force myself to breathe in.

My mother's been medicating me. On top of everything else. She's risked everything, even my baby – the baby she claims to love. Now, I know I have to get out, using whatever means necessary.

CHAPTER SEVENTY-TWO

Angela

Something wakes me with a jump. All my synapses are firing. My senses are on high alert. I'm immediately aware that Eli isn't in the bed beside me. Maybe she's just gone to the bathroom. That's the most likely explanation.

I tell myself not to worry while at the same time cursing myself for falling asleep. I should've tried harder to stay awake. But I'm just so tired – burned out from living on my nerves.

I listen, trying to pick up the familiar sounds of my house. The rattle of the loo roll holder. The clinking and clanking of the old pipes as the bathroom taps are switched on. The creak of the floorboard just to the left of the bath, beside the towel rack. Nothing.

I swing my feet out of bed, crane my head so I can see through the door. The bathroom door is ajar, the light off. I should've locked the bedroom door while Eli was sleeping. Locked us both in. I have the key with me, in the pocket of my dressing gown. I hear the creak of a door, followed by a loud sigh, and I know it's coming from downstairs.

I try to hold on to whatever sliver of calm I can. There are any number of reasons why she could be downstairs. I should've given her more sedative before bed, but I was scared after she'd been so sick. It was the first time I'd used the syrup; I hadn't expected it to work so quickly or so violently. I'd just hoped it would make her a feel a little out of sorts. Nauseous. Make her think that pregnancy sickness thing she had was flaring. Make her a little needy, but not too needy.

Maybe now she's just hungry. Or thirsty. Or unable to sleep and watching TV. It doesn't have to mean anything bad . . .

Except that it does. I know it. I feel it and I know whatever happens next will define everything going forwards.

Sliding my feet into my slippers, I stand, pull my dressing gown on. I think of where I've put Eli's things – her keys and purse in my car, in the glove compartment. If she's looking for them, and I suspect she might be, she'll never find them.

Not that she'll be able to get out of the front door. The keys for that are safely in my dressing gown pocket too.

I creep out of the room, stand at the top of stairs and listen. I can hear the door to my study open. She'll find nothing in there. I've deleted any files, any information at all that could link me to any recent events. I've filed Peter's email in a secret online folder.

I hear another loud sigh, her footsteps in the hall. I stand back, just at the corner so she can't see me, and listen as I hear her lift the phone from its cradle.

Damn it. I feel the adrenaline surge through me. Who's she calling and why had I not thought to pull the phone from its socket? Hide the damn thing. I listen as she taps at the numbers. I have seconds, just seconds to stop her from contacting someone. I have a choice. I can stand here and wait, see who she's calling and listen to what she has to say.

I can listen as she brings our worlds crumbling around us. Betrays me. Leaves me.

Or I can make a move.

I decide I simply can't take any more chances. I can no longer pretend she doesn't know something is very wrong. There's no way whoever's on the other end of the line will tell her my desperate actions have been normal. But they are normal, aren't they? A mother's love . . .

A bomb is about to go off in my world and I have to stop it.

She's given me no choice.

'Eli!' I shout, my voice shaking. 'Stop.'

I watch as she jumps, my voice startling her. Her eyes widen as she looks at me. I see fear then. For the first time – real, stark fear. I notice the hand she's holding the phone with is trembling.

'Put the phone down, Eli,' I say as firmly as I can.

I have to draw on every ounce of my strength to keep my voice from shaking. Oh, Eli, I think, why are you making me do this?

I can see the hesitation on her face. She doesn't move. Not an inch. The phone is still in her hand.

'Put it down,' I say, harsher this time.

She doesn't move her eyes from mine. My heart thumps against my chest. I will her to drop the phone. To say something. To look less scared. To look less horrified by me. I don't want to have to shout. I don't want to have to take this further.

But I will, if I need to.

Nothing's going to take her from me.

I watch her slow but shaky inhalations of breath. Watch as she starts to shake her head slowly. But she places the phone down and I momentarily sag with relief.

'What have you done, Mum? What *have* you done?'

There's fear there, but anger, too. Sadness. Pain. I'm starting to realise there's no coming back from this.

'The first thing you need to know, Eli, is that everything

I've ever done has been for you, and because I love you. Everything.'

I watch a tear slide down her cheek. This is her moment of weakness. Her softening. I have to take every advantage of it.

I take one step towards her, start to walk down the stairs.

The strength of her voice, the volume of it, shocks me.

'*Don't!*' echoes around the hallway, bouncing off the walls. 'Don't take one more step!'

'Eliana . . .' I'm pleading.

'Don't Eliana me!' she says, her face contorting with grief.

'I love you,' I say, my own voice cracking.

'No!' she shouts. 'No, you don't love me. You can't love me. You've been drugging me! You've been drugging my baby!' She points her finger at me, her hand still shaking.

'No, no, I wouldn't. That's absurd, Eliana.'

'*Don't lie!* Why is everything a lie? I found the drugs. I found the fucking syrup! Making me sick? As if I haven't been sick enough! As if it hasn't been hard enough. And Martin hasn't been cheating, has he? No one has been throwing rocks through my windows – no one but you! You! The cufflink? I know that was in my house when we were there. You're the only person who could've lifted it. It's been you all along. Having me on edge and terrified and sick and feeling like my entire life is one big catastrophe. And my marriage . . . and my work . . .'

I watch as each realisation comes to her in waves like contractions, bending her in two with grief. I watch my daughter detach herself from me, step by painful step. It's more painful than the cutting of any umbilical cord. Any birth. Any labour pain.

But she doesn't understand. If I can only make her understand. If she does, she'll be on my side. She'll see how I love her. She'll appreciate that I'm just being a good mother.

'It's *because* I love you, you have to let me explain,' I say, taking another step.

'You can't explain this away, Mum. This isn't excusable or forgivable. Are you mad? Are you actually insane? Why anyone would behave like you have . . .' Her voice drifts off as if she's trying to process it all.

'But . . . you need to know. It was because I was scared . . .'

I'm laying it on the line. Being honest. Hoping she'll see just how scared I am. How I'm terrified of losing her.

'Scared? Scared! Of what? That I might, just might, be happy? Have a life independent from you. Jesus Christ, Mum. Were you scared I'd have a baby of my own? A happy marriage.'

'That you'd have a new family, away from me. You said you wouldn't leave me. You said you'd live near me and with me . . .'

'So that made it okay to launch a nuclear attack on my life?'

'Eliana, please.' I take one more step. I'm losing her.

'*No!* I don't want to know. Just tell me where my keys are and let me go. I don't want to be anywhere near you. I don't want to listen to your lies any more.'

No, I think, taking one more step. That isn't going to happen. She isn't going to leave me. Not now.

'I can't do that, Eli,' I say and take another step, and then another and another.

CHAPTER SEVENTY-THREE

Eli

I don't know her any more. I don't recognise the tone in her voice, the look on her face. She looks the least like my mother than she ever has. She's a stranger in front of me and now she's walking down the stairs, glaring at me.

'I'm not giving you the keys, Eli. I'm not letting you leave.'

I stand my ground. 'You can't keep me here. I'll break a window if I have to.'

'And what, Eli? You'll squeeze that pregnant tummy of yours out through a narrow window with broken glass. You're being ridiculous. Why not just sit down and I'll make us a cup of tea and we can talk.'

She's talking differently now. Her voice isn't shaking. She's calm and it's more terrifying than when she was shouting and screaming.

She's delusional if she thinks there's any chance any of this could be talked about over a cup of tea! As if I'd trust her to prepare anything for me any more. She *drugged* me, for Christ's sake! As if I'd even want to be in the same space as her any more.

I feel a cold sweat break out again at the back of my neck,

my legs weak. I need out of here before I faint again. I just want to go now. To get to Martin, or Kate, or anyone who'll keep her from me.

I'd dialled Martin's number before my mother had shouted at me. I hadn't hit the cancel button, but I don't know if it's connected. I don't even know if he has his mobile switched on. If he can hear our conversation or if any or all of it is being recorded on his voicemail while he sleeps.

I reach my hand across to lift the phone, to see if he's there or to try to hit the redial button. But just as I lift it, my mother's in front of me, her eyes blazing, her voice fierce, her hand raised. I close my eyes, awaiting the impact of the palm of her hand on my face, but the crash comes to my right.

I open my eyes to see the phone is on the floor, the handset smashed. But just in case, just on the off-chance that it hasn't blocked my access to the outside world, I watch as my mother pulls the phone lead from the socket.

'I told you, Eliana, I'm not letting you leave. I can't let you leave.'

'You can't stop me!' I shout as I turn and pull at the door again, the futility of my actions not deterring me from trying. I need out.

I feel her hand on my shoulder and I do my best to shrug her off.

'Don't touch me!' I shout, turning to try to push her away from me.

The blow to the side of my head comes as a surprise. I haven't time to turn properly to focus on her before I feel a weight crash into the left side of my skull, dull and heavy. I hear a crack, a buzzing, a noise without noise. I see her face as I fall. I can see fear in her eyes. She knows she's hurt me.

She *has* hurt me.

Confusion washes over me, along with the pain and along

with the blackness. The darkness. A distant voice mutters something about just doing what's good for me. She's sorry. She's so sorry.

I reach one hand out to the wall, to try to steady myself, stop the fall, but I'm already on my knees. My other hand is on my stomach. My baby. Hang in there, baby. My daughter. I have to protect my baby. This baby I'd struggled to bond with. This child who I'd even resented at times. I can't let anything happen to her. Mummy bears have to protect their baby bears.

Then there's blackness.

CHAPTER SEVENTY-FOUR

Angela

I have just minutes to decide what to do. I hadn't meant to hit Eli so hard. I hadn't really meant to hit her at all, but she was pulling at the door and screaming like a woman possessed and I didn't want the neighbours to hear. To wake and realise something was badly wrong. Not until I'd had a chance to make it better.

And I was sure I could make it better. Only now, in the hall, with my daughter unconscious on the floor beside me, the base of the lamp I'd hit her with stained with her blood, her hand draped protectively over her stomach, I'm not sure I can make it better any more. Oh, Eli, why did you make me do it?

I drop to my knees, almost too afraid to get close to her. But I know I have to find out if she's breathing. Jesus, if she isn't breathing, what will I do? Will I be able to get the baby out of her before her blood stops circulating completely? Will I lose them both? The baby's too young anyway. Too small. Like Noah.

Thoughts of him swim before my eyes. How small he was. Those tiny hands, translucent skin, fingernails that were microscopic. Maybe it was always meant to come to this. From that day, things had been set in motion. I stole Eli from her family, and now it's just karma in action that I'll lose her, and her child, and have to live with it.

I'll have to bury yet another baby.

But maybe it isn't too late. I hold my face to Eli's, try to hear or feel for breath. It's hard. My own heart is beating so furiously that it drowns out every other noise in the world. I'm shaking so violently I don't know if it's her breath I can hear or if it's just my own hyperventilation.

'I'm so sorry, Eli. I'm so, so sorry. But you wouldn't listen. Get better and you can listen and I can make it up to you. Live, Eli, please . . .' I beg, and I'm almost sure I feel the faint wisp of her breath on my face.

I put my fingers to her wrist, feel for a pulse. Panic when I find nothing then almost weep with relief when I locate it. Weak but there. She's with me. I touch my hand to her head, pull it away sticky with her blood.

'You'll be okay, pet. I'll make sure you're okay.'

I turn around and look for the phone to call for help, forgetting that I smashed it off the wall only minutes before. I wail with despair when I see it on the floor.

'I'll get help,' I say to her. 'I'll get help. Don't worry, my darling. Don't worry, my sweet child. I'm here. Mummy's here.'

I rock over her, desperate to go and get help but not wanting to leave her at the same time. She needs me, you see. Her whole life, she'd never really known just how much she needs me, but she does. Just like I need her.

I rock back on my heels and pull myself to standing, running to the kitchen and grabbing some tea towels from the corner cupboard. I run one of them under a cool tap, just to dampen it, and then I run back to her, gently sliding a towel under her head and pressing another on her head wound.

'Stay with me,' I whisper again.

I know I should get help, but it dawns on me what that'll mean. Grief overwhelms me as I realise I'll never be able to make her understand. I'll be arrested. Everything will come out. What Peter knows . . . There'll be no coming back from it.

I realise I can't let that happen. No matter the price.

I wasn't with her when she came into this world. Maybe it's my job to be with her as she leaves . . .

To hold her. To nurse her. To care for her. To keep her comfortable – just like she does for her patients. Hadn't she helped Mrs Doherty have a more peaceful death in the end? This can be the same. I can stop Eli from being hurt any further – from learning the truth about me. About us. From ever knowing the dichotomy of joy and pain that comes with being a parent. She won't have to leave me then, you see. Not ever. And her child will never leave her, or me . . . We can just be together. All three of us.

And Noah, too.

And all those other lost souls.

I feel every muscle in my body relax. There's a peace that comes with making a decision.

I think of the boxes of sedatives I have in the kitchen. I could be asleep soon. *We* could be asleep soon.

Sure that I'm doing the right thing, I kneel over my daughter and kiss her forehead. Closing my eyes, I'm back in that moment. When we first arrived in Scotland. When I could breathe out. When I held her in my arms in front of the small window in the room that would be our world and I'd kissed her, revelling in the feel of my lips against the soft, warm skin of her forehead. How I loved her then more than anything I could ever love. How I promised in that moment that I'd also be her mother and that I'd never let anyone break our bond.

'I love you, Eliana Johnston,' I whisper. 'I love you with every breath in my body.'

300

I stroke her hair, watch as her skin pales in front of me, and then I pull myself to standing again. I walk to the kitchen, find the tablets where Eli has left them on the worktop.

I take an old pint glass from the cupboard and fill it with water, then I walk back to the hall, where I can see my daughter's blood seeping through the tea towel. I change it for a clean towel, sit down beside her and, one by one, take the tablets in front of me while I tell her over and over again how I love her. How she was and is my miracle. My rainbow after the storm. How I know I'm flawed and messed up and how I didn't get everything right but that every action has been borne out of pure love. She's my sunshine. My starlight. The love of my life. The apple of my eye.

Then I lie down on the floor beside her and rest my hand on hers, on the hand that rests on her swollen tummy. I feel my eyes flutter closed as I'm pulled from this world . . .

CHAPTER SEVENTY-FIVE

Eli

Something is just out of my grasp. Everything is blurred. Light. Colour. Noise. Voices. It's all a blur. None of it makes sense. The world around me comes to me in colours. Bright white. Green. Yellow. Blurring into each other. Blue, bright. Warm hands on me.

I try to reach out. Try to move. Blue again. Yellow. Green. Bright white. Then the pain hits in screaming shards of red and purple until I pray for the blackness again. Just let me go. Just let me be. Sensations, pressure, throbbing, scratches, something on my face and I can't breathe. I can think of nothing but the pain. The pain and my baby.

I try to scream, 'Take care of my baby. Save my baby. Don't worry about me. My baby.'

My baby.

My words won't come. My voice remains pathetically silent. My eyes won't open. I can't get through the pain to scream. Nothing works. My stupid body. Nothing makes sense. There are voices but I don't know what they were saying. It's just noise.

And fear.

And then blackness again.

★

I'm alive. I can breathe. I can see the colours again but they've started to come into focus now. My head hurts. I try to reach up to touch it but my hands won't respond. Not yet. My eyes flicker open, the bright colours hurting them. I fight the urge to close them again. Try to move my hand. I'm sure my fingers are wiggling. If I could just talk . . .

Noises come into sharp focus. Footsteps. People talking. The beeping of machines . . .

A hospital. I'm in a hospital. Something bad has happened. I feel tears spring to my eyes even though I can't remember what it is that's actually happened. All I know is that my head hurts and my hands aren't moving as they should. I want to speak. My mouth is so dry. My lips cracked. I can hear voices but they aren't beside me.

I feel a hand take mine. I can feel the warmth and pressure of another person's hand. I try to turn my head to see who it is.

'Mum?' I mutter, but it's Martin who I see looking down at me.

His face is strained with worry. Dark circles. Scratchy face. He hasn't shaved. His eyes are streaked with red.

'Are you back, Eli?' he asks, blinking back tears.

I see one fall, feel it land on my face. Mingle with my own. 'Martin?' I say.

My voice is weak but it's there. I'm coming back bit by bit.

'I'm here, darling. I'm here. And you're going to be okay,' he says, his voice breaking.

I can't remember, can't touch the memory of what's happened . . . But in a flash of consciousness, I remember my baby. Oh

God, my baby. I try to move my hand to my tummy, but my arms are so leaden.

'The baby?' I mutter to Martin.

'She's fine. She's a fighter and she's doing really well.'

She's here? I couldn't hold on to her. I start to cry. She's too young. Too small. This isn't right. This isn't how it was meant to happen.

'What happened? Where's Mum? What happened?' I scream, feeling myself growing more and more hysterical.

I see Martin shake his head and pull away. 'I can't . . .' he says as he sobs.

I see Kate come into view. Feel her take my hand in hers. Oh God . . . it's starting to come back to me. My mother. What she did. What she did to us. To me. To my baby. To my daughter. To Martin, my beloved Martin. Do they know? Is she here?

They need to keep her away from me. I don't want her near me. I feel panic surge through me. I try to pull myself to sitting.

'You need to try to stay calm,' Kate says. 'The main thing is you're safe.'

But the pain grows with my panic. I hear a doctor approach and maybe a nurse and they talk, but all I can hear is Kate telling me it'll be okay. I'm safe now. I feel my eyes flicker closed again as I fall back into the darkness.

★

I open my eyes again and it's different. It's dark. The voices are still here but they're hushed now. I can still hear the beep of the machines. Can feel the warmth of a hand on mine. I move, my fingers responding. Martin's voice.

'You're awake.'

'I think so,' I say.

My mouth is still so dry. I ask for water, let Martin hold a cup and straw to me so I can sip it. The slightest movement of my head causes more pain, but I'm able to reach my hand to my head. It's bandaged. The memory of the impact of something. My mother. My baby. My brain tries to piece it all together. I put my hand to my stomach again, look to Martin.

'Is she still okay?'

Martin nods. 'The doctors say she's doing really well. *Really* well. They're going to reduce her oxygen tomorrow, see how she tolerates it.'

'I'm sorry,' I mutter. I hurt our baby. I've failed to keep her safe. I took my mother at her word and believed everything she told me. 'I'm so sorry.'

'It's not your fault, Eli,' Martin says. His voice sounds so sincere. 'You did everything right. And you're here. You're both here, and that's all that matters to me. All that matters full stop.'

'Mum?' It's the only word I can mutter.

He takes a deep breath. 'She's alive,' he says. 'Under police guard.'

I sag with relief. She can't get to me now. She can't get to us.

'What happened?' I ask.

He looks pained, but I need him to fill in the puzzle pieces for me.

'I called the police,' he says. 'I heard your call, heard everything – well, up to the point where there was a loud crash . . . Then I didn't know. But I could hear how scared you were, Eli. It almost killed me. I was an hour and a half away and I couldn't get to you. I didn't know what I'd find when I got to you. What the police would find.

'They found you on the floor. Your head . . . she fractured your skull, Eli. She left you for dead. You were bleeding and your pulse was weak. They didn't know if you'd make it. If the baby would make it.

'They had to operate and I just had to sit and wait and I

couldn't make any sense of it. Not knowing, Eli, if I'd lost everything. You had swelling on your brain. The baby was in distress and they had no choice but to deliver. You've been unconscious for three days, Eli. Our girl is three days old.'

I blink back tears. See the pain in his face but also the love. And I wonder how I ever doubted him. How my mother had made me doubt this man who's never shown me anything but love. What has he been through these last three days? These last few weeks.

Will I ever be able to get him to forgive me?

'I'm so, so sorry,' I say, using what little strength I have to squeeze his hand.

'Please. You don't need to say sorry. She . . . she was so devious. So manipulative.'

'Didn't she call for help?' I ask him. 'Where was she when the police arrived?'

I see something shift in his expression. He moves in his seat and rubs my hand gently. I feel my heart start to beat faster.

'They found her unconscious,' he says. 'She'd taken an overdose, Eli. Rather than get you help – you and our daughter help – she took an overdose and lay down beside you to die.'

I feel my stomach turn. She'd have let us all die? All of us? For what? Because she didn't want me to have a life of my own? Because she was jealous of Martin and me? Because she wanted our baby for herself?

'She's a very sick and troubled woman, Eli,' Martin says, cutting through my thoughts. 'But she'll recover. Physically at least. Try not worry about her now. Let's just focus on us. And our little girl. She's so tiny. So beautiful. Do you want to see a picture? I have one on my phone.'

I didn't expect that the first time I'd see my child it would be on the screen of a phone.

Nor, if I'm honest, did I expect to fall absolutely, passionately and wholeheartedly in love with her the first time I saw her. But I do. I feel a connection with her so deep and so primal that I can feel my heart swell and my body physically ache to hold her.

And in that moment, I know that I'll never, ever be able to understand why my mother did what she did.

CHAPTER SEVENTY-SIX

Angela

I can't so much as move without someone watching me. If I go to the bathroom, the door has to be left open. If I move to the chair by my hospital bed, someone'll come in and check that I'm behaving. They'll be able to move me soon. To a secure ward.

The madhouse, I suppose.

None of them understand that I'm far from mad. I'm just a mother who loves her child. I hadn't meant to hurt her. Of course I hadn't. And I hadn't left her. I'd cared for her until I couldn't any more.

There was no one as shocked, surprised or upset as I was to wake up in hospital – my throat raw from having my stomach pumped. Tubes and wires going in and out. My wrist aching from the handcuff that attached me to the hospital bed.

A hospital gown. My free hand had gone to my neck to find my crucifix, but it was gone. Could be used as a weapon to hurt myself or others, they said. How cruel of them to take my comfort from me.

I wept then. Because I don't want to be here any more. I should've been gone. With Eli and the baby. With Noah. With the others. Those who'd never had a chance. Could they not have just let me go to be with them?

I tried asking the nurses about Eli. I wanted them to let me know where she was. I felt a palpable fear that Martin would bury her in Derry. So far away from me. Too far away.

After a day and a half, someone let slip she was still alive. My grandchild was alive. But they wouldn't tell me any more. No matter how much I pleaded. And when I became angry and irate, they sedated me. Let me slip away for a while.

Now, the police have come to see me. To ask me about what I've done. Martin has filled them in, it appears, on all the details. I have the good grace to blush as a ruddy-faced officer with red hair that sticks up in every direction imaginable asks me again and again about what's happened. He throws phrases at me: perverting the course of justice, wasting police time, breaking and entering, harassment, attempted murder.

Attempted murder? That one makes me angry. That's not what it was at all. I shake my head.

He gets increasingly frustrated when I stop answering his questions, choosing to sit in silence and stare out of the window instead.

They send in another police officer after that. A woman. She sits in her nicely pressed suit, her hair iron-straight, a trace of slut-red lipstick across her lips, and tells me she's a mother. That she understands a mother's love can be all-consuming but, if she's to help me, she needs to know more.

She's lying. She doesn't want to help me. She must think I'm stupid as well as mad. She reads the list of allegations against me and can't hide the shock from her voice, no matter how she tries.

I just stare at the window again. It's clear she's never going to understand. Just as it's clear she's made up her mind that I'm guilty. There's little point in me adding anything to the conversation.

Another day passes, and another officer arrives. Tall. Handsome. Flecks of silver through his hair. He has the weather-beaten look of a man who enjoys an outdoorsy lifestyle. Crinkles by his eyes. Tanned hands. I always notice a man's hands. A simple gold wedding ring glinting on his left hand. A nice suit. Freshly pressed.

He seems friendly as he sits down beside me. Calls me Ms Johnston. Not missus. That earns him some points straight away.

He introduces himself as DS Bradley, from Strand Road PSNI in Derry. I imagine he's here to talk to me about the break-in at Eli's house – the one for which I'd been responsible.

'I'm terribly sorry you've come all this way,' I tell him. 'But I've said as much as I'm going to say about the whole thing already to your colleagues. Everything else, well, that's between my daughter and me.'

He shifts in his seat. 'Actually, Ms Johnston, I'm not here to talk to you about recent events. This would be more an historical matter.'

I feel my nonchalance slip.

'Can you tell me, does the name Louise Barr mean anything to you?'

I shake my head, hoping my momentary pause, the slight widening of my eyes, hasn't given away that I'm lying. I can feel my palms moisten with sweat. Oh, Peter, what have you done?

'Does the name Carys Kearney mean anything to you?'

I haven't heard that name in a long time. Not since the day I turned up at her doorstep and left with my heart and my arms full.

I shake my head.

Deny everything, isn't that what they say? If they have any real evidence they won't ask questions. They'll just arrest me.

'Are you aware that on 24 November 1984, a female child

– an infant – of Mrs Kearney was taken from its home by a woman claiming to be a health visitor?'

'You don't expect me to remember every missing child of the last thirty-odd years, do you?' I ask.

'No, Ms Johnston, I certainly do not. But we have reason to believe this particular case might be one you'd remember. Just as we have reason to believe that you're familiar with Louise Barr, née McLaughlin.'

'I was living in Scotland in 1984,' I said. 'I can prove it. Sure, that's where my daughter's registered.'

He shifts again in his seat and clears his throat. 'If I can be perfectly frank with you, Ms Johnston, it would be easier for everyone, your daughter included, if you just came clean now. The Kearney family have been through enough trauma in their lives, and your daughter has been through enough over the last few weeks by the sounds of things. I understand life was tough for you then. I don't believe there's anyone who wouldn't be sympathetic to that.'

'Are you a parent yourself? Do you know what it feels like?'

He shakes his head. 'Not yet.'

'But one day?'

'This isn't really about me. This is about baby Kearney. Olivia. That was her given name.'

'I don't know what this has to do with me,' I lie, but I can feel the net closing tighter and tighter. It's clear Peter's spoken to them.

'We've taken blood tests,' he says. 'Within a short time we'll have a definitive answer one way or the other. It'll look better for you if you come clean before we present you with all the evidence. Eliana is the Kearney baby, isn't she? And you are or were Louise Barr. She was never really yours to begin with.'

I wanted to scream that of course she was mine. God had brought her to me. She was more mine than Carys Kearney's.

She's more mine than Martin's. She belongs to me more than she does to that baby lying in the NeoNatal Intensive Care Unit. She's the only thing in this entire world who's ever truly been mine.

But no one else will understand that. Not DS Bradley. Not the nurses. The doctors. All the Kates and Martins and friends and family in the world.

But that doesn't mean it's not as true as the sky being blue or the sea being wet.

'She was always mine,' I tell him, and as what little that was left of my heart crumbles away to nothing, I turn to look at the window again.

Biology might say one thing. The law might agree. But Eliana is my daughter.

CHAPTER SEVENTY-SEVEN

Eli

'This will come as a shock,' a kindly faced nurse had said before a policeman came into my hospital room and told me the 'truth' about my mother.

Not that she *is* my mother. Not biologically, anyway. Martin holds my hand as the words wash over me, one by one. The new information overwhelming me.

Olivia Kearney. That's my name. My first name. My real name. I have another mother. Carys. I have a father, Tom, who's alive and real and who'd wanted me. My 'mother' had taken me from my home, in Derry. Where I have set up home. There's an irony in that, I suppose. It was where my mother had been from all along. And her family.

'We were contacted by Ms Johnston's ex-husband. He'd seen an article about you in the local paper, put two and two together.'

She'd been married. My mother. What life had she led before me?

'He'd tried to contact her directly but she never replied, so he came to the police. When we ran a check on our systems, the incident in which you were injured in her home showed up. That's when we looked further.'

All this time, my mother's carefully constructed world was just one person away from falling down around her ears.

'Can I see her – my mother, Angela?' I ask.

The police officer looks surprised at my request. Martin is vocal in his shock. He doesn't want me anywhere near her. Not now. Not ever. They don't understand how I need to see her face, to see the truth of what she's done in her expression. Perhaps even to hear her say she's sorry.

'She's been moved to a secure location,' DS Bradley says. 'Awaiting psychiatric assessment, to see if she's fit for trial. I think, maybe, in time . . .'

'I just want to ask her why,' I say to the police officer, who looks at me sympathetically.

'We're still piecing together what happened,' he says. 'But it seems she lost a child, a son, in the year before you were born. Very late in her pregnancy. She'd suffered a series of losses before, most in the early stages, but this one affected her more than the others.

'She asked one of the police officers to bring her a storage box from her study, said she needed it with her. We didn't, of course, but we were able to open it – found a locket with a curl of baby hair, a little pot with soil, some footprints . . .'

I think of my baby. Our baby. Clara. Already, the thought of something bad happening to her is unbearable. Even though I haven't yet been well enough to hold her in my arms, have only been able to stroke her hand through the incubator, watching her tiny chest move up and down, her body fight for life, I know it'll kill me, too, if she doesn't make it.

My love for her exceeds each and every expectation I've ever had in my life about motherhood. I feel a pang for my mother, for Angela, or Louise, or whoever she is, for her loss.

But to inflict that loss on another woman?

'We've made contact with your birth parents,' DS Bradley

says softly. 'Informed them that we suspect you to be their missing child. I know this is a lot to take in, but we'll have a family liaison officer and social workers to help you all through this process.'

'Do they want to meet me?' I'm scared. My whole life has turned on its head.

He nods. 'But it doesn't have to be rushed. I think everyone's trying to process what's happened. I think it's important you all take time to try to come to terms with things.'

I wonder how I'll ever – can ever – come to terms with everything. With the fact my whole life has been a lie. And those poor people. What must they have been going through all these years?

I feel my husband squeeze my hand softly. I look at him. His face is so filled with love, even after all that he's been put through. I know he'll be by my side through it all. Every step of the way. Through every challenge life will throw at us. And I know that Clara will help us both to heal and move on.

EPILOGUE

Eli

I stand in the sunlight. A soft breeze is caressing my skin. I hold Clara close to me. Even though she's safely ensconced in her baby sling, I feel the urge to wrap my arms around her, so I do.

Martin's waiting in the car, the window down, looking in my direction, but we both know this is something I need to do myself. Well, it's not so much that I need to do it, but I want to.

This was a place of so much sadness, but it feels so very peaceful all the same. I look at the small white headstone in front of me, inscribed: Noah Barr, Born Sleeping.

I'll never meet him. He was gone before I was even born, but our lives will always be intrinsically linked. Had he breathed, would Angela have been okay? Would I have had a good life with Carys and Tom?

I've met them twice now. Emotional, strange meetings where we're trying to suss each other out. I look like her. My mother. And I'm sure Clara has my father's eyes. But it will be a slow, delicate process. We're trying so hard to get our heads around everything. I'm hopeful one day we'll be in a room together and be able to talk without thinking, first of all, of all that was robbed from us.

I kneel down on the soft patch of grass, lovingly tended, where he lies. A fresh posy of yellow roses has been placed on his grave. I leave them just as they are as I put my own flowers, soft white roses, set in baby's breath, in front of his headstone.

I sit there for a moment and think about Clara. And about Noah. And of course about Angela, who's still in custody in a psychiatric unit. She's not yet fit for trial. She still refuses to talk except to ask where I am.

I changed my mind; I haven't been brave enough to see her yet. Or maybe it's just that I'm too angry to see her, knowing what she tried to take from me. I'm not sure I'll ever be ready to see her again.

I've met her ex-husband, though. Peter. A nice man. A caring man. A man who blames himself for not doing more back then. As if it were his fault for not doing more to get her help.

He's gone on to have two more children – two daughters – both grown women with children of their own now. But when we talked and he told me about Noah and that devastating heartbreak, he looked broken.

'It was more than she could bear. It was more than anyone should have to bear. To lose her baby and, well, to lose her womb, too. All she ever wanted was to be a mother.'

'She was a good mother,' I said wryly, because she had been, until it had all gone so horrifically wrong.

'I think she could've taken one loss, but there were so many. Noah was the last in a long line. Maybe she would've been able to live with losing him if it hadn't been for the others,' he said. 'We really thought he'd make it. He'd got so far along. Much further than the others, even . . . even our daughter.'

'You lost a daughter?'

No one had mentioned this to me before. Yes, I knew there

were other losses, but I'd never been told any details. Assumed they'd all been early miscarriages.

Peter had looked uncomfortable. 'A little girl. At five months. Just the year before Noah. She didn't have a chance. Louise wouldn't even talk about her. Refused to. She fell pregnant with Noah so quickly afterwards that she said she was sure that this baby would be God's way of making up for the heartache of losing our little girl. She had always, always longed for a daughter.'

I had wept with him. Walked away stunned. Horrified. Overwhelmed with all the emotions.

It's taken me a further two months to find the strength to come here.

A tear rolls down my cheek, landing squarely on Clara's soft downy hair as I trace the second name on the small white headstone: Eliana Barr, Born Sleeping.

Acknowledgements

First and foremost I must thank my editor Phoebe Morgan, whose guidance and insight has turned a challenging first draft into a finished article I'm proud of, and whose belief in me – and willingness to challenge me to move outside of my comfort zone at times – has meant the world.

In addition, the entire team at Avon Books have made me feel so welcome and I am eternally grateful for all the hard work they have done on my behalf. In particular, thank you to Sabah, Elke, Dom and Anna. I owe you all more chocolate.

Thanks to Claire Pickering, whose all-seeing eye during copy-edits smoothed all the rough edges. Apologies for all the Northern Irish turns of phrase which make no sense to anyone elsewhere in the world!

Thanks also to Mary, Tony, Eoin and Ciara - the brilliant team at HarperCollins Ireland who held my hand through the launch of *Her Name Was Rose* and helped me enjoy my moments in the sun.

And to the HarperCollins teams around the world who have championed *Her Name Was Rose* and who will hopefully champion this book just as much!

As always, my thanks goes to my agent Ger Nichol who is my first sounding board, my cheerleader and my friend. I am lucky to have had you on my side for the last twelve years.

Writing is a solitary business, but it's also conversely a very supportive one and I'm blessed with some truly wonderful author friends who make me feel a little less alone in my madness.

Thanks to all of you who came out and supported *Her Name Was Rose*, saying exceptionally kind things.

Special thanks go to Margaret Scott, Caroline Finnerty, Anstey Harris, John Marrs, Louise Beech, Cally Taylor, Brian McGilloway, Marian Keyes and Liz Nugent.

The most special thanks of all goes to my beta-reader, my friend and my soul sister Fionnuala Kearney who has taken every step of this journey with me.

Thanks to all the booksellers who have supported my books, with special mention to David Torrans of No Alibis in Belfast, and Jenni Doherty of Little Acorns in Derry. Also to the brilliant booksellers in Eason, Waterstones, Dubray and Argosy. And to librarians everywhere, but most especially at the Central Library in Derry.

Thank you to all the bloggers, reviewers and journalists who have given me the time of day and lovely reviews. With special love for Margaret Bonass Madden, who has been championing my work for many years.

Sincere thanks to Ruth Underdown, Sarah Rushton, Laura Hopwood and Katherine Lawson who provided information on end of life care. Any mistakes are entirely of my own making.

Writing over the last couple of years has brought a lot of things into focus in my life – not least the importance of having a good 'tribe' on your side. To you who pick me up when I (frequently) fall down, thank you.

Especially Vicki, Erin, Catherine, Carey-Ann, Sandra,

Marie-Louise and Bernie. You ladies show what it's like when women support women in the best way possible.

And to my 'stunt hand' and road-trip partner who just understands, Julie-Anne – you are shaping up to be a first rate 'herself'.

My family as always, Mum, Dad, Lisa, Peter, Emma – assorted nieces and nephews and in-laws, thank you with all my heart. To Auntie Raine and Mimi who have provided practical and emotional support.

To my long-suffering and mostly understanding husband and children – thank you for letting me live my dream. I owe you a holiday and then some.

And to all my readers, and all those lovely Twitter friends of mine. I will never be able to adequately express my gratitude.

Finally, while this book was being written I lost one of my greatest champions. My granny, Mary McGuinness, who had been so incredibly proud to have an author in the family, whose love of reading rubbed off on me and who came to every launch and event with a proud smile. You will be missed always, but forgotten never. This book is for you.

Read on for an extract of Claire's first thriller:

Her Name Was Rose

Chapter One

It should have been me. I should have been the one who was tossed in the air by the impact of a car that didn't stop. 'Like a ragdoll,' the papers said.

I had seen it. She wasn't like a ragdoll. A ragdoll is soft, malleable even. This impact was not soft. There were no cushions. No graceful flight through the air. No softness.

There was a scream of 'look out!' followed by the crunch of metal on flesh, on muscle, on bone, the squeal of tyres on tarmac, the screams of onlookers – disjointed words, tumbling together. The thump of my heart. A crying baby. At least the baby was crying. At least the baby was okay. The roar of the engine, screaming in too low a gear as the car sped off. Footsteps, thundering, running into the road. Cars screeching to a halt as they came across the scene.

But it was the silence – amid all the noise – that was the loudest. Not a scream. Not a cry. Not a last gasp of breath. Just silence and stillness, and I swore she was looking at me. Accusing me. Blaming me.

I couldn't tear my gaze away. I stood there as people around me swarmed to help her, not realising or accepting that she was beyond help. To lift the baby. To comfort him. To call an ambulance. To look in the direction in which the car sped off. Was it black? Not navy? Not dark grey? It was dirty. Tinted windows. Southern reg, maybe. It was hard to tell – muddied as it was so that the letters and numbers were obscured. No one got a picture of the car – but one man was filming the woman bleeding onto the street. He'd try and sell it to the newspapers later, or post it on Facebook. Because people would 'like' it. A child, perhaps eight years old, was screaming. Her cries piercing through all else. Her mother bundled her into her arms, hiding her eyes from the scene. But it was too late. What has been seen cannot be unseen. People around me did what needed to be done. But I just stood there – staring at her while she stared at me.

Because it should have been me. I should be the one lying on the road, clouds of scarlet spreading around me on the tarmac.

★

I stood there for a few minutes – maybe less. It's hard to tell. Everything went so slowly and so quickly and in my mind it all jumps around until I'm not sure what happened when and first and to whom.

I moved when someone covered her – put a brown duffle coat over her head. I remember thinking it looked awful. It looked wrong. The coat looked like it had seen better days. She deserved better. But it broke our stare and an older lady with artificially blonde brassy hair gently took my arm and led me away from the footpath.

'Are you okay, dear?' she asked. 'You saw it, didn't you?'

'I was just behind her,' I muttered, still trying to see my way through the crowds. Sure that if I did, the coat would be lifted in a flourish of magic trickery and the lady would be gone.

Someone would appear and shout it was an elaborate trick and the lovely woman – who just minutes before had been singing 'Twinkle Twinkle' to the cooing baby boy in the pram as we travelled down in the lift together – would appear and bow.

But the brown coat stayed there and soon I could hear the distant wail of sirens.

There's no need to rush, I thought, she's going nowhere.

'I'll get you a sweet tea,' the brassy blonde said, leading me to the benches close to where the horror was still unfolding. It seemed absurd though. To sit drinking tea, while that woman lay dead only metres away. 'I'm fine. I don't need tea,' I told her.

'For the shock,' the blonde said and I stared back blankly at her.

This was more than shock though. This was guilt. This was a sense that the universe had messed up on some ginormous, stupid scale and that the Grim Reaper was going to get his P45 after this one. Mistaken identity was unforgivable.

I looked around me. Fear piercing through the shock. There were so many people. So many faces. And the driver? Had I even seen him? Got a glimpse? Could it have been *him*? Or had he got someone else to do the dirty work, and he was standing somewhere, watching? It would be more like him to stand and observe, enjoy the destruction he had caused. Except he'd got it wrong. She'd walked out in front of me. I'd let her. I'd messed with his plan.

I'd smiled at her and told her to 'go ahead' as the lift doors opened. She'd smiled back not knowing what she was walking towards.

A paper cup of tea was wafted in front of me – weak, beige. A voice I didn't recognise told me there were four sugars in it. Brassy Blonde sat down beside me and nodded, gesturing that I should take a sip.

I didn't want to. I knew if I did, I would taste. I would feel the warmth of it slide down my throat. I would smell the tea leaves. I would be reminded I was still here.

'Let me take your bags from you,' Brassy Blonde said. I realised I was gripping my handbag tightly, and in my other hand was the paper bag I had just been given in Boots when I'd picked up my prescription. Anxiety meds. I could use some now. My hands were clamped tight. I looked her in the eyes for the first time. 'I can't,' I said. 'My hands won't work.'

'It's the shock. Let me, pet,' she said softly as she reached across and gently prised my hands open, sitting my bags on the bench beside me. She lifted the cup towards me, placed it in my right hand and helped me guide the cup to my mouth.

The taste was disgustingly sweet, sickening even. I sipped what I could but the panic was rising inside me. The ambulance was there. Police too. I heard a woman crying. Lots of hushed voices. People pointing in the direction in which the car had sped off. As if their pointing would make it reappear. Beeps of car horns who didn't realise something so catastrophic had held them up on their way to their meetings and appointments and coffees with friends. Faces, blurring. Familiar yet not. They couldn't have been.

The tightness started in my chest – that feeling that the air was being pushed from my lungs – and it radiated through my body until my stomach clenched and my head began to spin just a little.

He could be watching me crumble and enjoying it.

The noise became unbearable. Parents covering the eyes of children. Shop workers standing outside their automatic doors, hands over their mouths. I swear I could hear the shaking of their heads – the soft brush of hair on collars as they struggled to accept what they were seeing. Breathing – loud, deep. Was it my own? Shadows moving around me. Haunting me. I felt sick.

'I have to go,' I muttered – my voice tiny, distorted, far away

– as much to myself as to Brassy Blonde, and I put down the teacup and lifted my bags.

'You have to stay, pet,' she said, a little too firmly. I took against her then. No, I wanted to scream. I don't have to do anything except breathe – and right now, right here, that was becoming increasingly difficult.

I glared at her instead, unable to find the words – any words.

'You're a witness, aren't you? The police will want to talk to you?'

That made the panic rise in me more. Would they find out that it should have been me? Would I get the blame? Would I become a headline in a story – 'lucky escape for local woman' – and if so, what else would they find out about me? I couldn't take that risk.

I consoled myself that I probably couldn't tell them anything new anyway.

No, I didn't want to talk to the police. I couldn't talk to the police. The police had had quite enough of me once before.

Chapter Two

A hit and run, they said. That was the official line. A joyrider, most likely. Joyrider is such a strange name for it, really. There was no joy here. The words of the police did little to comfort me. After I ran from Brassy Blonde, I checked the locks three times before bed, kept the curtains pulled on the windows of my flat and for those first 48 hours I didn't go out or answer my phone. The only person I spoke to was my boss to tell him I was sick and wouldn't be in. I didn't even wait for him to answer. I just ended the call, crawled back into bed and took more of my anti-anxiety medication.

I tried to rationalise my thoughts and fears in the way my counsellor had told me. A few years had passed since Ben had made his threat; five to be exact. Life had moved on. He had moved on. Moved to England, if my brother Simon was to be believed. Simon, who I secretly suspected believed Ben about everything that went wrong with us.

Simon, who most definitely, did not believe that his former friend was waiting in the wings to destroy my life for a second time in his twisted form of revenge.

'You're letting him win every day,' my counsellor had told me. 'You're giving him power he doesn't deserve.'

But she didn't know him. Not the way I did. I spent those two days in a ball in my bed, sleeping or at least trying to sleep, and compulsively checking Facebook to find out as much as I could about the woman who had died when it should have been me.

There was no fairness to it. She had everything going for her while I, well, if I evaporated from this earth at this moment no one would really notice. Except perhaps for Andrew who would be waiting to give me a final written warning.

I had to go to the funeral. I was drawn to it. I had to see the pain and let it wash over me – to salve my guilt perhaps or to torture myself further? See if she really was as loved as it seemed.

I needed to remind myself just how spectacularly the gods had messed this one up.

Perhaps I was a bit obsessed. It was hard not to be. The story of her death was everywhere and I had seen her life extinguished right in front of my eyes. Her eyes had stayed open – and they were there every time I closed mine.

Her funeral was held at St. Mary's Church in Creggan – a chapel that overlooked most of the city of Derry, down its steep hills towards the River Foyle before the city rises back up again in the Waterside. It's a church scored in the history of Derry, where the funeral Mass of the Bloody Sunday dead had taken place. Thirteen coffins lined up side by side. On the day of Rose Grahame's funeral, just one coffin lay at the top of the aisle. The sight stopped my breath as I sneaked in the side entrance, took a seat away from her friends and family. Hidden from view.

All the attention focused on the life she'd led, full of

happiness and devotion to her family and success in her career. I thought of how the mourners – the genuine ones dressed in bright colours (as Rose would have wanted) – had followed the coffin to the front of the church, gripping each other, holding each other up. I wondered what they would say if they knew what I knew.

I allowed the echoes of the sobs that occasionally punctuated the quiet of the service to seep into my very bones.

I recognised her husband, Cian; as he walked bowed and broken to the altar, I willed myself not to sob. Grief was etched in every line on his face. He looked so different from the pictures I had seen of him on Facebook. His eyes were almost as dead as Rose's had been. He took every step as if it required Herculean effort. It probably did. His love for her seemed to be a love on that kind of scale. His grief would be too.

He stood, cleared his throat, said her name and then stopped, head bowed, shoulders shaking. I felt my heart constrict. I willed someone – anyone – to go and stand with him. To hold his hand. To offer comfort. No one moved. It was as if everyone in the church was holding their breath, waiting to see what would happen next. Enjoying the show.

He took a breath, straightened himself, and spoke. 'Rose was more than a headline. More than a tragic victim. She was my everything. My all. But even that isn't enough. As a writer, you would think the words would come easily to me. I work with words every day – mould them and shape them to say what I need to say. But this time, my words have failed me. There are no words in existence to adequately describe how I'm feeling as I stand here in front of you, looking at a wooden box that holds the most precious gift life ever gave me. When a person dies young, we so often say they had so much more to give. This was true of Rose. She gave every day. We had so many dreams and plans.'

He faltered, looking down at the lectern, then to Rose's coffin and back to the congregation. 'We were trying for a baby. A brother or sister for Jack. We said that would make our happiness complete – and now, knowing it will never be, I wonder how life can be so cruel.' He paused again, as if trying to find his words, but instead of speaking, he simply shook his head and walked, slowly, painfully, to his seat where he sat down and buried his head in his hands, the sound of his anguished sobs bouncing off the stone walls of the church.

There was no rhyme or reason to it. No fairness in it. I tried to tell myself that Rose had just been spectacularly unlucky. I tried to comfort myself that on that day luck had, for once, in a kind of twisted turn of fate, been on my side. I needed to believe that – believe in chance and bad luck and not something more sinister. I had to believe the ghosts of my past weren't still chasing me.

I tried to tell myself life was trying to give me another chance – one that had been robbed from me five years before. It was fucked up. George Bailey got Clarence the angel to guide him to his second chance. I got Rose Grahame and her violent death.

I got the sobs of the mutli-coloured mourners. And I got the guilt I had craved.

It might have helped if I'd have found out Rose Grahame was a horrible person – although the way she sang to her baby and smiled her thank you to me as I let her go ahead of me out of the lift and into the cold street had already told me she was a decent sort.

I wondered, selfishly, if this had been my funeral, would I have garnered such a crowd? I doubted it. My parents would be there, I supposed. My brothers and their partners. My two nieces probably wouldn't. They were young. They wouldn't understand. A few cousins, a few work colleagues there because they had to be. Some nosy neighbours. Aunts and uncles. Friends – maybe, although many of them had fallen by the wayside. Maud may travel over for it from the US, but it would depend on her bank balance and the cost of the flights. They would be suitably sad but they'd have full lives to go back to – busy lives, the kind of life Rose Grahame seemed to have had. The kind of life that allows you to pick up the pieces after a tragedy and move on, even if at times it feels as if you are walking through mud. The kind of lives with fulfilling jobs and hectic social calendars and children and hobbies.

Not like my hermit-like existence.

Five years is a long time to live alone.

Of course, being at the funeral made me feel worse. I suppose I should have expected that. But I hadn't expected to feel jealous of her. Jealous that her death had had such an impact.

I crept from the pew, pushed past the crowds at the back of the church, past the gaggle of photographers from the local media waiting to catch an image of a family in breakdown, and walked as quickly as I could from the church grounds to my car, where I lit a cigarette, took my phone from my bag and logged into Facebook.

Social media had become my obsession since the day of the accident. Once I had got home, and I had crawled under my duvet and tried to sleep to block out the thoughts of what I had just seen – what I had just done – I found myself unable to let it go.

I didn't sleep that day. I got up, I made coffee and I switched on my laptop. Sure enough the local news websites were reporting the accident. They were reporting a fatality – believed to be a woman in her thirties who was with her baby at the time.

A hit and run.

A dark-coloured car.

The police were appealing for witnesses.

The family were yet to be informed.

The woman was 'named locally' as Rosie Grahame.

No, it was Rose Grahame. Not Rosie.

She was thirty-four.

She was a receptionist at a busy dental practice.

Scott's in Shipquay Street.

The child in the pram was her son – Jack, twenty months old.

She was married.

Believed to be the wife of local author, Cian Grahame, winner of the prestigious 2015 Simpson Literary Award for his third novel, *From Darkness Comes Light*.

The news updated. Facebook went into overdrive. People giving details. Offering condolences. Sharing rumours. Suggesting a fund be set up to pay for the funeral and support baby Jack, despite the fact that, by all accounts, Cian Grahame was successful and clearly not in any great need of financial support.

Pictures were shared. Rose Grahame – smiling, blonde, hair in one of those messy buns that actually take an age to get right. Sunglasses on her head. Kissing the pudgy cheek of an angelic-faced baby. A smiling husband beside her – tall, dark and handsome (of course). A bit stubbly but in a sexy way – not in a layabout-who-can't-be-bothered-to-shave way. He was grinning at his wife and their son.

It was all just an awful, awful tragedy.

Someone tagged Rose Grahame into their comment saying, 'Rose, I will miss you hun. Always smiling. Sleep well.' As if Rose Grahame was going to read it just because it was on Facebook. Does heaven have Wi-Fi?

Of course I clicked through to her profile. I wanted to know more about her – more than the snippets the news told me, more than the smile she gave me as I held the door to let her through, more than the gaunt stare she gave me as she lay dead on the ground, the colour literally draining from her.

I expected her profile to be a bit of a closed book. So many are – privacy settings set to Fort Knox levels. But Rose clearly didn't care about her privacy settings. Perhaps because her life was so gloriously happy that she wanted the whole world to know.

I found myself studying her timeline for hours – scanning through her photo albums. She never seemed to be without a smile. Or without friends to keep her company.

There she was, arms thrown around Cian on their wedding day. A simple flowing gown. A crown of roses. A beautiful outdoor affair. The whole thing looked as if it could be part of a brochure for hipster weddings.

There she was, showing off her expanding baby bump – her two hands touching in front of her tummy to make the shape of a heart. Or standing with a paint roller in one hand, the requisite dab of paint on her nose, as she painted the walls of the soon-to-be nursery.

There were nights out with friends, where she glowed and sparkled and all her friends glowed and sparkled too. Pictures of her smiling proudly with her husband as he held aloft his latest book.

And then, of course, the baby came along. Pictures of her, perhaps a little tired-looking but happy all the same, cradling a tiny newborn, announcing his birth and letting the world know he was 'the most perfect creature' she had ever set her eyes on.

Pictures of her bathing him, feeding him, playing with him, pushing him in his buggy, helping him mush his birthday cake with his chubby fists. Endless happy pictures. Endless posting of positive quotes about happiness and love and gratitude for her amazing husband and her beautiful son.

The outpouring was unreal – I hit refresh time and time again, the page jumping with new comments. From friends. From family. From colleagues, old school friends, cousins, acquaintances, second cousins three times removed.

And then, that night, at just after eleven – when I was considering switching off and trying to sleep once again, fuelled by sleeping tablets – a post popped up from Cian himself.

My darling Rose,

I can't believe I will never hold you again. That you will never walk through this door again. You were and always will be the love of my life. My everything. My muse. Thank you for the happy years and for your final act of bravery in saving our Jack. I am broken, my darling, but I will do my best to carry on, for you and for Jack.

I stared at it. Reread it until my eyes started to hurt, the letters began to blur. This declaration of love – saying what needed to be said so simply – made me wonder again how the gods had cocked it up so spectacularly.

Poor Cian, I thought. Poor Jack. Poor all those friends and family members and colleagues and second cousins twenty times removed. They were all plunged into the worst grief imaginable. I felt like a voyeur and yet, I couldn't bring myself to look away.

So that was why, then, even outside the church, fag in my hand, smoke filling up my Mini, I clicked onto Facebook and loaded Rose's page again. The messages continued. Posts directly on her timeline, or posts she had been tagged in.

'Can't believe we are laying this beautiful woman to rest today.'

'I will be wearing the brightest thing I can find to remember the brightest star in the sky.'

'Rose,' Cian wrote. 'Help me get through this, honey. I don't know how.'

I looked to the chapel doors, to the pockets of people standing around. Heads bowed. Conversations whispered. A few sucking on cigarettes. I wondered how any of us got through anything? All the tragedies life throws at us. All the bumps in the road. Although, perhaps that was a bad choice of words. A black sense of humour, maybe. I'd needed it these past few years. Although sometimes I wondered if I used it too much. If it made me appear cold to others.

Cian had changed his profile picture, I noticed. It was now a black and white image – Rose, head thrown back, mid laugh. Eyes bright. Laughter lines only adding to her beauty. She looked happy, vital, alive.

I glanced at the clock on my dashboard. Wondered if I should wait until the funeral cortège left the chapel to make their way on that final short journey to the City Cemetery as a mark of respect. I could probably even follow them. Keep a distance. Watch them lay her to rest. Perhaps that would give me some sort of closure.

I took a long drag of my cigarette and looked back at my phone. Scrolled through Facebook one last time. A new notification caught my eye and I clicked on it. It was then that his face, his name, jumped out at me. Everything blurred. I was aware I wasn't breathing, had dropped my cigarette. I think it was only the thought of it setting the car on fire around me that jolted me to action. I reached down, grabbed it, opened my car door and threw the cigarette into the street; at the same time sucking in deep lungfuls of air. I could feel a cold sweat prickle on the back of my neck. It had been five years since I had last seen him. And now? When my heart is sick with the notion that he could finally be making good on the promise he made to get back at me, he appears back in my life.

A friend request from Ben Cullen.

In a panic I looked around me – as the mourners started to

file out of the chapel. I wondered was he among them. Had he been watching me all this time? I turned the key in the ignition and sped off, drove to work mindlessly where I sat in the car park and tried to stop myself from shaking.

The urge to go home was strong. To go and hide under my duvet. I typed a quick email to my friend Maud. All I had to say was 'Ben Cullen has sent me a friend request'.

Maud would understand the rest.

Andrew – my line manager in the grim call centre I spent my days in – wouldn't understand though. He wouldn't get my panic or why I felt the need to run home to the safety of my dark flat with its triple locks and pulled curtains. As it was, he thought I was at a dentist appointment. He had made it clear the leave would be unpaid and it had already been an hour and a half since I'd left the office. I was surprised he hadn't called to check on me yet. If I were to call him to try and verbalise the fear that was literally eating me from the inside out, he not only wouldn't understand, he would erupt. I was skating on perilously thin ice with him as it was. My two days' absence after Rose's death had been the icing on the cake.

But my head hurt. I saw a couple of police officers in uniform as I drove and momentarily wondered whether to tell them Ben Cullen had sent me a friend request and I thought there might be a chance he was caught up in all this. Saying it in my head made me realise how implausible that would sound to an outsider; but not to me, I knew what he was capable of.

I had to get away from here. I wanted to go home but I needed my job. Maybe I would be safer at work anyway? Desolate as it was, we had good security measures. I made sure all the doors on my car were locked and I drove on, the friend request sitting unanswered on my phone.

If you loved *Apple of My Eye*, try Claire's first thriller!

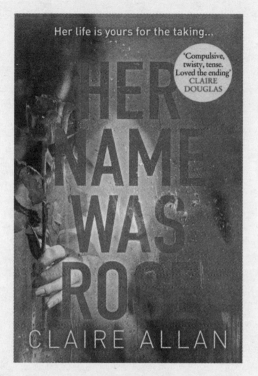

Not everyone's life
is as perfect as it seems . . .